'Elise Esther Hearst's impressive debut *One Day We're All Going to Die* is introspective, evocative [...] simplicity. Hearst is a fresh and exciting voice and easily draws readers into a relatable, at times uncomfortable, exploration of identity, love and the pursuit of personal fulfilment. This must-read is for Sally Rooney, Ottessa Moshfegh and Meg Mason fans, but Hearst's ability to embrace brevity while packing emotional depth and capturing aspects of the female millennial experience is also reminiscent of Japanese authors Meiko Kawakami (*Breasts and Eggs*) and Emi Yagi (*Diary of a Void*). *One Day We're All Going to Die* reminds us that even in the face of uncertainty, there are moments when you know you're exactly where you're meant to be.' —*Bookseller + Publisher*

'A remarkable debut from an enthralling storyteller. I didn't want it to end.' —Sarah Krasnostein, author of *The Trauma Cleaner*

'Sharply witty and sharply real in its mixture of tears and laughter and lust and (the very Jewish art of) sighing, Elise Hearst's debut novel is a compelling, immersive, utterly absorbing read. There are no taboos in *One Day We're All Going to Die* – families, romantic love, identity and sexual politics, money, the Holocaust even, nothing escapes her laser-clear eye. Hearst's arrival on the literary scene is a triumphal one. I cannot wait to see what she writes next.' —Dr Lee Kofman, author

'An absorbing debut novel about lust, grief, and the traumatic weight of the past that's carried into the future. Hearst's novel is a boldly frank, visceral and darkly humorous coming-of-age story. A striking and vivid new voice on the literary scene.' —Marija Pericic, *Australian/Vogel's Award* winner, author of *Exquisite Corpse*

'Captures the essence of life perfectly – its humour, pain, frustration and often hideous awkwardness!' —Sonia Henry, author of *Going Under*

'For fans of Ottessa Moshfegh and Sally Rooney. As a straight non-Jewish white male in my 30s these sorts of books are surprisingly entertaining, and the writing/mood here is just spot-on. Must read when it pops up in bookstores. Plus, that title is just *chef kissy fingers*' —Goodreads

Elise Esther Hearst is a Melbourne-based playwright and author, working and living on Boon Wurrung country. She studied Creative Arts at Melbourne University and playwriting at the Royal Court Theatre in London. Her work has appeared at Melbourne Theatre Company, Red Stitch Actors' Theatre, Arts Centre Melbourne, Griffin Theatre and Melbourne Jewish Book Week. *One Day We're All Going to Die* is Elise's first novel.

One day we're all going to die

ELISE ESTHER HEARST

FICTION
H Q

First Published 2023
First Australian Paperback Edition 2023
ISBN 9781867251279

ONE DAY WE'RE ALL GOING TO DIE
© 2023 by Elise Esther Hearst
Australian Copyright 2023
New Zealand Copyright 2023

Published by
HQ Fiction
An imprint of Harlequin Enterprises (Australia) Pty Limited (ABN 47 001 180 918),
a subsidiary of HarperCollins Publishers Australia Pty Limited (ABN 36 009 913 517)
Level 19, 201 Elizabeth St
SYDNEY NSW 2000
AUSTRALIA

® and TM (apart from those relating to FSC®) are trademarks of Harlequin Enterprises (Australia) Pty Limited or its corporate affiliates. Trademarks indicated with ® are registered in Australia, New Zealand and in other countries.

A catalogue record for this book is available from the National Library of Australia
www.librariesaustralia.nla.gov.au

Printed and bound in Australia by McPherson's Printing Group

FSC
www.fsc.org
MIX
Paper | Supporting
responsible forestry
FSC® C001695

This story was written on the traditional lands of the first storytellers of this place, the Boon Wurrung and Wurundjeri peoples of the Kulin Nation. Sovereignty has never been ceded and this always was and always will be Aboriginal land. I pay my respects to Elders past and present.

For my parents, whom I love.

In memory of Maria Kamm, my grandmother.
Without her, nothing.

Cookie

'Your mother was murdered and now she's dead, darling. That's what I said to her. Exactly.'

My grandmother's mouth, like a malformed wire hanger, bent from a grimace into a smirk. I watched her add two Equals to her coffee, stirring haphazardly with the spoon in her better hand. Coffee mud gushed over the sides onto the saucer.

She was referring to a conversation she'd had with the woman in the unit next door, who had been searching for her mother's phone number in the White Pages. That same lady came knocking the day before, asking if anyone had seen her dead relatives wandering the halls of the home.

'It's not nice to tell someone that their parents have been murdered, Cookie,' I said. My grandmother's name is Carolina, but somewhere between Poland and Melbourne, and her daughter and two granddaughters, and the eternal hope for great-grandchildren and all the children after that, she became known as Cookie. I asked her once if she'd ever considered changing her name by deed poll. 'I'm going to have Cookie

1

on my gravestone? Pft.' And then she'd rolled some phlegm around in her mouth, spat into a hankie, reapplied her lipstick, and followed up with, 'Don't be ridiculous.' That phrase, 'don't be ridiculous', was one my grandmother repeated frequently, in particular when she was the one being ridiculous. My mother liked to borrow it from time to time, and I had the feeling it would reside among the fragments I was destined to inherit.

Now Cookie was scowling. 'Ha! Everyone in this place has parents who've been murdered. She's an idiot.'

'Shush,' spat David, my grandfather, peering up momentarily from his sudoku. 'She can hear you.'

'You shush,' Cookie spat back. 'The idiot is deaf. She's completely deaf.'

I was due back at work soon. I snuck my phone out of my pocket to check the time. I loved my grandparents and couldn't imagine a life without them. However, each time I visited the home there was a part of me that hoped they wouldn't be there. Not dead, but at lunch, in the arts and crafts room, asleep in front of a film.

'She's been hitting the nurses,' Cookie said to me, sucking in a breath. 'Though apparently only the men. I don't blame her.' Cookie pushed a plastic container under my nose. 'Eat one.'

I removed the lid of the container and found a few digestives cascading out of a ripped packet. I scanned unsuccessfully for a use-by date. I'd already refused tea and coffee. Cookie never washed her cups properly. They were discoloured and lipstick stained. My repulsion was bratty, but I couldn't help it. I bit into a biscuit (it was stale) and was careful to wince without her noticing. 'What's wrong with the male nurses?'

'They're rough.'

'No, they're not,' muttered David.

'Except the Filipino boy. I can't understand a word he's saying, but oh! Beautiful face. Like a dolly.'

'His name is ...' David said. 'Wait. It will come ...'

'Finish your puzzle!'

David shook his head and closed his eyes.

Cookie leaned in so close to me that I could smell ninety-five years on her sour breath. 'David's been at that puzzle all morning.'

Not many couples made it together to the Remi Zalcberg Home for the Aged. It would be nice to say that Cookie and David's was a great love story and they had stayed alive for each other, but it was perhaps more accurate to say they had been soldered together by age, time, grief, soup.

It hadn't been Cookie's choice to move, rather it had been thrust upon her by gravity: the pull of all things towards the centre of the earth, that caused the bricks in her driveway to shift and jut out like a shattered block of chocolate, that so callously brought her smashing to the ground when she tripped over one of those bricks and broke her hip and a couple of ribs and her right arm. It was a few months after her ninetieth birthday and her bones were wafer brittle. It was fortunate that David was there and promptly called the ambulance. When

Mum had heard the news she'd screamed, thinking Cookie had died, until she realised it was only a fall. A fall. Something retrievable. Not irreversible. But it was irreversible. After a long stint in hospital, and then rehab, and fraught discussions with aged care consultants, doctors and real estate agents, they sold the house. Cookie only returned there once, to collect some cuttings from her beloved garden, which she would then stick in emptied pickle jars that sat on the windowsill of the one-bedroom unit in the Remi Zalcberg Home for the Aged and mournfully watch their roots splay.

David was now snoring and a string of drool was connecting him to the newspaper. If he slurped upwards he'd swallow a clue to the cryptic crossword. I looked away. I was mentally out the door and heading back to work. I just had to get up, though it was always hard when she was holding my hand because she wasn't really holding it, rather attempting to affix me to the indentation on the faded tan velvet of her couch. And she could. She was strong.

Cookie caressed a fake pearl on her necklace between her fingers, rolling it back and forth, back and forth. She often gloated about how everyone at the home thought her pearls were real.

I took Cookie's hand. I stroked her big purple veins. Cookie's hands were cold. They were always cold. She studied my manicure and pressed her index finger hard on my thumbnail, as if to test the strength of the light blue polish.

'From the Vietnamese?'

'I don't know.' I shrugged. 'Do you want to do something for Shabbat this week?'

'What for?'

'Mum's going away.'

'Hmph.'

'We could go out for dinner?'

My parents' social life never used to bother Cookie as much when she too had a social life, lived in her own house and had a car, a theatre group and a book club. But now, in the home, she detested Mum being more than a five-minute drive away. She took it as a personal affront. Mum, knowing this, left me to do the heavy lifting when she wasn't around. There was no way she was asking my sister, Melanie, who was forever occupied. With what exactly I was never quite sure of.

Cookie looked at David and then back at me. 'What time will you pick us up?'

'6.30. Okay?'

Cookie reached over to the wooden side table. Her hands wafted over everything on it like a fortune teller with a crystal ball – the big button phone, large-print murder mystery, mug full of blunt pencils and warped nail files, and personalised stationery pad with her former address printed at the top (now when she wrote letters she crossed the address out and put a question mark beneath it). She landed on a bottle of marbled nail varnish.

'$4.95 at Priceline,' she said. 'How much did yours cost?'

*

The first time I stepped inside the collection storeroom of the Museum of Jewish Heritage, I lost my breath for a moment. Perhaps it was from the stinging chill. Or maybe it was the fluorescent lights, the metal drawers and trays, or the squeal of rubber-soled shoes on the linoleum floor. A sense of dread and excitement intermingled there. It reminded me that I was due for a pap smear.

The museum was located at the tail-end of the Balaclava shopping strip – an expansive mid-century home designed by a prominent Jewish architect in the 1950s, which, since being acquired by the founders of the institution in the early 1980s had been retrofitted for purpose. The front of the building housed a permanent gallery documenting Jewish life and ritual, and a large contemporary extension at the back held temporary exhibitions that changed biannually. The home's original kitchen displayed traditional Jewish foods amid warm wooden panelling and *Do Not Touch* signs: petrified matzah balls floating in plastic soup, a papier mâché challah, paint-chipped wooden dates and pomegranates. The staff worked upstairs in a maze of rooms, some formerly bedrooms. When I started here last year I'd researched whether anyone had died here, because to me it felt full of ghosts.

The building was south-facing, always cast in shade and its insides were too cold: ideal conditions for the preservation of artefacts. Once in the midst of a heatwave, I'd driven home to collect a jumper and shawl. My boss, Josh, had teased me about this, said how it reminded him of his wife. I'd wanted to say, yes, I know – in everyone's relationship there is always one who is hot and one who is cold, and if I were to be in a relationship then I would be the cold one. But seeing as I was single, I'd said nothing, and fanned the shawl over my legs and arms like a blanket.

I realised I had forgotten to bring lunch, but the visit to my grandparents had exhausted me and I couldn't be bothered heading out again. I was hopeful for leftover challah or matzah in the kitchen from a school group, who were due to visit me soon in the library. 'Now, children,' I'd overheard from the education room down the hall, 'we eat this plaited bread on Shabbat to thank God for the manna sent down from heaven. And this matzah we eat on Passover. We are told it is the bread of affliction, of slavery, of suffering. Now who can tell me, what does affliction mean?'

I ignored the pit in my stomach, put on white gloves and proceeded to remove a 230-year-old Haggadah from its box and place it on a white cloth.

My mother would say that the commitment I showed to the museum's artefacts was in direct contrast to the ambivalence I showed to the rest of my life, which tumbled about me like an upturned bedroom. In fact, she had said something of the sort when she'd come to visit last week. She'd run her fingers over the various piles of paperwork and books on my desk as if she were playing piano.

I had hoped to work at the museum since seeing the Diane Arbus exhibition there a few years ago. A postcard of her identical twins had been Blu Tacked to my bedroom wall from then on, and when I moved out of my parents' house I made sure to keep the Blu Tack on and transplanted it from one wall to another.

Some visitors to my bedroom had found the photograph unsettling: two seven-year-old girls, four pairs of eyes, so similar and yet the girl on the left's eyes are smaller, less bright, dissatisfied, compared to her sister, whose eyes are happy and open. I liked the photo for its endless possibilities – how we can all be so similar and we can all be so different. How we can make so many deductions about someone but the truth of a person lies with them and we, on the outside, can only wonder.

I expressed this sentiment (with great embarrassment) in my job interview. It served me well, and I got the job that I had long coveted.

I was careful and methodical in my work. I wasn't clumsy. I'd only broken something once – the clasp of a necklace, which was deemed of little value to the museum anyway. But I was hesitant when dealing with objects – always anticipating things slipping from my fingers, fearful of causing an accident. I was efficient with other aspects of my job though, for example dealing with emails, even tangly ones that required well-researched responses. But when it came to the seemingly simple task of tagging a new acquisition and placing it in a box, I was slow, like a child writing the alphabet for the first time. Even Josh said I didn't have to be so cautious, which seemed an odd thing to say considering we were tasked with the grave responsibility of preservation.

The Haggadah I was about to show the children had been donated by a guy who had found it beneath the floorboards of his mother's house after she had died, along with some buttons and a lock of hair. When I met with him, he sat too close to me while we slowly sifted through his objects, which had been unceremoniously chucked into a Coles shopping bag. Eventually I got up for some water and when I returned I sat myself on the other side of the table so there was no way our legs could touch. He believed the hair was his – that his mother had kept his hair long until his third birthday when a rabbi he'd never met appeared and proceeded to cut it all off. He remembered screaming as the rabbi recited the prayers (for what he later learned was an upsherin) and approached with sharp scissors and a beard peppered with birthday cake crumbs. He told me how odd this all was: how they were not religious, not kosher, never went to synagogue and yet intermittently throughout his life his mother would silently foist certain aspects of Jewish ritual onto him without comment or explanation. 'Maybe she was religious in Poland,' I had offered. The man had wiped away a tear, shrugged and said he didn't know. And his mother never spoke about Poland anyway. I told the man that the museum would gratefully acquire the Haggadah, but that he should keep the buttons and the hair.

There was a knock at the door. 'Ready for us?' Marilyn, Director of Visitor Services and anything else that needed attention at the museum, entered the library without waiting for my response. 'Come inside, children. Quietly.' She ushered in ten six-year-olds and two teachers. Maybe it was the reverence for a room full of books or Marilyn's schoolmarm demeanour, but silently, and without being told to, the children all lined up in front of me.

School groups always made me feel self-conscious, like my teeth were unbrushed or I'd slept in my clothes and they could all tell.

The kids were from a Jewish school. I had been to a similar school. I'd thrived there because I had always found academia easy and had no great social ambition. Sometimes I wished I'd gone to public school, or at least a non-religious private school as my sister had done. Maybe this would have somehow allowed me to move through the world in a more regular way. I'd be better at small talk. I'd have left home sooner. Throughout my whole school career, I'd been dimly aware of a whole other world out there, beyond the community. A less sheltered world that was at once appealing and scary. It wasn't until I got to my second last year of high school and the biology teacher was dismissed for having an inappropriate relationship with a student that I could entertain the idea that Jews could commit crimes. No one had ever explicitly told me that all Jews were law-abiding good people, yet somehow I had internalised this notion. By now, in 2009, at almost twenty-seven, I knew this was a falsehood. I had seen Jews shoplift in the local supermarket. I had heard of Jews beating their wives, of committing crimes against humanity. Jews are, after all, human. Indeed, part of my role at the museum required me to enforce that notion.

I looked up at the children. 'So, this is a very special book. Does anyone know what it is?'

'A really old book!' a girl said and started giggling.

'Millie,' a teacher warned.

'That's right,' I said softly, feeling bad for Millie. 'It is a really old book. It's a Haggadah. And when do we use the Haggadah?'

The children all knew the answer and responded in unison.

My family had many versions of the Haggadah that would all be brought out at Passover. My favourite one had an orange tree on the cover and told the ancient story of the Exodus, depicting both Moses and God as women. Melanie liked to joke that God had turned all the Egyptians' wine to blood because God was on her period, which I had found funny at first, but later was agitated by. Melanie loved to minimise tradition and symbolism, whereas I took great comfort in story and ritual regardless of the preposterousness of the content.

'We think it's about 230 years old,' I continued. 'And it came from Poland. And the pages are made from some sort of animal skin. Maybe a goat?'

'Isn't that interesting, children?' Marilyn enthused.

'How did they draw on the goat?' asked Millie, scratching her nose.

'Well, they would have had to kill the goat first. And then, uh, skin it. And then use its skin as parchment. Paper. Sorry. It's not very nice.'

'I don't care,' Millie said. 'My shoes are made from a cow.'

'Right.'

Millie stuck two fingers in her mouth, took them out and inspected them, and then looked at me and said, 'But how did it get here? How did it get here from Poland?'

'We're not really sure. Probably on a boat.'

'Why?'

'Because it meant something to someone. It meant enough for them to keep it.'

I went upstairs to the office with a piece of challah stuffed in between my lips. Josh was just finishing up.

'How'd you go?'

'Fine,' I said, putting one hand over my mouth. Bits of the sweet dough were clumping in my teeth. 'They were cute.'

'I should really come and do one of those talks.'

'The kids would like you. Probably more than me. I don't know how to talk to kids.'

'You talk to me,' he said with a wink, and then picked up his bag and tucked his chair beneath his desk.

I watched him leave. It was always a relief to see him go, as if I'd been holding something in the whole time he was there.

I refreshed my inbox. One new enquiry: someone researching their family history. I closed the email and flicked down to the one my mother had sent me about Whatshisname. His name was in fact Adam but, when chatting about the proposed blind date, Mum and I had referred to him as Whatshisname. She did that to appear uninvested. I did it to take the sting out of it.

I hated being the one to initiate contact. I thought about ringing Gemma, my housemate, but I knew she'd tell me I was overthinking, and I would say just because I was in a high-school musical doesn't mean I can dance, and she would say you can't dance, and I would say that's why I was in the chorus.

I blinked my eyes shut until they watered. I opened them and blotted them with a tissue. I sucked in my stomach as if I were being watched, and texted: *Hey Adam. I got your number from Helen. Just wondered if you'd be interested in having a drink or something. Naomi.*

Reply dots appeared almost immediately. *Hey Naomi. Sure. I'd be up for that. What about tonight?*

I looked him up on Facebook. Four mutual friends. It was hard to tell what he looked like. He had sunglasses and a hat on in his profile pic. Sunglasses and a hat on top of a mountain somewhere. A good Jewish boy on top of a mountain. I replied because I didn't know what else to do.

OK. Can do. Where are you thinking?

Do you know Bella Bar on Chapel? 7 pm?

Sounds good. See you then.

Distinguishing features?

Brown hair. Jewy nose.

13

I regretted sending that immediately, but before I could figure out if there was a way to possibly unsend it, there appeared a new message from Whatshisname. *Ha ha. See you at 7.*

I'd had half an hour to go home after work and change, though I'd left my jeans on as they hugged my bum nicely. I opted for a tight black T-shirt with a scooped neck pulled directly from the laundry basket and a red lip. I got to the bar first, which made me feel stupid, so I panicked and went to the 7-Eleven a few doors down. The fluorescent lights made me feel uneasy and ugly. I perused the aisles, pausing at the tampons. My period was due soon. Maybe I'd buy some. I settled on gum instead because it was directly in front of me when I circled back to the counter.

'Good flavour,' said the cashier, as I pushed the gum towards him. I gave a polite smile, which I instantly regretted, and inserted my credit card. 'I like your hair,' he continued.

The automatic doors opened. I surged through and almost straight into a group of women loudly banging along the footpath. I trailed at their rear in a cloud of candy-wrapper perfume until I was back in the bar.

I looked around. He still wasn't there. I sat at the bar and ordered a pinot noir from a tanned bartender with hefty biceps. He winked and said 'bella' and I couldn't tell if he was using the word as a noun or an adjective, or if it was for me or just a signature greeting given the name of the bar.

My stomach made a noise that I couldn't really hear over the loud music, but I could feel. I regretted buying the gum and not a bag of chips.

Then Whatshisname walked in. His eyes darted around and fixed themselves steadily on me. I waved timidly. He came over and rushed in for a cheek-kiss but overreached and faintly kissed my ear and a bunch of hair. He then proceeded to tell me that my nose wasn't as Jewy as he'd been expecting. I laughed and told him that his nose was more Jewy than I was expecting, and then he said, 'You're funny,' and I uncrossed and recrossed my legs while he fumbled for a coat hook under the bar. 'What are you drinking?' He put his nose in my wine. 'Hang on, I'll see if I can sniff it out with my, ahem, large schnoz. Hm.' He flared his nostrils. There was something obscene about it, and about him, but it didn't stop me from having the thought that I could grow to like it. 'Cab sav?'

'Pinot.'

'Shit! My schnoz failed me. Okay. I'll have one too.' He tapped the bar as if it was his and then his eyes were on me but also everywhere else, as if in search of someone he might recognise.

He told me he worked for one of the big banks in a role I couldn't name even if I was asked moments after he'd told me. I nodded and smiled, deciding I'd invest more in his job description should the date progress to something further. Then he said, 'I've heard you're really creative.'

I wondered what my mother had told Helen, and what Helen had told him. Earlier in the week, when my mother had dictated Whatshisname's number to me over the phone, she had told me not to be negative. 'Don't be negative,' Mum had said over the noise of the waste disposal. 'I think you'll like Whatshisname. He's very nice. Good fun.'

'Good fun?'

'You know. Easygoing. A real laugh. That's what Helen said.'

'Sure. Has Helen dated him?'

'Don't be ridiculous. Call him.'

'Call him? I'm not going to call him.'

'Naomi. Seriously.' Mum sucked her teeth. 'He sounds great on paper.'

'On paper. What paper?'

'I don't know what you're waiting for. What are you waiting for?' I resented her insinuation that it was somehow my fault that I was still single, that I purposefully hadn't met someone, and that this perceived personal failure was an attack on her.

Whatshisname was looking at me intently. I didn't know what to say. It was hard not to feel that his comment was a kind of slur. I'd known boys like him my whole life. He'd gone to university, got a job and stuck with the same group of boys from school. Generally speaking, I dreaded parties or social gatherings where the cool boys from high school would appear. They never gave me much, maybe a smile, while checking me out and wondering whether since seeing me last they'd consider fucking me, or not.

'Did Helen say that I was creative?' I asked.

'Helen's awesome.'

'I don't really know her. She's a bit gossipy, isn't she?' I probed at the back of my head and pulled at a knot until the hair snapped.

'Ha.' He sat up straight. 'Never thought about it.'

He ordered more wine for the two of us, tried to ascertain which people we had in common and how closely or distantly related we were likely to be, and then told me about all the countries he'd visited. He showed me some photos on his phone, which reminded me of his Facebook picture.

I had to piss and look in the mirror. I felt off-balance getting to the bathroom. After that second glass I really needed to eat but I didn't feel I could articulate my need for food, even though the date had been for seven pm and, surely, he hadn't had time to have dinner. I sank onto the cold toilet and I started giggling to myself at something he'd said. About on his travels ordering pancakes and getting chicken feet and eating them anyway. I wasn't sure which part of the story I'd found funny, if any of it, or whether I was simply giddy with a sense of helplessness for what might follow. I checked myself in the mirror and noticed my lips, plum-stained. I pressed them hard on a swab of toilet paper, but the stain was still there.

When I got back, he had his jacket on and said he lived close. He reached for my hand and I followed him out into the night. The man in the 7-Eleven watched us go by.

People watching

I knew I looked hungover because Josh said to me, 'Big night?' and I blushed and touched my finger to my lips, which were still a little purple from the wine, or bruising, I couldn't be sure.

'Hot date?' Josh asked again, trying to get my attention.

'No!' I said, and tucked my hair behind my ears. 'Not really.'

'Not really?'

'Hey, I can't seem to find the candle images,' I said.

'Oh sorry, I must have moved them to another folder.' Josh walked over to my desk and leaned over my shoulder, all long legs and arms, grabbing the mouse and clicking through the folders. I caught a glimpse of him in my peripheral vision, a look of fixed concentration. Anyone else fumbling around on my computer would have been infuriating, but I forgave Josh a lot of things. I liked him. He was a good boss. Or maybe it was the hair. Josh had floppy brown hair that was neither cool nor uncool, but it worked.

His arm was touching mine, and I felt panicked that he could smell sex and disappointment.

'Here. They're on your desktop.' Thumbnails of ornamental Iraqi candle holders appeared on the screen. It was a new acquisition for which we were trying to raise funds.

'Sorry. I must have moved them out by mistake.'

'All good.' He dragged them back into the shared drive. 'I read your intro. It's good, but can we throw in a reference to the Babylonian stuff?'

'Yes. Sorry. I was going to do that.'

'You need to stop saying sorry, Naomi.' Josh moved back to his desk and sighed into his phone. And then he sighed again.

'Everything okay?' I asked as I stared at the screen, reordering the candle images in date order.

'Yeah. Kimiko can't pick the kids up tonight. And I'm meeting with Adele at five.' Adele was the museum's director.

I turned to him. 'Can you cancel?'

'I really don't want to. Kimiko's checking with our babysitter ...' He tapered off, looking at his phone. Then he looked up at me, as if he was using my face to process information.

'What?' I asked.

'Nothing.' He continued to stare.

'Can I help at all?'

He blinked twice and then said, 'Nah, nah. I can't ask you to do that.'

'I like kids.' I wasn't quite sure why I said that. I always imagined I would have kids, but my attitude to other people's children was at best curiosity, at worst indifference and irritation.

'Really? Okay, well, can I let you know?'

I swallowed some air and repressed the urge to burp. 'Sure. I mean, whatever.'

The afternoon passed slowly. I was cutting and pasting from a previous grant application and my enthusiasm for the Iraqi candle holders was waning. *The acquisition of these unique Sephardic artefacts would be a coup for the museum, dedicated to representing all aspects of Jewish …*

I flicked over to a proposal I had been working on, a retrospective of an obscure Jewish photographer from Vienna, Paula Hohenberg. She and her family had fled far and wide before the war, but she returned to Vienna in 1955, alone, and began photographing Austrians going about their daily life; sitting in cafes, eating strudel, wiping their mouths. She took a series of self-portraits in a bathroom mirror, wavy hair that might have been black or brown or auburn. Two years later, in 1957, she obtained a gun and shot herself in the head in that same bathroom. (Strangely enough, Diane Arbus had also killed herself, not that that had been the thing to entice me to either photographer.) Paula's negatives and photographs were discovered in her apartment by her surviving brother, who had ended up in Melbourne. He brought them home with him and subsequently bequeathed them to the museum in his will, along with a copy of her passport, stamped with a large red *J*, some correspondence between them and her death certificate. In an accompanying statement he wrote that he'd never intended to return to Vienna after the war, that Paula's suicide had forced an 'unwanted reckoning'.

On my first week at the museum, I had been given a long list of potential exhibition ideas left by the last curator. On the last page of this extensive document I saw Paula's name, an afterthought perhaps. Curious, I tracked down her photos in the collection storeroom and was struck by their beauty. Streets of a city rendered in black and white, no longer inhabited by people she knew.

I thought I could soft pitch this proposal to Josh and see what he would say before taking it further to the museum director. It would be a battle. No one had heard of Paula. I'd only managed to find her in the footnotes of a post-war photography book. And yet, her pictures were undeniable, arresting. And perhaps coupled with a story about the family, her brother who had sought refuge here in Melbourne, there might be enough of a hook for us to mount a small exhibition in our minor gallery space.

I lingered over one of the self-portraits I had scanned onto my desktop. Paula was looking through the mirror, directly at the camera, directly at her audience, directly at me. She might have been smiling or grimacing. It was hard to say. A strip of shadow fell across her forehead. It felt deliberate. I wanted to say something about it, but I wasn't sure what.

I closed the proposal and got up to stretch my legs down the stairs and through the permanent gallery space. Quiet as usual. A volunteer guide was drifting in and out of sleep, seated in a corner hunched over a clipboard. I stopped in front of a painting donated by my parents. It was entitled 'Hope' and was by a local Jewish artist who had painted a field, wild grass and in the distance a man and a woman dancing and rejoicing. The inscription beneath it read, *In loving memory of Mark, Henrietta and Marta Kalman. May their memories be a blessing.* Cookie's parents and sister.

Marilyn tapped me on the shoulder, startling me. 'There's cake in the kitchen,' she whispered.

'Why are you whispering?'

She pointed at the volunteer guide and told me that she hated waking them up. It was her job to train the guides, but also her job to keep them happy. The guide opened one eye and beckoned Marilyn over. I could hear her telling him there was cake in the kitchen.

I returned to my desk to find a missed call from my mother and a follow-up text: *How was the 'date'???*

Mum had a habit of putting things in quotation marks when she was trying to intimate nonchalance. It wasn't that she couldn't understand the ways of young people, she'd just, from what I could understand, never really dated. Mum and Dad had been together forever, apart from a brief separation in 1994 when Dad moved out, only to return a month later as quietly as he'd left. My mother cried for four weeks. She cried brushing her teeth. She cried pouring cereal. She cried when I started doing my homework and she cried when I finished. I distinctly remember hating my sister all through that period because she was always on the landline speaking to friends from high school, and for all I knew Dad was trying to ring to speak to me. Though I have no evidence to say whether he ever rang or not. When he came back, my mother stopped crying and never spoke of it again, and so I knew never to speak of it either.

Separation aside, my parents experienced similar childhoods of Australian sunshine and dark bread, and darker nights where, once in bed, grown-ups would speak in heavy sweated tongues about the things they didn't want their children to know. They were both only children. Though my father did have a sibling – a brother called Samuel – who died in a displaced persons camp before Dad was born. My father said his mother was extremely strict with him, whereas my mother said he'd been coddled.

My parents met at a Jewish club on the grounds of Melbourne University. My father was studying law and my mother arts. They married just after turning twenty-two and went honeymooning in Israel, visiting distant cousins. They returned and my mother was already pregnant with Melanie. Five years later they had me, and when I'd ask why there was such a gap between us my mother replied that life was easier with one child. She hadn't said this to hurt me (though it did).

When Melanie turned three, my father took six months off work and they drove around Australia. Imagine that! And when Melanie began kinder my mother said she felt liberated. She could read and work. She could sleep long enough to dream. So I had been an accident, I deduced. 'No,' she'd told me, definitively. 'We knew what it was to be only children. It's lonely. Neither of us wanted that for your sister.' And yet, growing up, I often felt so alone. And I hated it. Again and again I would question whether there was some seismic event I'd forgotten about that had made my sister so acrimonious towards me, as if I should be able to pinpoint the very bubble that I had burst. Perhaps it was simply my arrival into the world from between my mother's legs. As small children, we only seemed to exist in parallel. If I went to sit next to Melanie at dinner, she would scowl and tell me that Jane was sitting there already (Jane was an imaginary friend who only ever seemed to make an appearance when I was around). Mum never liked to acknowledge our dysfunctional relationship. When I would raise the subject, she'd feign ignorance, saying, 'I don't know. I was never lucky enough to have a sibling.'

As a baby, I had a weak cry and a strong latch; my sister, the opposite. I grew up in my mother's skirts and Melanie hated me for it. She and my father were closer, I think because he quietly respected her resilience and independence. He said if they had dropped Melanie on her head she would have bounced, whereas they knew to never let go of me in the first place.

My name meant 'pleasantness' in Hebrew, and my mother said she liked the sound of that; a pleasant child. When I was in a mood in my teenage years my parents would remind me of this. My middle name was Marta after my grandmother's sister. I was never told much about her – only that Jews didn't name their children after the living. As well as my name, pretty much everything I had my parents had given me. My house, my car, my computer, even my underwear. When I'd started developing, Mum told me, 'Bras from Target won't be any good for breasts like those.' My museum salary covered everything else. Gemma and I split the bills and Gemma paid me a nominal amount of rent, though I didn't need it and felt guilty taking it. I was embarrassed by my parents' success and had always been convinced that people wouldn't like me because of it. Gemma sometimes called me Princess, and even though this was said with affection I overcompensated by paying bills outright without telling her.

I had always wanted to live north of the city, but when, a couple of years earlier, my parents had offered to buy me something I knew it was on the condition that nobody would be required to cross the Yarra. They'd found me a two-bedroom house within view of the old St Kilda Cemetery on Alma Road. My parents wanted to do the same for my sister, though Melanie refused the offer, which I thought was silly and had hurt my parents deeply. At the time, Melanie had been married, so it's possible that it was her husband who hadn't wanted the help. I didn't know. Like most things, we'd never discussed it.

At first, I thought the cemetery might cause me some disturbance. I had always been prone to bad dreams, 'the terrors' as Mum used to call them. These were mostly about my mother dying, or my father, or both of them together, or me. I still had these dreams, also, more recently, nightmares involving hungry sex with repulsive scabby individuals, Nazis, from which I would wake incredibly horny and deeply ashamed.

It turned out I enjoyed the cemetery. At the entrance was a small Jewish section, and it was always fascinating to see the same names there as people I'd been to school with. I never tired of reading the gravestones – many so old that no one was remembering them. Many so old that they had devolved into disrepair. Sometimes I'd pick flowers on the way through and lay them at the long-forgotten graves of babies and children.

'So, you said you were free tonight?' Josh swerved around in his desk chair. For a moment I felt strangely excited and then he said, 'And that you might be able to look after the kids?'

'Oh,' I said, and then forced a cough. 'Yeah. Sure. Okay.'

'You don't seem too sure.'

'I'm sure. Seriously, I can handle it.'

'I know you can handle it. I just. Feel bad.'

'Don't. No. It's okay.' The third button down on his shirt had come undone and some coiled hair was poking through. I thought to say something but didn't.

'They're super easy. And a friend is going to pick them up from the school so all you have to do is go to the house. You can dump them in front of the TV, they'll fall into a coma. It's super easy.'

'You said that.'

He tapped his foot against one of the wheels of his chair. 'Are you sure?'

'Yes. Yeah. I'm sure.' I glanced down at the chipped polish on my index finger, which before last night had looked great until Whatshisname had bewilderingly scraped it off with his teeth. I looked back at Josh. 'Like, when are you thinking?'

'Uh … like now?'

'Now?' I half turned back to my computer and the grant application.

'You can finish that next week. I still need to do a budget for it anyway.'

'Oh. Okay.'

'I've texted you the address.'

'Cool,' I said, grabbing my bag. 'What are their names again?'

'Ava and Ollie. Ava's three, but a mature three. Ollie's five. Like I said. Super easy. And I'm buying you a huge bottle of wine.'

'A huge bottle of wine?'

'Yes. Huge. I'm gonna rush to get home. I'll be there by six. I promise.'

'Okay.'

'You're a lifesaver, Nay.'

He'd never called me Nay before.

*

I had been curious about how Josh lived, though I hadn't imagined ever stepping foot in his house. Maybe just to drop something off. Something work-related. Or to pick him up on the way somewhere, though I couldn't really imagine that either. I'd seen him a handful of times in the local shopping strip. I'd never said hello and neither had he.

There was a gunmetal-grey picket fence and a creaky wooden gate, which I pushed open and promptly shut behind me. I didn't want to be responsible for letting anything out, or in. A scooter straddled the path and little shoes lined the verandah. A deflated balloon was sticky taped under the doorbell – limp remnants from a birthday party. Above the doorbell was a faded handwritten sign, *Do not ring bell. Please knock. Baby sleeping!* I knocked. There was no answer. I checked the address he'd given me and walked back out to see the house number again. I went back and knocked again and waited. I pressed my ear to the door, listening for signs of life. After another minute, I shut my eyes tightly and pressed the doorbell.

Now I could hear footsteps. The door opened and I braced myself to be reprimanded. A woman with thick frizzy hair – not Kimiko – opened the door, her bag already over her shoulder. 'Naomi?' I nodded. 'Tom, we're going!' she yelled down the hallway. She turned back to me, blowing hair from her face. 'I'm a friend from the school. So, the kids are watching telly. Only ABC Kids, I'm told.' I nodded obediently. 'Tom!' the

28

woman yelled again. A boy stormed towards the door. 'Get your shoes. Where are your shoes?' The woman shook her head and momentarily smiled at me. 'Come inside.'

I followed her down the hallway. I got a glimpse of a bedroom to the right. Large bed. Unmade. Further down, a family bathroom and a children's bedroom with bunk beds. I came to the kitchen, which overlooked an open-plan living space with large glass doors facing onto a backyard with a trampoline, more scooters, gumboots. I couldn't quite picture Josh in gumboots, but maybe they were Kimiko's.

'Guys,' the woman announced to the back of the couch. 'This is Naomi.' She bent down and breathlessly jammed her son's feet into runners. 'So, do you babysit in the area?'

'Oh, no. I'm— I'm Josh's colleague. At the museum. I'm just doing him a favour.'

'Oh, yeah. Nice favour! Kimiko said something about that. Sorry I can't stay. But Fridays are basketball days. Anyway. Okay. We're going. Help yourself to whatever. Josh and Kimiko are super chilled. Oh, of course, you know them. Okay. Bye, Ava! Bye, Ollie!' I watched the woman and her son close the front door with a jerk.

I turned to the children. Ava had her thumb in her mouth and was fondling a well-loved colourless rag. Ollie picked his nose and ate his snot. They were irrefutably good-looking with dark brown wavy hair and large eyes.

It felt weird being in the same space as the children and not saying hello, even though my natural instinct was to ignore them completely and it seemed so was theirs. So I said hello in an unintentionally sing-songy way, but they took no notice of me and I slunk over to the kitchen happy to be rejected and ran my hand over the marble island bench. I opened the pantry and poked my head in. There was good olive oil, organic soba noodles, wholemeal pasta and an abundance of fresh fruit. No half-eaten packets of crackers like at home, which I would forget about and so buy another packet exactly the same. Here, everything had its place. Glass jars full of oats, flours, quinoa and rice. Containers for crackers and biscuits. One drawer for condiments and another for spices. Suddenly I really did start to feel hungover from the night before. I reached for a square tin and opened it. Home-made muesli bars? It made me wonder what sort of mother I'd be.

I self-consciously sat on a stool and ate one of the muesli bars quietly. It was delicious. I didn't want the kids to see me eating. I wasn't sure what they'd report back to Kimiko.

Kimiko had moved to Melbourne from Kyoto as a child, or something. Josh had mentioned it a couple of times but I couldn't quite remember. When I'd first met her (and I'm ashamed to admit it) I was overcome with envy. It wasn't just that Kimiko was pretty – her short black hair cradling her face like a hug – it was that she was all the things I felt I could never be: I would never have a delightful gap between my two front teeth (braces had corrected that); I would never speak a second language so effortlessly (thirteen years of Jewish education had resulted in an ability to read Hebrew prayer but understand little of it); and I'd never marry Josh (and probably not even a Josh type), who was kind, intelligent, handsome and Jewish. I had always assumed that I'd end up with someone Jewish. Mum said I wasn't trying hard enough, though I wasn't quite sure how to try any harder at something like that.

My parents never said to me 'don't marry out'. Not in any direct way. But once I was born they made the decision to raise us in a consciously Jewish environment; attending Jewish schools, making Jewish friends, learning Hebrew (a language that neither of my parents understood, though my father was proficient at colloquial Hungarian, and my mother high-school French), understanding Jewish practices and values, and therefore I was left to interpret these values as ones I would inherit and pass on. When I asked her why she wanted to raise us this way, when her own mother ate bacon more regularly than she hosted Shabbat, she said she wanted to give us everything. What did she mean by everything? Financial stability – yes, but more so a cultural and religious framework to hold dear, lest some unforeseen natural disaster or genocide occur and then everything else is suddenly gone.

My parents were lower-case liberal, upper-case Labor voters, who applauded multiculturalism and more than once a year used the phrase 'melting pot'. In terms of intermarriage, I'd never forgotten a story they had told me once, of a distant cousin who they invited every few years to Jewish New Year (out of pity), who I found both repulsive and terrifying. This cousin had fallen in love with a non-Jew. Her parents – both Auschwitz survivors – had not only threatened to disown her, they were prepared to recite Kaddish for her, metaphorically burying her, turning her to ash. Their survival hadn't lessened their faith; rather, solidified it. They were unbreakable. Not only did the marriage never go ahead, she never married anyone else, bore no children, and instead cared for her parents until they died (they both lived past a hundred), and had remained in their house ever since. 'Such a sad, sad story,' my mother had said.

'Yes,' my father agreed. 'Especially since all they'd been through.'

I had always held on to this story about the cousin, and my parents' response to it, as evidence of their unwavering love for me. That no matter what I did, or who I loved, they would hold me and not let go.

Now here I was, in Josh's house, and somehow his marriage to Kimiko inadvertently felt like a personal rejection. Kimiko and I had met each other a few times, though at work events we'd barely acknowledged one another. It was not out of malice – just shyness on my part and, well, I couldn't speak for Kimiko. I figured Kimiko didn't remember me.

Suddenly, the girl spoke. 'I want. I want …' I hovered back over to the couch, fishing out an oat and a cranberry stuck in the back of my teeth.

'Can I get you something to eat?' I offered. 'A muesli bar, maybe?'

'We're not allowed those after school,' the boy reprimanded.

'Okay, maybe some fruit?'

'Oh yuck, Ava!' The boy sprang up. 'She's peed on the couch.' He grumpily moved to a single chair and resumed watching TV, his look of disgust reverting to nothingness.

I looked over at the small child who was sitting in a dark wet patch. She didn't seem at all bothered by it. 'Oh. Okay. No problem. I'll just—'

I made my way to the bathroom and saw a pink hooded towel. I grabbed it and another towel and brought them back to the girl. 'Okay, Ava. Stand up.' She obediently did as she was told, and I peeled the wet pants and undies off her. I wrapped her in the towel and lay the other towel on the couch. I felt a great sense of achievement. Maybe I would make a good mother after all.

I picked up the wet clothes and made my way down the hall, looking for a laundry or a washing basket. I poked my head inside the master bedroom. Two pairs of Ugg boots next to a disused fireplace. A pile of books on one side of the bed and reading glasses on top. On the other side, an empty glass. A photograph of the four of them in the snow – the children barely visible beneath their ski gear. I heard the lock turn in the front door.

'Hey!' Josh sang out. He walked past his bedroom. 'Oh, hi,' he said, smiling and taking off his shoes without undoing the laces. I couldn't help but look beyond him to see if Kimiko was with him. She wasn't.

'Hi. Sorry. Ava wet herself. I was just looking for your washing pile.'

'Oh, shit, I'm so sorry. I should have told you that she's not fully toilet trained. Did she cry? Here, I'll take those.' He grabbed the soiled clothes and threw them in a basket to the side of the room. He had a stupidly big grin on his face. 'Other than that, no dramas?'

'No, they were easy.'

'Wow. Perfect.' He headed out of the room and I dumbly followed him. I started to ask him if it was a shoeless house but the children rushed at him, Ava half naked. He started kissing her face and patting her bottom playfully. Ava's bare legs were curled around his hip. I looked away apologetically, feeling like an imposter. Feeling that I shouldn't have been privy to such an intimate moment between father and daughter.

'Anyway, I should go,' I said.

'Oh, really? Stay for a glass of wine.'

'Oh, I—'

'If you like.'

I paused for a moment, and then said, 'Okay.'

He told the kids they could watch one more show before dinner. Ollie and Ava cheered. Apparently they weren't usually allowed to watch one more show before dinner.

'Now,' he said. 'What was I saying?' Josh had his head in the fridge.

'I'm not sure,' I said, sitting up at the bench.

He put some hard yellow cheese on a chopping board,

along with some crackers from the pantry. 'Thanks so much for this. Seriously. And sorry about Ava's little accident.'

'Don't be silly. All good.'

'Now,' he smiled like we were friends, 'red, white or pink?'

'Um. Whatever's open.'

'Nothing's open.'

'Whatever you want.'

'I want ...' He tapped the bench. One. Two. Three times. 'I want red.'

We sat side by side on the stools and he told me about the meeting with Adele. He was busy putting together a pitch to bring a small retrospective of Modigliani paintings to the museum, which was well beyond the museum's budget and probably never going to happen. 'But,' he said, with strong emphasis, 'the National Gallery have three Modiglianis, so they could potentially loan us at least one from their collection. It's got great partnership potential.'

I wondered whether Kimiko would be getting home soon. 'Sure. It's ambitious,' I said, 'but it would attract a large audience.'

'Exactly,' he said.

'I'd love the chance to work on it.'

'That goes without saying.' He pulled at his stubble.

'I didn't know you liked skiing,' I said through a sip of wine.

'Skiing? What? Geez, you're random sometimes.'

'Am I?'

'Yeah.'

I felt hot and ran my hands through my hair. 'No, just the photo next to your bed. Sorry, I was being nosy.'

'Oh, that. Yeah. The skiing's amazing in Japan.' He clinked his wedding ring on the side of his glass. He started telling me about the ski trip, but I was only half listening, looking around, wondering how a person living in the same city as me, in the same job as me, could come to have all of this and know what to do with it – not just the kids or the house, but the utensils, the artwork, the locks on the doors.

I wondered if this was my opportunity to tell him about Paula Hohenberg, here, in his kitchen. I was about to but my phone started ringing. And then I remembered Cookie and David. It was 6.40 already, and I'd totally forgotten about taking them for dinner.

'Oh. Shit.'

Josh watched as I turned and scrambled for my phone in my bag on the floor. I answered it without turning back around, staring into the wall.

'Where are you? We're waiting in reception for you.' Cookie was mad.

'Sorry, Cookie,' I murmured.

'What!?'

'I'll be there in ten minutes,' I blurted, louder this time.

'Ten minutes! Why?'

'I got held up at work. I'm on my way.' I fingered a tiny spot in the wall where the paint was chipped.

'Fine.'

I ended the call and turned around. Josh was smiling at me. 'I'm so sorry. I completely forgot I'm taking my grandparents out for dinner tonight.'

'Oh. Oops. Sounds like you're in trouble.'

'My grandmother's going to kill me.'

'Nah. You're a good girl.'

I thanked Josh for the wine, and mouthed a small bye to the children, who didn't look back. He walked me to the door.

'Thanks again. You're a lifesaver.' He hugged me then. Possibly our first hug. It felt strange but nice. Like approval from a big brother. Or a friend's big brother who you might have a bit of a crush on. Josh stayed on the porch while I got in the car, and when I started the engine I looked up and he was waving at me. I waved back and drove off.

Cookie was waiting with arms crossed, though David seemed pleased to see me. She was wearing one cardigan on top of another, each with large pearly buttons competing for attention. I had forgotten how to collapse Cookie's walker so I jammed it in until the boot of my car clicked shut. The rubber handle squeaked against the rear window for the entire journey to the restaurant. Cookie was terse and cleared her throat deliberately from time to time. It was too hard for David to hear in the back seat, so no one spoke.

We were the first customers at the Chinese restaurant and were seated on display in the window, right next to the fish tank.

I was relieved to not have to talk about work. They rarely asked me anything about it anyway. For whatever reason, Cookie found it extremely perplexing that I worked in a Jewish museum. When I had explained that the very mission of the museum was to celebrate Jewish culture and tradition, she questioned why a culture needed to draw attention to itself, that no good ever came of that. Wasn't it enough that we just were? Why did we need to bang on about it.

David pushed the spring rolls towards me. 'Try one. They're very good.'

'That's okay, David.' I scrunched my face involuntarily. 'They've got meat in them.'

'Not really,' retorted Cookie.

'Yes, really. They've got pork.'

'You call that pork? They're delicious.' Cookie wiped her mouth with the serviette leaving an oily bright pink blotch of lipstick. 'Or are you kosher now?'

'Well, I'm basically kosher, because I don't eat meat.'

'Leave her alone, Cookie.' David laid his hand on top of Cookie's and patted it gently, as if he could smooth out the wrinkles and unseize her joints.

'I didn't say anything. I just don't want her to be hungry.' Cookie rummaged through the handbag on her lap, took out a lipstick and a little mirror, and reapplied. She thrust the lipstick towards me with unintentional aggression and told me I could use some. Cookie had a knack for unintentional aggression because the world owed her all the good things –

cheap lipstick, fried dinners, the unconditional love of a granddaughter ...

I took the lipstick, which was whittled down to a stub. 'You need a new one, Cookie.'

'What for?'

I didn't answer, opting to eat the last bit of gloopy tofu instead. My grandmother's mood had lifted with a full stomach and she now stroked the tablecloth affectionately, removing the spring roll flakes and sprinkling them back onto her plate. She began stacking the finished plates on the table while David removed cash from a black leather bag he took with him on outings. It was only 7.30 pm and that was dinner. Done. I kept thinking back to Josh and that it was Friday night and wondered what he was doing. Would he be having Shabbat? I wasn't sure how things worked in their household. I was pretty sure that Kimiko hadn't converted. I strained to think whether or not I'd spotted any Judaica in their home, but then my mind went back to their bedroom – the Ugg boots, the ensuite. I gave the hairs on the back of my hand a little tug. I checked my phone to distract my fingers. There was a text from Whatshisname: *Thanks for last night. Xx.*

On the way home Cookie asked me to drive slowly. 'I like to watch the people out and about,' she explained. At a red light she yelled, 'Look at that one!' referring to a young woman in a very short dress and high heels, waiting at the crossing. David must have heard her because he suggested that we offer to pick up the woman and drive her home.

'She'll be right,' I said, yawning. The light turned green and I hit the accelerator.

I lay on top of my bed with my shoes still on and began scrolling through a celebrity's Instagram feed, fighting the urge to head to my favourite website full of clothes I couldn't afford. Gemma knocked on my door gently and opened it.

We had met studying arts at uni. Initially I was enrolled in arts/law, but after first semester I realised I didn't have the same competitive drive as the others, and was much more at home in the arts faculty where I would meet Gemma. Gemma now worked in marketing at a digital agency and loved it. She was a head taller than me, and though we looked nothing alike, the volume of our hair was similar in texture and weight and sometimes we were asked if we were sisters. At uni, I was drawn to Gemma because of her deep voice, which I found both commanding and reassuring, in the same way one might feel about a newsreader. It suggested that even though we were the same age, she knew far more about the world than me and I would be wise to follow her lead. And so I did, allowing her to advise me on what to wear, what music to listen to and who to kiss. When Gemma wasn't around, I would try to imitate the way she interacted with people, shifting my voice to a lower tone, making deliberate eye contact, jutting out my chin. The first time we spoke, she was sitting next to me in an ethics class. I knew I could no longer be in this class without saying something about the lecturer, who had a habit of shifting whatever was between his legs. After I said it, she squeezed my forearm that was draped over my notebook, looked at me with an expression of incredulous agreement and mouthed *I know*. We quickly learned that we found the same things funny, and could pivot seamlessly between discussions about Judith Butler and gender theory to *Buffy the Vampire Slayer* fan fiction to the mystifyingly bad hairstyles of the entire cast of *The OC* in seasons one and two. She'd surprised me when she'd told me she was into women because I'd never met a lesbian before. I think this was partly due to the fact that I'd finished high school in 1999 and coming out then was rarely worth the social sabotage. She always had women around, sometimes men too, though not to sleep with. She just enjoyed flirting, and the attention even more.

'We should go out,' Gemma said. Gemma often went out at night with the people she worked with. She would invite me, but I would decline or make up an excuse because I wasn't crazy about the people she worked with.

'I've already been out.'

'Dinner with your grandparents doesn't count. Anyway, I've just landed a big fuck-off client and celebrations are in order.'

'You're very impressive,' I said.

'I know,' she said, pinching itinerant hairs near her ankles. 'What about you? Is Joshy grooming you to become the senior curator, so he can bump off the all-powerful director?' I thought about telling Gemma about the whole interaction at

Josh's house but decided against it. There was nothing to tell anyway, and Gemma would only ask questions that I couldn't answer. I knew Gemma would much prefer an anecdote about Whatshisname's black leather couch and framed autographed footy posters.

Gemma had grown up in Bendigo and only moved to the city for uni. Maybe once a month I would bring Gemma along to a Shabbat dinner at my parents' place. My family wasn't religious. We were cultural Jews, 'prawn cocktail Jews' (my mother's little joke), who didn't talk about God and still had Shabbat dinner each week and said prayers by rote without thinking about what they meant. Even though my parents rarely attended, they still paid their membership fees to the local Reform synagogue, which ensured recognition on special occasions and my father a High Holy Day ticket for Yom Kippur, where he would pray, fast doggedly, and then return to his position of religious ambivalence the following day. But when Gemma had first come for Shabbat, I lamented my family not being more observant, because if they were the Shabbat would have been more of a spectacle. I wished my parents had more clutter – more tchotchkes – and didn't live so tastefully. Cookie made up for it though, telling Gemma that she was insulting us by not eating enough. Gemma had smiled gleefully at that and spooned more potatoes and sweetened carrots onto her plate.

'Come on, Princess. Get up.' She threw a pillow at my head.

'Do I need to change?' I asked her.

'Just put on some lippie and you'll be sweet.' She winked, pulling me upright.

At the venue we ordered gin and tonics. I rested my back against the cool soft edge of the bar and surveyed the scene. A guy whose lack of hair made it hard to distinguish an age range glanced at me and smiled. I smiled back momentarily, turned to Gemma and asked when the band would start. When I looked back, Bald Guy was still staring at me. Gemma waved to someone she knew and we moved towards a group sitting in a booth.

After another drink Bald Guy was still hanging around and came up to speak to me. His name was Dave or Gabe or Craig. We chatted and sort of danced (but more like swayed) as we spoke, the third gin and tonic helping me move and nod my head with conviction. At some point Gemma moved past me, squeezing my shoulders as she floated by, mouthing *go for it, he's hot* or something to that effect.

I followed Bald Guy into the alleyway and smoked a bit of his cigarette. It was a warm night and the smells from the alleyway were vivid and rising up from the bluestone. He asked if he could kiss me and I said he could. He softly bit at my bottom lip and sucked it with his mouth. It was nice at first but the sucking quickly escalated. I felt as though I was being pulled underwater with the forcefulness of his tongue. I wondered whether it was something I could grow to like. He asked if I would go back to his place and I said 'okay'.

I went inside to find Gemma and tell her, but when I went back outside he was gone, the alleyway empty like the tide had come in and washed everyone away.

I left Gemma at the bar and caught a taxi. She pouted when I told her I was leaving but the lure of the night kept her there just as the lure of my bed brought me home. I had no trouble falling asleep but woke up at 12.30. Gemma still wasn't home.

Gemma and I had been sharing my bed. It began when the air conditioner stopped working in Gemma's room and I felt guilty and offered her the use of the left side. Neither of us said it out loud, but we both found it comforting. Me especially. And maybe that's why I hadn't rushed to sort out the air conditioning, even though I had mentioned it to Dad and he'd promptly texted me the number of his guy. Now, when Gemma stayed out late, I found I couldn't sleep without her, anticipating the front door waking me up when she returned.

I reached for my phone and found a text from Josh: *Hey. Thanks for babysitting.*

I sat up and thought for a while what to reply, before writing: *No worries.*

He replied instantaneously: *Also your face at that programming committee. I'm still laughing.*

I thought of him in his own bed with the lights out, glued to his phone while Kimiko slept beside him. I smiled: *What about my face?*

I'm not telling you.

Tell me. I should know if I'm doing something with my face.

You're always doing something with your face.

I thought my face game was strong.

You have a good face.

I let some time pass before I responded, and then when I thought enough time had passed I didn't know how to respond, so I left it there with me having a good face.

It was around one am when Gemma turned the key in the lock and shuffled into the house quietly. I put the bedside light on. Gemma poked her head through the door. 'Oh hey. You're up. I'm busting to pee.'

Gemma returned minutes later with her teeth brushed and nightie on. It was a black silk slip with a lacy edge and it covered barely any of her. She hopped under the covers and I felt the middle of the mattress dip slightly, causing my side to slope inward. I showed her the message exchange between Josh and I.

'Ha. I think he's into you,' mumbled Gemma, opening one eye.

'No, he isn't,' I whispered, reaching to turn off the light. I edged my pillow closer to the dip in the mattress.

'What happened to the bald guy?'

'Good question.'

Gemma murmured something indecipherable, yawned and drifted to sleep.

Samsonite

'So where are you going anyway?' Mum asked, her head in the cupboard under the stairs.

'Geelong.'

'Geelong?' she repeated. 'What's in Geelong? Will this do?' she said, dragging out a medium-sized black Samsonite.

'A conference. Yeah. That looks good.'

'But you're only going for three days.'

'And?'

'This suitcase is too big.' Mum shook her head. 'It'll be warm. What are you going to take? A couple of dresses. Thongs.'

'It'll be air-conditioned.'

'Even so.' Mum had her head back in the cupboard.

'I'm not going to be wearing thongs at the conference.'

'Are you presenting?'

'No, Josh is doing the presentation.' I felt for my phone in my pocket, thought of the text exchanges between us, which over the last few weeks had become a nightly occurrence. I don't know why standing there with my mother I had the

46

sudden urge to delete the message thread. But what or who for? The messages were innocuous, hardly flirtatious, standard colleague banter.

'Oh,' Mum said, unable to hide her disappointment, as if she was remembering what a good speechmaker I had been at high school and thinking how all my talent was going to waste. She couldn't accept that, like most high-school extroverts, I was fast becoming a twenty-something introvert. 'Do you have sandals? Come and look at mine.'

I followed her to the bedroom and lay down on her bed. I could hear Classic FM playing in the study, which meant Dad was home and probably head-deep in the Sunday papers. I let my eyes close and began wondering how much money my parents had spent to have a bed that was so comfortable. Mum emerged from the walk-in wardrobe with three pairs of sandals. 'Get under the covers if you like,' she said. 'You're tired.'

I inelegantly flipped myself beneath the summer-weight quilt they liked to use between the months of October and February, while she tried on each pair of sandals to demonstrate their look and versatility, saying things like 'you can wear these with blue or black jeans, or maybe that pleated skirt I bought you'. She arranged her feet in various poses and looked effortlessly elegant and stylish, which now made me unsure whether I could pull off wearing anything of hers.

People often said we looked nothing alike. Mum had olive skin, while I was creamy. We both had a lot of hair, but Mum's was curly, dark, tight and springy, and my hair was long and straight, a light brown that garnered natural blonde streaks in the summertime. A mouse in the shadow of a raven's wing. She was thin and flat-chested and always skirted around the edges of her meals, always feeding people but seemingly never eating herself. I inherited stubby feet from my father and full breasts from the paternal grandmother I never knew, which was a bit of a family joke. Mum declared often, and unprompted, that daughters look like their fathers. And Mum insisted (as if by way of offering comfort) that she herself looked nothing like her mother either. I had asked her who she looked like, if not Cookie, and she had replied that she presumed she looked like her father, though she couldn't remember him, nor were there photos of him to prove it. He was a troubled man, had left the family home when Mum was three and never returned. When I asked Cookie about him, I was met with silence. She insisted that David was all my mother had ever needed in a father figure. When I asked Mum about him, she said much the same, though I did find it curious that she only ever addressed David by his name, never Dad, Daddy, Papa.

Growing up, Mum and Cookie lived in a one-room flat and, until Cookie met David, they'd shared a bed. One morning, when my mother was five, Cookie dropped her off at a neighbour's for the day. The neighbour was an elderly Irish woman who had an aggressive ginger cat, and Mum said she spent most of the day hiding under a table counting blemishes on the tiles. She was collected in the afternoon and introduced for the first time to David, Cookie's newly appointed husband. Over the next few days, they packed what few belongings they had and moved into a slightly larger place a couple of kilometres away. And so began their life with David, who had been a kind and benevolent stepfather, a godsend, really.

Unlike me, Melanie was often heralded as the younger version of our mother. And again, Mum insisted (as if by way of offering comfort) that it was a blessing that her daughters looked nothing alike, because otherwise people would have compared us, and nothing good ever came of that. 'Anyway,' Mum had said once, 'when I was at school, kids would call me a wog and a reffo, so enjoy being as fair as you are.' Regardless, I would never have been called a wog at school. Almost everyone I'd been to school with was the same as me, descended from Ashkenazi Jews who'd arrived in this country and did what epigenetics taught them to do best – establish community institutions, synagogues, schools, museums, establish a sense of permanence with the inherent knowledge that all things, livelihood, safety, breathing, were also malleable and impermanent.

There was a pair of leopard-print Birkenstocks that Mum had worn all summer (and I had coveted), but they were absent from the pile. 'Can I try on the Birkenstocks?'

She paused. 'They're not really appropriate for a conference, darling.' She unfastened a black strappy leather sandal. I sighed and slumped back into the pillow. Mum sat down beside me and squinted her eyes, as if to bring something on my face into sharper focus. 'Do you want me to take you shopping?'

'Yeah, but I don't have time,' I said, pulling the quilt over my face. 'Where did you buy this mattress?'

'You couldn't afford it,' Mum said, patting my leg. 'What's wrong? Is it a boy?'

'No.'

'I can't hear you.' Mum yanked the quilt off me with a sudden jerk. I looked up at her, batting my eyelashes. 'That's better,' she said.

'I'll take the black strappy ones, please.'

I got up and went to the full-length mirror. Mum came up behind me and ran her hands through my hair. We really didn't look anything alike, though we did have some things in common – a pointed nose, a weakness for salt and vinegar chips, how our ankles crack the same way when we walk around the house late at night. I knew she had tried to imbue me with her confidence, but I think she feared she'd passed all of it on to Melanie, leaving me timid and wanting. I had never seen my father flirt with others, only my mother. She'd owned and ran an art gallery for many years, and I'd always found it comforting observing her at openings, surrounded by jacketed men and short-haired women. My parents had never been overtly demonstrative with their affection for one another, but I always had the sense my father was watching her, appreciating her.

'Did you get the money in your account?'

I nodded, and said, 'Yes, thanks.' My parents put money in my account once a month. They'd done so ever since I'd been at uni and Mum would always ask me whether I'd received it. I found this extremely annoying. She was always babying me while at the same time telling me to be more independent.

'Good. Go say hi to your father. Melanie's here too.'

I found Dad and Melanie seated at opposite ends of the couch in the study. I said hi from the doorway and went to sit myself in between them. Dad leaned in and said, 'All good, my darling?'

I nodded and we pecked on the mouth, and he went back to reading an article about the spending habits of millennials in the *Financial Review*. Melanie was looking at the engagement and marriage listings in the *Jewish News*. 'Anyone we know?' I asked.

Melanie turned the page without letting me see it and said, 'Did you hear about Dov Bennett?'

'Who's that?' I asked.

'Carly Bennett's older brother.'

'Terrible story,' Dad said, licking his finger and turning a page of the newspaper.

'Why? Is he dead?' I asked.

'For God's sake, Naomi,' Melanie said and sighed dramatically. 'Yes, he's dead. Diving accident in Bali. He had a two-year-old.'

'Shit. When?'

'Last week. Didn't Mum tell you?'

'No.'

'You know, I dated him in year eight.'

'Did you? I don't remember that.'

Melanie shot me a sour look. 'He was in love with me.'

'I don't remember that either,' Dad said.

Melanie's first marriage was to a Dov Bennett type. They had a huge wedding for four hundred people at the casino. I had been a bridesmaid in canary yellow – Melanie's favourite colour, which didn't flatter any of the eight women in the wedding party. All the boomers danced exuberantly, a hot wind under their skirts and pants, egged on by speeches where there was weeping and laughter. My father might as well have said, 'Look at us now, Hitler, look at this sixty-thousand-dollar wedding. Watch us dancing on your grave'. Melanie divorced after only two years, and this was not something that was often spoken about in the family, among other things, like the fact that Melanie had declared that she wasn't interested in having children. When Cookie had heard this particular revelation (Melanie was prone to revelations), she'd threatened to kill herself. But she'd also threatened the same thing when I cut my hair boy-short in year twelve. And when her favourite underwear had been discontinued.

My parents had quietly grieved the failure of Melanie's marriage and the unborn children. They knew better than to grieve it loudly, though they still had a framed photo of Melanie in her wedding dress on their bedroom wall. I was expected to grieve also, and so would vacillate between comforting my parents, consoling them with my implied fertility and desire to be partnered, and feeling resentful of the pressure that Melanie had so resolutely thrust upon me.

What my parents didn't know was that Melanie had been pregnant at the time of her divorce and had had an abortion. I knew this because I was the one who had driven her to the clinic. I could never understand why she'd asked me, of all people. Had her friends been busy that day? What happened to the seven other bridesmaids? Or did she just want someone to take her who wouldn't try to talk to her about it (or out of it)? She'd made me wait in the car and told me not to worry. And just like that, I was expected to hold the weight of her choice and my family's grief in a heavy black box in my heart.

'They had the funeral yesterday,' Melanie said. 'There's a minyan tomorrow night. I might go.'

'Should I go?' I asked.

'That would be nice,' Dad said.

'She doesn't even remember him,' Melanie said.

'Oh, shit. I can't. I'm going away.' I could smell fresh bagels in the kitchen and wanted one.

'Tell your mother to get you the black Samsonite,' Dad said, looking up briefly. 'The zip's broken on the grey one.'

Melanie stood up and flung the *Jewish News* on the coffee table. She put her sunglasses on her head and turned to me. 'Do you seriously not have your own suitcase?'

*

The next day Josh pulled up outside my house and beeped the horn. I poked my head through the shutters in the front bedroom and saw him sitting in a black Volkswagen hatchback. I made one more dash to appraise myself in the bathroom mirror – resisting the urge to redo my make-up and change outfits – before triple-checking the locks to the house. Gemma's agency had just sent her to Sydney for a month and before she'd left she'd asked me if I would be okay in her absence. 'Of course I will,' I'd told her. 'Why does everyone think I'm incapable of being on my own?'

'I don't know,' she'd said, making up her side of my bed. 'You tell me.'

I tapped on the passenger window of Josh's car and he looked up with a goofy grin. I opened the boot thinking I could find space for my suitcase between the pram, nappies, box from Ikea, packet of unopened socks. He shouted through the fort of stuff for me to chuck my bag in the back seat.

'Sorry about that,' he said as I got in. He was wearing shorts, which surprised me. I don't think I'd ever seen his naked legs before, and they were hairy. We stopped at a cafe down the road from my house. I waited in the car and after a few minutes he returned with coffees and some pastries in a bag, one in his mouth. 'Mm. So good,' he said, dusting icing sugar from his chin. 'Okay. Let's go.'

54

As he drove, he told me that he had gone to Dov Bennett's funeral. I was surprised and then wasn't surprised that he knew Dov. They were a similar age and had played for the same Jewish football club. They hadn't kept in touch but if they, say, bumped into each other in the playground with their kids, they would be pleased to see each other and would hang out at the park longer than normal.

'I feel bad. If I had known in time I could have gone to the funeral,' I said. The night before, I had clicked on a fundraising page that had been set up in Dov's name. There were photos of him with his wife and daughter dressed in football jerseys, pink-faced and happy. There were hundreds of comments. I read them all and looked for the names of people I knew. Melanie had donated $180 and written *wish you long life and peace xx*.

'Nah. It was packed,' he said.

'I would have gone to the minyan, but ...'

'You're here? With me?'

'Um ...'

'Forget about it. It's all too depressing. No one needs that. You don't need that.' He smiled at me. 'I'm planning on never dying.'

'Sounds reasonable.'

We were moving fast now, up and over the Westgate Bridge, an industrial world below, a brown river, a pink lake. Josh was sticking to the far-right lane, riding up the backs of other cars until they felt pressured enough to move aside. He used one hand to steer, cruise control on, the seat low and far back. He might have been on a deck chair. 'So tell me, Nay,' he said. 'Where do you see yourself in five years?'

'Jesus!' I laughed.

'I'm genuinely curious.' He looked over at me for long enough that it felt necessary to gesture towards the road and remind him that it was there.

'Well,' I said, looking down at the pastry in my lap. 'I guess I see myself doing your job.'

'Ha!' He slammed the wheel with the palm of his hand. 'I love that for you.'

'You do?'

'Seriously. I was hoping you'd say that.'

'So where do you see yourself?' I asked. 'Obviously not at the museum.' I prodded the jellied apricot in the pastry on my lap and watched it jiggle.

'Can you just eat that apricot already?' he asked.

'Why? Do you want it?' I picked it up in my fingers and held it out to him. He shook his head. I ate it and licked some jelly off my fingers. 'Sorry, that was gross.'

Josh laughed. 'Have you met my children? Nothing grosses me out.'

I felt pleased with myself and crossed my feet at the ankles. I thought about removing my shoes but that seemed too much. 'I actually have an exhibition idea I'd like to run by you, if that's okay.'

'That's what I'm here for.'

'Have you heard of Paula Hohenberg? Austrian-Jewish photographer. She was mentioned in that exhibition document?'

He shook his head.

'She took a great series of photos after the war. Then killed herself.'

He squinted his eyes with an all-knowing certainty. 'Sounds about right.'

'I just— For me— There's an urgency to the images. All shot in Vienna. You can't look away. There's something very powerful in her femininity. Against the harshness of this city in denial that there had been a war, that Jews had ever lived there in the first place.' He stared ahead, sped up and switched lanes again. I was certain I had said too much, and wished I hadn't used the word femininity.

After what felt like ages he said, 'Let's set up a discussion when we're back. I love that you're thinking about this stuff. But you can't let it make you too sad.'

'Oh,' I said.

'No. It's a beautiful thing. In our work. To be feeling the objects we are working with. You have that sensitivity. I can't say that I do. But again, that helps me to focus.'

I inhaled deeply and caught his scent, familiar from work but thicker here in the space of the tinted windows. 'Do you think I'm unfocused? I— I don't think I'm too sensitive.'

'You misunderstand me. It's a good thing. You pore over materials, words. It's rather endearing, actually. Me, I just blunder through.'

'Hardly. You're great at your job. Everyone says so.'

'Thanks. That means a lot. Now, I hope you like Billy Joel.' He put on the stereo and 'Only the Good Die Young' started playing. He wanted to tell me that he knew it was daggy, but he really believed Billy Joel was one of the great storytellers of our time. His earlier work anyway. I told him Billy Joel was fine, and that he was one of my dad's favourites. Josh then told me that made him feel old. I had said it knowing it would, which made me smile. And that made him laugh.

Then we spoke about what to expect at the conference, which had been paid for by a philanthropic funding body invested in furthering the development of Australian culture and diversity. He seemed excited to be presenting. I'd read his presentation the night before, expecting greatness, and it was very good but I was also somehow relieved to discover that I could have easily written it myself. At one point Kimiko rang to check whether or not he'd remembered to cancel Ollie's footy practice on the weekend, to which he replied that he had forgotten. She then asked if she was on speaker, to which he replied that she was and then she said 'hi' to me and I said 'hello' back. Before he hung up, Kimiko told him she loved him, and he said 'I love you' back.

At that moment I was grateful for the monotonous landscape of farms and gumtrees and bush and road, which I had been taking note of in order to distract myself from a nausea rising in my belly. 'Do you mind if I drive, actually? I think I'm getting a bit carsick.'

Josh pulled over on the side of the freeway. We both got out, and I sat in the driver's seat. In the rear-view mirror I could see he was taking a piss. There was no tree to go on, just dusty gravel, and his piss scorched the dirt, hot and steaming.

We arrived in Geelong at around three pm, checked into the motel, and were allocated rooms next to one another. We arranged to meet up at five pm and walk together to the conference.

The Museum of Jewish Heritage had a good reputation and people were interested to meet us. When I made a somewhat facetious comment about the two of us getting a lot of unwarranted attention, Josh looked at me earnestly and said, 'We may be a small museum but we're still well respected, you know?'

'Sorry,' I said.

'Don't be sorry. Just know you're in good company here. You can be proud.'

There were delegations from other ethno-specific museums, each of them working within the constraints of tight budgets and the previous government, conservatives who excelled at cutting financial support to cultural institutions, knowing full well that communities would fight to preserve their cultures regardless of how little funding they received.

After the opening speeches and dinner, we were invited to go for a drink at a pub within walking distance. We sat around a table beneath a large mirror. I was next to a guy called Phillipe who worked as a researcher at the Greek museum, and on the other side of me was a woman from the LGBTI archival centre. Every now and then my eye would drift to the mirror, where I intermittently found Josh looking at me and we would smile at each other. After a while I found this completely embarrassing, made worse by my lipstick that had faded in the plump area of my lips and left a rim around my mouth. I wasn't sure if this was appealing or looked tacky. I did all I could to focus on the stickiness of the table and the smoke-coloured carpet and the latest gossip about the CEO of a major museum who was renowned for his casual racism and sexually inappropriate comments. Everyone was poised for his imminent removal, though also doubted it would ever eventuate. At one point, Josh excused himself to take a phone call, probably from Kimiko, and when he returned announced his departure. I was unsure of whether to stay or go. I started to shift in my seat and Josh told me I should stay. So I did. When dancing was mentioned I felt tired and knew I couldn't drink enough to keep up with the group. Phillipe said he'd leave too and walked back to the motel with me, for which I was thankful as I truthfully didn't have the bravado to walk back alone in the heat of the night and the strangeness of the town.

Phillipe had dark hair and eyes, was of a Lebanese background and lived in Coburg. I told him how I'd once done a day's work in Coburg, on the reception desk of a stationery business, back when I used to temp. I enjoyed it there. It reminded me of a holiday I'd taken to Israel with my parents:

older men grouped around tables in hazes of cigarette smoke, drinking little cups of coffee and playing backgammon.

I liked Philippe's name and thought about kissing him as he walked me to my door, imagining what our respective families would make of our union. In the midst of this fantasy, he started doing an impression of the MC at the conference dinner and I laughed inelegantly and too loudly. At that, Josh opened his door, looked at the two of us, apologised and closed the door. Then Phillipe politely said goodnight and left.

It was a relief to be inside the motel room. Through creamy plasterboard I could hear muted sounds of what I presumed was Josh's television or computer. I had a shower and got into bed.

There was a single black hair on the adjacent pillow. I turned away from it, closed my eyes and wondered about those sounds from the room next door, not sure what I was listening to, or for.

The next morning, I went to Josh's door and knocked gently. I waited for what felt like a minute though it was probably far less, fidgeting around my floral dress for pockets but there were none. I knocked again, a little less meekly, before concluding that he either wasn't there or wasn't answering. I shrugged my shoulders to no one and walked away.

The conference room was already full of people milling around an eight-slice toaster and a push-button coffee machine. Without Josh, I felt like a hanger-on at a party and had begun to pivot out the door when I bumped into Phillipe, who was heading inside.

'Morning. Coming in?' he asked, smiling his friendly smile. I nodded in surrender and went to a circular table covered in a white cloth, while he grabbed us coffees. I began reading a leaflet detailing the day's agenda.

10 am – Museums and community
11.30 am – Morning tea
12 pm – Exhibition storytime
1 pm – Lunch
2.30pm – Mindful guiding
4pm – Rest
6pm – Keynote and dinner

Phillipe returned and peered over my shoulder. 'What do you think mindful guiding is?' he asked.

'Um,' I said, and accepted a mug of watery coffee from him. 'Like, museum meditation?'

'What's that?'

'I dunno. I made it up.'

'This coffee is tragic,' he said. I nodded. 'How did you sleep?'

'Not great,' I said, avoiding eye contact and the proposed intimacy of the question. 'But I'm not a great sleeper.'

'Oh, yeah. One of those.'

'One of those? What's that supposed to mean?'

'Bad sleeper. Inherited trauma.' He winked.

'Seriously?'

'Probably everyone in this room.'

I drank the coffee down to the last residue of dirt in the mug. 'I need more bad coffee before I can discuss intergenerational trauma.' I spotted Josh in conversation with another curator. He looked back and gave a little wave. It was already very hot outside and Josh was wearing a pale blue linen shirt and beige trousers. I could see little sweat patches had already formed under his armpits.

'I slept great,' Phillipe said, getting up. 'The bed was awesome, didn't you think?' He took my mug. 'I'll get you more bad coffee.'

Josh finished up his conversation and wandered over to me with a wry expression. 'Made a friend?'

I laughed awkwardly and shook my head. 'Where were you this morning?'

'Where was I?'

'I knocked on your door.'

'You did?'

'Is that okay?'

He half smiled and said, 'I went for a run. Next time I'll tell you. Is that okay?'

'You don't have to tell me,' I said quickly.

Josh grabbed the leaflet out of my hand. 'Oh, shit. What the fuck is mindful guiding?'

*

I didn't see much of Josh throughout the day, apart from his presentation, which was met with a very enthusiastic response. Afterwards, there were a lot of people wanting to speak to him. I saw him briefly and he gave me an adrenaline-fuelled hug, and then I left to give the mindful guiding session a go and fell asleep to a lamentation on meaning-making. At dinner I sat with Phillipe and a bunch of others from the night before, and everyone was heady and drunk. The heat of the day had settled into our skin and made the alcohol absorb faster. Josh seemed to have connected with an older crowd – which was fine. He was networking. And I was just … There.

I went back to my room, half expecting Phillipe to follow, but he didn't and I was half relieved. I turned the air conditioning to low and as I sat on the bed there was a knock at the door. At first I thought it was the rumble of the minibar, but then I heard it again and realised it was coming from outside the room.

'It's me,' Josh said in a loud whisper.

I opened the door, and his face was flushed and grinning. 'Hey. I just wanted to say hey.'

'Hey,' I said.

'Can I come in?' He floated past me, suddenly easy in my presence. He picked up my book from the bedside table, scratched his freshly curated stubble and put it down again. 'I'm a bit drunk,' he said.

'Okay.'

'And … I just smoked a joint with the Iranians and the Maltese.'

'Jesus.'

He had two bars of chocolate in his pocket that he threw on the bed. 'Kimiko always packs me chocolate. Take whatever you want. Sorry.'

'Why are you saying sorry?' I caught a glance of myself in the mirror and noticed my eyeliner had smudged in the heat. I tried to smooth it out with my forefinger.

'Because you don't want to hear about my fucking wife.'

'Um,' I said, staring at the chocolate, thinking about his wife. 'Okay …'

'Fuck!' He started laughing and sat on the bed. I didn't know what to do so I sat down next to him and he ran his hand through his floppy hair and said 'fuck' again and again and again. I started laughing too.

'You have a bad mouth,' I said. He looked at me and showed his teeth. 'Good teeth though,' I added.

He swallowed and said, 'You're always funny.'

'Funny? Okay.'

'And clever. Too clever. Do you know how clever you are?'

'Um. I don't know.'

'And fucking hot. I mean. Sorry.'

'How much did you smoke?' I looked at him and his reddened eyes and then turned away to the oatmeal carpet, the crisscrossed indents left on my feet by my mother's sandals, the Samsonite.

'I'm a lightweight. Yeah. But no. I am sorry. Really sorry. I shouldn't say that shit.'

'Probably not.' My hands were resting in my lap. I suddenly felt like a schoolgirl waiting for instruction.

'I should go,' he said, not moving. Then he opened his palm for me to take.

My first boyfriend at age seventeen told me I should be the one to choose the names for body parts. Tits was an obvious choice, cunt instead of pussy (my vagina was not a cat), and cock because my favourite author at the time used the word a lot in her writing. This was supposed to give me some sort of agency in our coupling. I thought it did, but it was only at twenty-two when I'd purchased my first vibrator that I realised I'd never had an orgasm before. I'd placed the cool metal wand on my clitoris and shuddered under the covers, alone and quite frankly in shock. And then a vague sense of betrayal, that this was a secret that my sister and my mother had kept from me. Even with this discovery, it was hard for me to be any other way around sexual partners. Their pleasure was a given and mine a chore. Gemma told me this was shitty but not unusual and this somehow validated the way I was around men: eyes open, mouth open, legs open, agreeable in almost every way. But I also hoped for some sort of reckoning, where I might understand my own desires and relinquish myself completely. Maybe with a man like this, whose sudden desire for me was palpable, desperate even, but off-limits.

I took Josh's hand. He squeezed it. One. Two. Three pulses.

'So what is this, Nay?' He leaned in, bumped his shoulder against mine. 'I mean. I'm not imagining it. There is a *this*, right?'

'Is there?' I spoke quietly, feeling my heart pumping outside of myself.

My hair was in my eyes and he parted it gently and tucked it behind my ears. Dov Bennett's family photo from the fundraising website flashed into my mind. Dov looked fit, like he had been into sports and stuck to high-protein low-carb diets. In the photo, his arm was curled around his wife's waist, clutching her knowingly. The children they'd produced together squatted perfectly in the front. Was that what a family looked like, I wondered? Was that what Josh's family looked like? Like the photo of them in the snow, in his bedroom. Maybe one day Josh would slink his arm around my waist. I looked into Josh's eyes. He kissed my cheek, a little sloppily. I greedily kissed him on the mouth and he opened it wide and took in my tongue, cupped my face in his hands and said, 'Your skin is soft. Your skin is so soft.' He climbed on top of me, the collar of his shirt tickling my neck and the chocolate bar stuck to my hip. He kissed me and kissed me again and I grabbed the back of his neck and arched my body so he could feel it all, young and fuckable. A deep and guttural noise escaped from my mouth and he groaned and rolled off me and said, 'Fuck I'm stoned.' Then he got off the bed, walked to the door without looking back, and shut it behind him.

The chocolate bars had melted underneath me but I ate them anyway. I didn't sleep at all.

Wet carrots

The door to Cookie's unit was always unlocked. To be fair, there was not much of interest to be taken. What was most valuable to her were her photos, and no one wanted those.

When I arrived, David was out and Cookie was dozing on the couch with a book in her lap: a well-thumbed whodunnit from the library. I hated waking her up, so I sat in the worn velvet armchair opposite my grandmother, watching the rise and fall of her chest, the fluttering of her eyelids, the heaviness and softness in the flaps of her cheeks.

Eventually I gently whispered her name. I knew she wouldn't hear but tried it anyway. Then I got up and sat next to her on the couch and began to stroke the paper skin of her knuckles. 'Cookie,' I said again, more confidently. Cookie flinched for a moment and then resettled, still in her world. I felt guilty at disturbing the peace of it all. She'd told me once how, in Poland, her father was the only man in her street with a car. He was mad about it, she said. Would drive her mother and her sister and her all across town, just to show it off. Sometimes she would dream about her father and that car. Was she dreaming of it now? Were her dreams in Polish, Yiddish or English?

She startled and opened one eye and then the other, looking displeased.

'Hi, Cookie,' I said softly. 'Sorry I woke you.'

'From what?' Cookie reprimanded. She opened and closed her mouth and stretched out her tongue like a lion. 'I was just reading. God knows what it's about.'

'I've been away,' I said, winding a lone wiry hair around my finger until the skin turned white.

'That's right. Where were you?'

'Geelong.'

'Geelong. Nu? What's in Geelong?'

'A conference.'

'Ooh. And was it good?'

My skin prickled. I desperately wanted to tell Cookie everything: about Josh in my motel room; about the drive home from Geelong; how I'd already mentally prepared for us to drive back in virtual silence but he insisted on talking about the conference and asked me a few times if I had taken Phillipe's contact details, saying he was a cool guy; how when he dropped me at home and I took my things from the back, he looked down at his phone and said 'See you Monday' with a wave of his hand and I had slunk to my door and it took me a few goes to get the key in the lock; how I dumped the suitcase at the front door and went straight to my bed and under the covers and stayed like that till the urge to piss forced me out again, and that by then the weather had turned, and the sky was dark; how I had switched the light on and looked in the mirror and thought about the stupid noise I had made underneath him and put a hand over my mouth and then took it away again and said 'You're a fucking idiot'.

I wanted to tell Cookie everything. But I didn't. I crumpled into her and she moved the book to one side and I put my head in her lap and she said, 'Have a rest, darling. You're very tired. Have a rest.'

Outside Cookie's door I got a text. From Josh: *Hey. Good time to talk?*

I hesitated, for only a moment. *Sure.*

My phone rang. 'Hello?'

'Hi. It's Josh.'

'I know.' I was so relieved to hear his voice, I thought I might cry, or be sick, or both.

'I'm a piece of shit.'

I cleared my throat. 'It's complicated.'

'Yeah. I just think. I mean I know. For my sake. And I'm sure for yours. We just need to clear the air. If we're going to go on working together. Which is what I want. I love working with you. I should never have let myself get so … out of control. Well, wasted, either. I'm … mortified, actually.'

'It's okay.'

'I don't think it is.'

'I love working with you too,' I said quickly, smiling at a

grey elderly lady who was creeping slowly past. I headed out of Cookie's building onto the street and took a deep breath, shaking off the scent of hand sanitiser and wet carrots.

'Well, that's good.' He blew out into the phone. 'Anyway. I don't know if you have anything on tonight but I could pop by … or if you prefer, we can just do this over the phone.'

'I'm free tonight.'

'Okay. I'll organise it.'

I didn't ask what he needed to organise and hoped he wouldn't offer up the details. I really didn't want to know.

I had a quick shower and got changed into jeans and a black T-shirt. I blasted the air-con through the back of the house. I checked the time every few minutes. I brushed my teeth. I put on make-up in a way that made it seem like I wasn't wearing any make-up. I tried to eat but couldn't. I drank water. I pissed. I drank more and pissed again. I cleaned the toilet. I made the bed. I waited.

He turned up after eight pm with a bottle of red wine. He was wearing a T-shirt with holes in it, jeans and thongs. His casual wear unsettled me slightly.

He followed me down the corridor. We passed my bedroom and then Gemma's bedroom, and he paused to ask me whether we were alone. I told him yes, Gemma was away, and he shrugged and nodded as if it was fine either way. I found this confusing but soldiered on towards the couch, inviting him to sit, leaving a generous gap between us.

'Hi,' he said.

'Hi ...' I said.

He unscrewed the lid of the wine bottle and looked at me and smirked, before I realised we had nothing to drink out of. I returned from the kitchen with mismatched glasses, which he took from me, bemused, like he was remembering something from his youth. 'Before I drink too much,' he said, sinking into his seat and stretching both his legs out long in front of him, 'and please, don't let me drink too much,' he added, 'I want to say ... sorry.'

I took a sip of wine, giving pause to what I presumed was intended to be a moment of significance. 'I'm sorry too.'

He snorted and told me I didn't need to apologise for anything, as if his desire was uncontrollable and mine was inconsequential. 'But we were both there,' I responded.

'Yes.' He took a sip. 'Yes. We were. But the point is ... I am sorry. It's important to me that you know that.'

I nodded purposefully and slowly this time. 'I know.'

He took a deep breath and sighed. 'Fuck fuck fuck, this is hard,' he said, his free hand roaming through his hair.

'It's okay, really.' I suddenly couldn't tell which way this was going to go. Was he about to leave, or cry, or kiss me? I fingered an opening in the seam of the couch. A bit of foam was bulging out and I pressed it back inside. 'It's all fine,' I said. 'Nothing really happened.'

'You probably think I'm a middle-aged loser.'

'Are you middle-aged?'

'I'm thirty-nine'

'Oof,' I said, putting my hands on my cheeks and opening my mouth wide in fake shock.

'Fuck you.' He laughed. 'I just want to say … I respect you.'

'Okay. Fuck you, too.'

'But do you respect me?'

I shrugged. He smiled at me. I smiled back. He brought my hand up to his mouth and said, 'Oh no,' and kissed it. 'Are you sure?' he asked. I nodded, perhaps too eagerly. He moved my hand around his face and back again to his mouth and then he kissed me on the lips.

I wasn't sure about the after. After the kiss. After the fuck. After the orgasm (his, not mine – I'd been way too self-conscious for that). After the unrolling and untangling of the stickiness.

'Well …' he started to say, and then I knew that the after was entirely beyond my control. He looked over at me from my side of the bed, performatively biting his lip. His chest hair and armpit fluff were grotesque and arousing to me simultaneously. I looked back at him quizzically and stifled a laugh, putting my head in my hands and shaking it like a bad dog with its mouth on a shoe. 'That was—' He stopped himself, picked some lint off the sheet and rolled it around in his fingers. He sighed.

'Are you okay?' I asked him.

'Don't ask me that.' He stretched his salty fingers towards me, jiggled my breast playfully and smiled. 'So buoyant.'

'Shut up.' I slid under the sheets coyly.

'Are you okay?' he repeated back to me.

'Yeah.' I wanted to say, 'I've wanted this for a really long time and now I don't know what to do with it but please don't leave,' but of course I didn't.

'I want you to be okay,' he said.

'I'm great.'

'You didn't come though. Or did you?'

'It doesn't matter,' I said. His question filled me with dread. Did he usually make Kimiko come? Who else had he fucked since being married to Kimiko? Was I the first? I hoped he'd say, 'Oh well, there's time for that,' but he didn't say anything. He just closed his eyes and he looked peaceful and I was busting to piss so I pulled a T-shirt on and went to the toilet. I came back to the room hoping he'd be asleep but expecting the opposite: expecting that by the time I'd come back he'd be dressed, with his phone and keys in his hands, scratching his stubble or combing his stupidly floppy hair with his fingers. And he was.

A jungle inside

Over the next month, nothing really happened at work between us. Josh would always wait for quiet moments in the dark. Blinds drawn, under the covers, the shade of a tree, the end of a corridor. Not seen by anyone. Barely seen by each other. And very quiet. Or we were at my house, which was only a five-minute drive to the museum. That, combined with Gemma's temporary absence, had made it a haven for us.

At one staff meeting we were sitting side by side and our legs were touching and for a moment his hand was on my thigh. And then it wasn't. In our office with the door closed we might make an arrangement to see each other. It was easier like that: the luxury of being able to orchestrate a casual afternoon of fucking without the trail of incriminating evidence. He set the tone, of course. Made the rules. Sometimes he would bring up Kimiko like it was no big thing, though I noticed he spoke less about the children.

There were clear topics to avoid and topics to rely upon, such as the things that happened to Josh when he was my age or younger. Initially he'd wanted to study palaeontology, then archaeology, then geology, and then finally he settled upon art history. Art and curatorship were female-dominated industries and he made a point of telling me that this didn't bother him. He told me about his brother who lived in Austin, Texas, and refurbished vintage record players; how the two of them were healthily competitive, yet close. He told me how he had gone and spent time in Austin, and the amazing Mexican food that, for some baffling reason, couldn't be replicated here in Melbourne. He told me about his lazy-eyed grandfather, who survived the war on the outskirts of Budapest hidden in a pig farmer's cellar, and his blonde-haired grandmother who had travelled in broad daylight with false papers and a crucifix dangling from her neck. He told me all of this and I felt like I was the first person he had ever told these things to. I had to stop myself from asking what his parents thought of his intermarriage, and what, on a scale of one to ten, they would think of me as a potential replacement.

Some days at work I felt inspired and hardworking, and other days I felt my performance slipping. This didn't matter because I knew he would never say anything, but I was, undoubtedly, distracted, afraid to ask for anything. God forbid he should have thought I was entitled to any special treatment because we were sleeping together. I was happy. And then at once deeply unhappy. And I still hadn't told anyone. I knew I would tell Gemma about it on her return and was prepared to hold on to it – all of it – until then.

*

The next time I brought up my Paula Hohenberg exhibition idea we were on my couch.

I figured, because I had my period, it might be a moment of reprieve, a moment in which we could talk, connect. I began to flick through some of Paula's images that I had stored on my phone. He pulled the hair from the back of my neck to the side as I zoomed in on an ornate chandelier, the light catching each crystal. Shimmering movement in stasis. 'See how she is so deft with the light, here,' I said. He nodded and slipped his hand down my pants. 'Oh. I'm bleeding,' I said. And he kissed my ear and held me there and said, 'I don't know why but that makes me so fucking horny,' and slipped his fingers inside me and I came like that on the couch. After, I watched him scrub my blood from his fingers with the scourer in the kitchen sink.

I always felt terribly sad when he left, and lonely. It reminded me of being a child, lost in the supermarket aisle.

My mother said she'd knocked a few times. I hadn't answered because I hadn't heard. She used her spare key to find me braless, in a T-shirt and undies, clipping my toenails in the courtyard, Billy Joel playing. Josh had only left thirty minutes before and I hadn't changed or washed. This was deliberate. I needed his smell. She stood at the back door, watching me through the glass like a ghost, sunglasses and visor on.

'Don't cut the nail too short. You'll get an infection,' she called out, startling me. I dropped the clippers, crescent moons tumbling onto the courtyard bricks. 'I didn't mean to scare you,' she said in a way that implied she had meant to scare me.

I followed her into the kitchen, past the stack of unwashed plates in the sink, condiments without lids, unopened mail, straggly hair-ties.

'I walked here, you know,' she said. 'Can you turn that music off? Why are you moping?'

'You walked from home?' I pressed pause on 'Only the Good Die Young'.

'It's filthy in here, Naomi.'

'Filthy is a strong word,' I said. I turned on the sink taps and began moving dishes around.

She began rifling through the pantry. 'Don't you have any regular tea?' she asked.

'You know I only have herbal. Why didn't you drive?'

'Because Katie said I need to exercise more.'

'Who's Katie?'

'My doctor. You should see her about your eczema.'

'I don't have eczema.'

'But you used to.' She poured herself a glass of water. 'Anyway,' she said, gulping it down, 'you can drop me home if I'm too tired to walk back. Or your father will pick me up.' There was no way she was going to walk home, and it would be dark soon. And she had instilled in me never to trust the night. There were rapists and murderers behind every tree and stop sign. 'The garden's looking a bit drab,' she continued.

'Mm,' I said, and we both looked out the window to a fern that had been scorched in the last heatwave. 'I need Cookie to come and work her magic.' Cookie had a knack for not letting things die if she could help it (though sometimes she couldn't help it). Before moving to the home, she fought hard to keep her garden flourishing, experimenting with seaweed and coffee grinds and eggshells. These were little lives whose fortunes were at her mercy. But even the plants were vulnerable to the forces beyond us – the might of the sun, the secrets of the dirt. Maybe that's what was missing from my garden. I didn't have Cookie's horizonless need to keep things alive.

'Do you now?' Mum took her visor off. Sweaty ringlets clung to the front of her head. She scrunched her hair in her fingers and rubbed her moist hands down the front of her T-shirt. 'She's been missing you, you know.'

When I moved into the house a couple of years ago, Cookie helped me choose the plants for the small courtyard. She told me that if there couldn't be a jungle inside, there must be one outside, and vice versa.

I had spent a lot of time in Cookie's garden as a child, and it was a fecundant source of my earliest daydreams. It wasn't a big block of land, but everywhere there was ground Cookie had planted something in the hope that it would grow. And more often than not, it had.

Before I started my first year of primary school, Cookie would look after me on a Thursday. We would spend the mornings in the courtyard at the front of the house. She would busy herself picking dead, crinkled things off the bases of pots and repurposed ice cream containers, while I was small enough to make myself lost in between the larger plants growing by the fence, and then found, and then lost again. Meanwhile, David would go for a walk to a Polish/Russian/ Czech delicatessen, and return with caraway seeded rye, which I'd eat with butter and they'd eat with herring, and angel wing biscuits for something sweet.

It was around this time that I'd been told that Cookie was the only surviving member of her family. Cookie was eighteen when she left Poland. It was before the war, and a second cousin once removed wrote and urged her family to come to Australia, describing it as a quaint place where politics were of little consequence and the wildlife was terrifically bizarre. Over a few days of agonised deliberation and subsequent agonised planning, it was decided that Cookie should go first and then sponsor the rest of the family to follow. Cookie's younger sister Marta was only twelve at the time, and their parents thought it best if she remained in school as long as possible.

It took years to find out what had happened to Cookie's parents and sister. In the early days of dial-up internet, my mother sent an email to Yad Vashem with as much information about the family as was available to her (whatever Cookie was prepared to give over). Each night she turned on the computer, waiting while the beep-bop hum of the modem tantalised us all with hope for a reply. A few weeks later it came. Seeing it there, Dad clasped his hands together and marvelled at the wonder of the world wide web. Then we read the contents of the email and wonder quickly turned to sorrow. The Yad Vashem researcher had discovered Cookie's parents and sister's names on a deportation list to Chełmno extermination camp, some fifty kilometres away from their hometown of Łódź. The email provided closure without closure's usual promise of solace.

I was curious about Marta and asked my mother too many questions about her, which she couldn't adequately answer, which ultimately caused me nightmares. When I'd tried asking Cookie, her face turned lemon-sour and she couldn't look at me. When I turned twelve, my grandmother absented herself from the family Shabbat dinner with a stomach ache and my mother wept as I blew out the candles on my cake. As I wavered in and out of the thick shrubbery at Cookie's house, I was certain I'd seen Marta's ghost; a girl with a short, crimped hairstyle, hiding in the shadows and beckoning for me to let her out to play. I imagined Cookie had kept her there for safekeeping. Perhaps it was Marta who had made the soil fertile, the camellias burst in wintertime, the jasmine heavy and heaving on the back fence in spring.

'I've been busy,' I said. Of course I had been avoiding Cookie. I found it hardest of all to keep things from my grandmother.

My mother poured salt and vinegar chips into a bowl. 'Are these any good?' Mum asked, putting one in her mouth. 'Even Melanie's been to see her this week. She's interviewing her.'

'Interviewing her?'

'Apparently.'

'Why?'

'She's enrolled in a PhD.'

'Oh, sure she has. In what?'

'I don't know,' my mother said, raising her palms to the ceiling in a 'beats me' sort of a way. 'But I think it's fabulous that she's found something she's interested in. And look, she wants to get the family story down.' Mum found me the easier of her daughters but she would never admit it and would almost go above and beyond to defend Melanie just to curb any whiff of it. 'I told her it's a great idea and she could interview me next.'

'Interview you?' I asked, trying to mask my annoyance with a perfunctory hand to my chin and a smile.

'What? I don't have a story to tell?'

'Of course you do, but I thought you didn't like talking about yourself.'

'I don't. But Melanie is interested so—'

I curled my lip.

'Don't be jealous, darling.'

'I'm not.' I forced a smile. 'We can learn a lot from second-generation survivors.'

'Ugh,' she frowned. 'Don't call me that.'

Josh had only recently finished a proposal for an exhibition exploring the children of Holocaust survivors in Melbourne and their contributions to Australian society. I'd asked my mother if she had wanted to be involved in the exhibition, but she declined saying she was sure there were far better candidates than her, including my father. To that I'd said there were enough lawyers but so far no one who had run their own gallery. She'd shrugged her shoulders and changed the subject, so I had left it at that, wishing I'd never asked. That was the thing about my mother. She was as attached to her pride as she was to her shame. When I was eight, she told me off for telling a shop assistant that we were Jews, which I'd only done because the man had wished us a Merry Christmas. I still remember the harsh yank of my arm out of the shop, and then being told that certain information was private. Up until then I thought the only things one needed to keep private were their parts.

Josh and I had worked closely together selecting the subjects for the exhibition. He often deferred to me on matters of religiosity. Maybe, I wondered, he believed that, because he married out, his Judaism was now somewhat diluted. Regardless, I found his deference to me very sexy, and maybe Josh knew this and so indulged me slightly more by asking me to deliver the presentation to Adele, which I had done nervously, wanting desperately to impress them both. Adele was in her early sixties with a chic futuristic silvery bob. I felt that she must know my parents but was too embarrassed to ever ask. When the presentation was done, Adele praised our work and said we were a great team, to which I blushed recalling the things that were unknowable to Adele: the weight of me on him, his heavy cock drooping down towards the shower drain, the sound of his piss in the toilet bowl. When our exhibition proposal had been approved, Josh told me he wished he had some champagne to celebrate, but instead dragged me into the collection storeroom and kissed me between some eighteenth-century porcelain teapots and a boxful of illustrations drawn in the Theresienstadt Ghetto depicting barracks, huddled children and beech trees. An unarchived stack of photographs dislodged from somewhere above my head. He kicked them and they swished across the linoleum. Then he put his hand up my T-shirt and said, 'Well, you outdid yourself today.'

'Listen,' Mum said. 'The point is … Melanie's interested in something. In me! And I think that's lovely.'

'How did you know I'd be home, anyway?' I asked, changing the subject.

'You're always home.'

'No, I'm not.'

'Do you want me to leave? It's not like you were doing anything. You were half naked, for God's sake. Next time I'll call first, okay?'

His hand on her back

It was late at night when I collected Gemma from the airport. Over the Bolte Bridge lights pulsated below us. All over the city there were people on park benches and in apartments and in office blocks. People hitting return on keyboards, inhaling smoke or dope or someone's hair, or fucking people they were and weren't supposed to. People like me. Gemma said she had found the revelations about Josh both thrilling and completely predictable. I had told her everything with the standard qualifications: 'I am a terrible person' et cetera, to which Gemma had dutifully responded: 'of course you're not' and 'it's their deal so let them deal with it' followed by 'but you do know these things don't really end well, don't you?'

The details were gory and plentiful, and she consumed them with a voracity that only a best friend can manage. His mellifluous voice, left-leaning penis, a guileless obsession with my breasts.

She went to sleep in her own bed that night, which felt right. In the short time since Gemma had been away, I'd grown used to someone else in my bed, even if it hadn't been for sleep. I found the spectre of him soothing, feeling for parts of him that he'd unwittingly abandoned: skin, hair, sweat; closing my eyes and mimicking sensations – a thumb tenderly pressing flesh, the gnawing of preserved fruit.

Gemma's presence in the house was comforting to me, but as I lay in bed with her in the next room I was visited by tummy pain, sleeplessness. It had been one thing to think about telling her, and completely another having told her. The night air swirled, and I panicked. I lay awake thinking of the fable of the rabbi who told the town gossip to slash a pillow and watch its feathers fly through the street, and then instructed the gossip to retrieve the feathers one by one. But like gossip, the feathers were now strewn everywhere, irretrievable. Could whispers be carried on the wind? Could guilt?

I sat up in my bed and opened my computer. There were three new emails from Josh. I read them. They were flat and without feeling.

I opened Paula's self-portrait, which I had saved on my desktop. I studied her lips: neither a smile nor frown, but a knowingness. What did she know? What wouldn't she say? The portrait, cropped at the collarbone, offered an entire world of mystery below. I touched my own lips, pushed them back against my teeth, felt for sharpness, fragility. 'Oh well,' I said aloud, startling myself. What identity was Paula constructing through her images, I wondered? That of a woman, alone in a city, documenting her solitude until it became too much to bear? I googled her gravesite, and found her in the Zentralfriedhof, the central Viennese cemetery. Artists of much larger note were buried here too – Beethoven, Brahms, Schubert. Paula, however, was buried in Gate One, the Jewish section. Large trees shrouded the graves in forest light. Many of them were dilapidated and overrun with creeping plants, particularly the graves dating back to 1874 when the Jewish section was first established. The website promised a long overdue restoration, and there was a link to click to donate funds to the cause. It seemed Paula was buried on the outer perimeters, as is common for Jews who die by their own hand. Jewish law prohibits suicide and therefore forbids us from mourning for them. Though I had no doubt that Paula was mourned for. Here in my bed, I was mourning for her.

Eventually I fell asleep. When I awoke I rolled onto my computer, and there was Paula, her face gazing into an endless night on the pillow next to me.

I begged Gemma to accompany me to a fundraising event at the museum. I figured Kimiko would probably be there and I couldn't face the thought of going alone.

The last time Gemma had come to the museum, she had told me that she loved me dearly but just couldn't get excited about the sixteen Jewish convicts who'd arrived on the First Fleet. She'd also told me that a couple of paragraphs next to the exhibit acknowledging First Australians wasn't really adequate, and I felt flushed with disappointment, having written the text myself and being quite proud of it.

People were milling around the permanent exhibition space and we swiftly moved past them, grabbing two glasses of kosher wine. Gemma said the wine was gross and went to get some sparkling water. I continued drinking it because I couldn't taste the difference between good and bad wine, and while I wasn't sure that it would help calm my nerves, I hoped that it might. Gemma returned to me staring blankly at a mottled Iron Age terracotta vase I'd walked by hundreds of times before and said, through a mouthful of pretzels, that Josh was here. 'With the wife.' I turned and saw Josh and Kimiko amid a small group of sharp-suited men, and women wearing understated, overpriced garments. They were all in their mid-forties and had been strategically categorised as next-generation potential donors. Josh knew half of them. His hand rested on the small of Kimiko's back and seemed comfortable in the groove of it. An announcement was made, the speeches began and Josh moved to the front of the room. Gemma and I moved to the rear. I took little sips of wine, which met the back of my throat with a scratch.

Josh adjusted the microphone as if it were an old friend and began speaking about the museum's upcoming exhibitions, new acquisitions and restoration projects. He spoke with an ease that was disarming, and when I looked over to Adele I saw her head bobbing up and down in approval and admiration.

'Oof. He's so articulate,' Gemma whispered.

'I know,' I said.

'Like, I totally get it now.' Gemma squeezed my bum and we both giggled.

'How are you, Naomi?' I turned. Kimiko was standing right next to me, wearing a black and white striped shift dress. She wore pearl droplet earrings that dangled like cherries. On anyone else this outfit would have been mumsy. On her it looked contained, effortless. I, on the other hand, was wearing a dress with a sweetheart neckline that accentuated my cleavage, and now made me feel vulgar.

'Kimiko, hi!' I stumbled. 'I'm well,' I said, my giggles fizzling sharply into sobriety, and without thinking took Gemma's hand. 'This is my friend, Gemma.'

Gemma grinned and complimented Kimiko on her earrings, and they began talking about where Kimiko had bought them from. It turned out Josh had given them to her on their recent wedding anniversary. I stopped myself from asking when it was: whether it was on the Monday he'd taken off work a few weeks ago, or the night I'd texted him three times and he hadn't responded.

I released Gemma's hand and found my way to the back of my head, searching for knots. A piece of hair snapped and I rolled it back and forth between my fingers while Gemma and Kimiko whispered to each other under Josh's speech.

After some applause, Josh came over to greet us and, again, placed his hand on Kimiko's back. Kimiko smiled generously and said to me, 'Oh, I meant to say thank you, by the way.'

'For what?' I asked, vaguely panicked.

'For looking after the kids that time. Josh never should have asked you to do that. It's hardly in your job description.' Kimiko grabbed Josh's hand and smacked it playfully. 'Not appropriate, darling!'

I felt myself turning pink. Josh just looked on and smiled idiotically.

'I hope he paid you,' Kimiko continued.

'Oh, no. No, there was no need for that. Your kids are so sweet.' I emphasised the word sweet.

'Are you sure?' Kimiko fiddled with her earring and jiggled it in and out of the hole.

'Yes, it's totally fine.' I shook my head and looked at my feet.

'I've just been up to the office for a sneak peek of the new exhibition. You've both been working so hard on it.' The office. Bulldog clips. Plastic pockets. Underwear pulled to the side. Flesh against flesh.

'Yep, we have,' I said. And then quickly added, 'Apologies for my messy desk.'

I felt Gemma's hand reach for mine again. And then I felt Kimiko looking at our interlaced fingers. 'I didn't notice,' Kimiko said.

'It was so nice to meet you,' Gemma said. 'We've got a play to get to.'

I hesitated for a moment and then said, 'Yeah.'

'The night went great. I hope you raised loads of money,' Gemma said.

'Looking forward to receiving your donation, Gemma.' Josh winked. And the four of us laughed. I looked at Josh, and he looked back at me for just a moment as Gemma dragged me away.

Out the front of the museum she said, 'Well, that was awkward.'

'Holy shit, do you think she knows?'

'She doesn't know.'

'I should end it. Don't you think?'

Gemma shrugged. 'Probably.'

'I shouldn't have told you. I told him I wouldn't tell anyone, not even you.'

'Of course you were going to tell me. He's an idiot if he thinks otherwise.'

A group of people exited the museum and walked by us. An older, well-dressed man with wire-framed glasses, a friend of my parents, stopped to greet me and congratulate me on the event. I told him I hadn't really had anything to do with it, and he just smiled and said, 'You're looking great, sweetheart. Say hi to Mum and Dad.'

'Ugh, did you see the way he looked at you?' Gemma said, when they were out of earshot.

'He's harmless. Let's go home,' I said.

'No way! We're going to the play.'

'There's an actual play?'

'Of course there is, Princess. It starts in half an hour. We should be able to make it.'

I could feel the wind sneaking around beneath my dress and shuddered. Before I could say anything Gemma had hailed a taxi and we were on our way to a warehouse in Collingwood. In the car, she pinched my cheeks. 'Your face is pale like soap. This will be good for you.'

In the foyer we paid five dollars for a glass of cheap red wine and I told Gemma, 'By the way, I don't see how this wine is any better than the kosher wine', and Gemma said it wasn't and we squeezed through the crowd to find Liv, a friend from uni who'd invited us. Liv warned us that the play we were about to see was experimental, devised by the actors, but not to let that put us off. Her brother, Moses, was in it. Liv was originally from Tasmania and had recently moved back there to work in her boyfriend's family's business. She told us that Moses still used their childhood home in Launceston as his base, though he was so rarely there he might as well set up permanently in Sydney or Melbourne, 'if he really wants to make it as an actor,' she added, under her breath. She then insisted we both come and visit Launceston, at which point Gemma took out her phone and started looking at her calendar and they began throwing dates around.

I tried to enjoy the play but was distracted both by seeing Josh and Kimiko earlier, and by the fact that the actors barely engaged with each other and delivered their lines directly to the audience without emotion. I could feel Gemma trying to look at me and I had to clench every part of my body not to look back, knowing that we would both get the giggles and would likely be unable to stop.

There were ten thankful minutes where the actors interacted in a Christmas party scene with naturalistic dialogue. The music then became very loud and the lights flashed heavily and Moses made out with a man in the corner. Then he came to the front of the stage and crouched down. His face was half in light, half in shade, and his gaze appeared to land on me. The lights and music dissipated and the actors began addressing the audience all over again, but Moses kept looking in my direction, so much so that I felt that he was delivering his lines to me, and it made me feel very exposed.

After, I hoped we'd be able to leave straight away, but Liv said we must stay and say hello to her brother. 'Here he is now,' she said, waving at the actors emerging one by one into the foyer.

Moses walked towards us with his hands in his pockets. He was wearing a faded black shirt over black skinny jeans. He reminded me of one of the crew we contracted to help with exhibition installations at the museum.

'That was amazing!' Gemma said this with such insistence that I almost believed her.

'Oh, thanks.' He shrugged.

Liv handed him a beer and said, 'I loved the Christmas scene. Shame there weren't more people in the audience.'

'We'll get the word out, won't we, Naomi?' Gemma said to me.

'I liked the Christmas bit,' I offered.

Moses looked at me and smiled, and I felt ridiculous for thinking he had been delivering his lines to me. Then the actor he'd made out with came over and put his arm around Moses's shoulders and said in a deep voice, 'This guy, hey?' Moses kissed him on the cheek and they dinged their beer bottles together.

'We're not big on Christmas in our family,' Liv said to me.

'Neither,' I said.

'Aw,' Gemma said. 'My little Jewish princess!'

Just after midnight, Josh texted me: *How was the play?* I got up out of bed and put the kettle on. I considered not replying, but then thought better of it, in case he might turn off his phone and go to sleep. *It was good.*

He called almost immediately. 'What are you doing?' he whispered.

I thought about saying something clever or sexy, but instead I told him I was making tea, when in fact all I wanted was to tell him how awful it had been to see his hand on his wife's back.

'Did you like my speech?'

'Everybody liked your speech.'

'What are you wearing?'

'Josh ...'

'I know you wore that dress for me tonight, didn't you.' I couldn't say anything back. 'Sorry,' he said in a low voice. 'I'm a terrible person.'

A silence followed. I dipped my teabag in a mug and watched the water turn to rust in a steamy puddle.

'Are you there?' he prompted.

I took a deep breath. 'Yeah. I just … You can't say you're a terrible person.'

'Yeah,' he said. 'I know. I guess I … I don't always know what to say.'

I sipped the tea, knowing it was still too hot and that I would burn my tongue, which is what happened. He spoke fast as he told me that he and Kimiko rarely had sex. When the kids were born, they started co-sleeping. Ollie would breastfeed all night and even though it made Kimiko delirious with fatigue she would persist because she wasn't going to breastfeed forever. But then Ava was born, and she did the same. And Kimiko became the receptacle for all the children's touching, and heavy breathing, and clawing, and there was no longer space for Josh. He was there to play the monster at breakfast time who would hold the children upside down or chase them around the kitchen table in their urine-stained pyjamas and with half-wiped bums. The children still often slept with them at night. All they wanted was their mum in the night-time, and their dad, the monster, in the morning.

He cleared his throat a couple of times and then said, 'I'm not happy.'

I could hear him moving. Maybe he'd just stepped outside onto the verandah. 'Okay.'

'But I don't know what that means.'

I felt helpless and panicked. Like it was all going to end here, in this phone conversation, and I hadn't intended for that to happen at all. So I took another sip of the scalding tea, patted down my long-sleeve nightie, and told him the following: I was wearing nothing. I was completely naked. And I wanted him.

Visitations

In the morning Marilyn, cheeks puffy with adrenaline, found me in the staff kitchen. She told me that only moments earlier Derek, the security guard, had killed a spider the size of a regular stapler in the stationery cupboard. She knew this because she'd been in the cupboard at the time, getting a stapler, and had screamed so loudly that he came running and withdrew his gun. Of course, he hadn't killed the spider with the gun. He killed it with a ream of A4 paper.

The way she told me this story in a gossipy tone was indicative of how little action occurred at the museum. Derek had been stationed at the front door for the past thirteen years and in all that time there'd never been an incident that required him to handle his weapon. Occasionally there would be a nasty email or Facebook post and, since my period of employment, one bomb threat that saw the staff and a handful of American tourists huddled in the side street at the back of the museum waiting for the bomb squad to give the all clear. The lack of activity surprised if not disappointed people like my dad, who would regularly tag me in posts from the AntiSemitism Watch Facebook group. I could never quite get my head around being in such close proximity to a loaded gun at work. Maybe one day I'd ask to see it up close. Probably not though.

'Didn't you hear me scream?' she wanted to know.

'No, sorry,' I said, pouring my coffee from the French press into a mug that had *Coffee, Chocolate and Men. Some things are just better rich!* written on it in Comic Sans.

Marilyn opened the fridge and said, 'You should join the walking group at lunchtime. It's very energising. Josh won't be in today, and I know how you like to have lunch together.' She took out the milk, placed it on the bench and smiled at me. I smiled back. I tried to focus on the spiral brooch she pinned to every cardigan she owned. I tried to channel my annoyance with her for having been the one to tell me that Josh wasn't at work. I channelled it into the brooch, into the milk she was pouring, because otherwise I feared I might slap her in the face. There was no way she could know anything. We had been so discreet. Still. The way she smiled at me ... I felt as if I had just stepped in shit and dragged it through the house.

'Maybe,' I said. I took the French press to the sink and began rinsing it out, while Marilyn made tea behind my back. 'Where's Josh?'

'He didn't tell you? He's working from home. Ava's not well, little darling.'

*

There was an email from Josh waiting for me. *Working from home. Ava is sick and Kimiko working late today.*

I replied *Okay. Do you need anything?*

I stared at the screen for what felt like too long and when he didn't respond I felt sick and got up from the desk. I went to the toilet and stared in the mirror for a long time. The bathroom door opened and a modestly dressed woman in long sleeves and a floor-length skirt entered. I said hello and the woman nodded and paused for a moment in front of the mirror next to me, touching her hair. On second glance I realised it was a sheitel. She went into a toilet stall while I stood at the mirror with my pale reflection and touched my own scalp.

I came back to my office determined to finish responding to a backlog of email enquiries. There was a new email from Josh. *There are some forms I need to sign in my pigeonhole. Would you mind dropping them over to me at some stage.*

He had asked me to come to the side gate because Ava was asleep. The gate was tall and black and I stood there for what felt like ages waiting for him to appear. Finally he poked his finger through it and opened the latch. He was barefoot and talking to someone on the phone. He put two fingers up in the air and mouthed *two minutes*. He gestured for me to follow him inside through the sliding glass doors, saying things like 'I agree wholeheartedly' and 'I believe so' while rolling his eyes at me, and then winking, and then smiling. He had his laptop open on the kitchen counter and went back to it. Meanwhile,

I rummaged through my bag for the papers he'd requested and put them next to him.

I hadn't been to his place since the night I babysat. It felt odd to be back here. We were never here. 'Sorry,' he said finally, placing his phone face down on the bench. 'You want some water?' He headed for the fridge. This was always how things began between us. He'd pretend to be doing anything but trying to fuck me.

'No,' I said. 'I'd better get back to work.'

'Yeah,' he said, nodding his head. 'Okay.'

'How's Ava?' I had to force the words out.

'Oh. She's got a bad cold. Poor thing. She'll sleep for ages though.' He delivered this last sentence as a question and followed it with a sheepish look. His hand hovered without commitment over the counter and landed by my pinkie finger. This was his unspoken invitation for me to inch my hand closer to his. Only in this moment did I feel like I had any say in any of this. I held off touching him because it was his house and his daughter was asleep down the hall and if he wanted to touch my hand he'd better just touch my fucking hand, and said, 'You missed all the excitement at work today.' I told him about Marilyn and the spider, and he laughed. And then he got up and silently walked towards the laundry and signalled for me to follow. I did and he shut the door and laid a towel down on the tiles. He didn't say anything. Just pulled down my pants and kissed the top of my undies, and then pulled them down and put his mouth on me. His stubble was prickly and my skin bristled at his touch. I flinched then put my hands around his head to pull him in closer. He slipped a finger inside me and I arched my back and then together we lay down on the towel and he pulled down his shorts and showed me his erection. He entered me deeply and my body rocked back and forth and my head kept hitting the base of the washing machine and it hurt but I didn't care. He commanded me to touch myself and I obediently wedged my hand between his tummy and mine and rubbed myself till I came, and then he came on my stomach. For a moment neither of us moved and I fixed my eyes on a cobweb in the corner and the trapped black fly, still alive, straining against the lacelike snare, buzzing, pleading. Then he lurched himself up and used some of the towel that was beneath us to wipe the come off.

Then he heard something I didn't, pulled up his pants, went to the door and opened it a fraction. Ava was standing just outside. He went out to her and briskly shut the door behind him, leaving me in the laundry alone. I didn't know what to do so shoved the towel in the washing machine and waited for him to reappear. Minutes later the door opened. He signalled for me to come out. Ava was sitting in front of the TV and Josh quietly ushered me down the hallway to the front door like a ghost. He closed the flywire behind us and walked me to the front gate.

'Ah, fuck. Sorry,' he said. His top lip was sweaty. He looked beyond me to a van parked across the road and squinted and shook his head.

'It's okay,' I said without feeling.

'I'm sorry,' he said again. 'I just— We shouldn't have done that.'

I felt the weight of the word *we*. A word that I realised I'd been itching to hear. And now *we* felt dirty. Because *we* were dirty. I stepped backwards and tripped a little over some uneven paving.

'Sorry,' he said. 'I've been meaning to fix that. I'd better go back inside.'

'Okay,' I said and rummaged around in my bag for my keys. I walked to my car hearing the front door shut behind me.

There was a partner at my father's law firm who had a reputation for flirting with ('harassing', my mother had corrected Dad in the telling) junior lawyers. But eventually he got one of them pregnant. My parents, along with many of my father's colleagues, threw confetti at the wedding, and according to workplace lore the couple were still very happy together. I told Gemma this story and she said, 'Yeah, but I bet she's not a lawyer any more.'

Gemma was kind enough not to tell me what to do (end it), but as soon as I conceded that I couldn't see where my relationship – both professional and romantic – with Josh was going, she was quick to offer to take my phone and scour it of any romantic evidence of him. But I'd clutched my phone tightly to my chest and, when she'd gone to her own room that night, I sifted through our messages, digging out the crumbs.

When I finally lay my head on the pillow, I combed my fingers through my hair, pressing on the soft ridge of my skull, sore from the repeated banging against the washing machine.

I woke early with terrible stomach pain and sat on the toilet with diarrhoea. I thought about calling my mother and asking if it was real, but she would probably ask me what I meant by that and I would say that what I meant by that was did I really have diarrhoea or was it anxiety and I just didn't want to go to work. And then she would say 'well, what was your shit like?' and I would say 'it was a deluge' and she would say 'well, that sounds real to me'. Of course, I would never call her because she would want to know why I was having anxiety. In the end I felt obliged to show up to work so I did.

I was relieved to discover that Josh would be in meetings most of the day and so I muddled around with quick-response emails. Then there were the less straightforward ones that were gradually mounting in a folder I had titled *Stuff to Do*. I thought if I just answer one of these today, that will be an accomplishment. I randomly clicked on an email. The subject line read *Researching Buchner Family Tree*. I closed it as quickly as I'd opened it and flicked over to videos recommended to me on YouTube, and for a while watched a faceless person assemble a miniature apple pie using miniature utensils and baking it in a miniature oven. The video was one minute and thirty-seven seconds, and when it was finished I allowed it to roll into the next video, where the same faceless person made miniature chicken teriyaki with rice and miniature chopsticks.

At midday, the receptionist called to let me know that my mother and grandmother had popped in for a visit and asked if she could send them up to my office. A nagging panic rose in my throat. I looked at my calendar and realised that I'd completely forgotten about them coming. What else had I forgotten? I shoved things to one side of my desk, put the pens in the drawer, used a tissue to wipe off hair (his and mine) and dust (his and mine) and pencil marks and told the receptionist to send them up.

'So, this is where you work?' Cookie said, implying my work was something I'd been keeping from her, whereas in truth Mum had brought Cookie once before, but Cookie had either forgotten or was just intent on stirring.

Cookie kissed me, leaving a crayon-thick blotch of pink lipstick on my cheek that I tried to rub off without her noticing. She had dressed up for the occasion, wearing a silver blouse and a chunky gold necklace. She sat herself in Josh's chair and began swivelling it back and forth with her feet barely touching the ground. Cookie had worked for many years as an accountant in David's upholstery business, and while she'd never used a computer, she had likely sat in a chair that swivelled.

Mum placed a green shopping bag on my desk and took out three salad sandwiches. She was already unwrapping the first sandwich when she asked, 'Can we eat in here?'

'Yes, but don't touch anything,' I said. Mum shot raised eyebrows to Cookie and the two of them smiled.

I ate very quickly.

'Why are you so hungry?' asked Cookie, as I fished for wayward spinach in my teeth. 'You want some more? Eat mine.' Cookie pushed her sandwich towards me. The bread was stained with her lipstick and she had already begun to reapply the make-up she'd left on the sandwich.

'I'm fine,' I said, shaking my head. They began discussing how I never ate breakfast, which hadn't been completely true for a while, and then the door opened and in walked Josh. We all looked up at him and he stumbled. 'Sorry,' he apologised. 'I didn't realise you were having lunch.'

'Are we in trouble?' Cookie smirked. 'Are you the boss?'

He didn't say anything, and I realised he was waiting for me to speak. 'This is Josh,' I said slowly. 'He's the senior curator here. This is Viv, my mum, and Cookie, my grandmother.'

'We've met, haven't we?' my mother said.

'Oh. Of course,' I said, feeling the sandwich swimming inside me.

'Nice to see you,' Josh said to her, not skipping a beat.

'So, he *is* the boss,' Cookie said.

'Not really,' Josh said. 'Naomi is definitely the expert on most things.'

'It's very cold in here,' Cookie said.

'Ha. Naomi says the same thing all the time.' He smiled.

'Here, Cookie.' I reached into a drawer for my shawl and handed it to my grandmother. 'Josh doesn't feel the cold.'

'Neither do I,' my mother said, and winked at him.

'Oh, well. Nice to meet you both. I just came to get ...' He paused and looked around. 'Never mind. I'll leave you to it. I hope you'll stay and look at the exhibition.' And then, to my grandmother, 'Stay warm, Cookie.' He backed out of the office and shut the door behind him.

'He's very handsome,' Mum said.

'Very,' agreed Cookie.

'And cute,' Mum said.

'Very,' Cookie said.

'I don't remember him being so handsome,' Mum said. 'He's Jewish, isn't he?'

'From Perth, originally, I think.' I said this to stop her asking about his family. She didn't know Perth Jews.

'Perth? South African?'

'I don't think so.'

'Married?'

'What?' Cookie asked. 'What did she say?' She scrunched her face.

'Is he married?' Mum repeated.

'Yes. Jesus.' I looked away.

'To who?'

'No one you know.'

'Oh, so she's not Jewish.'

'No.'

'Who cares,' Cookie said.

'Do they have children?' Mum went on.

'Mum!' I said loudly, and looked to the door to ensure it was closed.

'What?' she smiled. 'It's just a shame.'

I sighed. 'What is?'

'When a guy like that marries a shiksa.'

'Mum, that is so rude. You don't know anything about him.'

'Leave her alone, Vivienne,' Cookie said.

'Men like him are the reason girls like her,' Mum pointed her finger directly at me, 'are still single. What is she? A tall leggy blonde? Or is she Asian?'

I lowered my head, looked down at my desk, and said quietly, 'She's Japanese.' I looked back at my mother and started giggling, and then so did she.

'Ha! I knew it!' She slapped her hands together. 'Men like him,' she continued, 'are never interested in girls like her.' She was still pointing her finger at me. This made me laugh even harder.

'What's wrong with you two?' Cookie said.

'I bet he likes you though,' Mum said.

'Of course he likes her,' Cookie said. 'What's not to like?'

I stopped laughing. 'Do you want to see the exhibition?'

'Of course we want to. What is it again?'

'Jewish Poetry Across the Ages.'

'Couldn't they have come up with a better title?' my mother asked.

107

'By they, do you mean me?'

'Leave her alone, Vivienne,' Cookie said.

'There's a nice Leonard Cohen soundtrack,' I mustered.

My mother grabbed her handbag. 'Are you coming, Mum?'

'Sounds boring,' Cookie said, and yawned without covering her mouth, her furry tongue in plain view.

'Oh, Mum, I thought that's why you wanted to come here,' Mum said.

'I can't be bothered. You go have a look. I'll stay with my Naomi.'

'Fine,' Mum said, grabbing her purse. 'Which way do I go?'

I dropped my mother off at the start of the exhibition, and then went to the staff kitchen to make Cookie a cup of weak tea. Josh was standing at the counter eating leftover pasta out of a plastic container. He started to say something. His mouth was full of food and he covered it with his hand, waving his other hand apologetically. I began to make the tea in silence when he said, half garbled, 'What does your grandmother make of the exhibition?'

'It's not really her thing.' I dunked a teabag in water momentarily, so it left a faint stain. 'I'd better take this to her,' I said.

He put his hand on my arm. 'I think we should talk.'

'About what?'

He grabbed a tea towel and used it to wipe his mouth. 'Oh, Nay.' He quickly kissed the top of my head and exited the kitchen, leaving the tea towel sitting on the bench.

*

Cookie was rifling through a plastic bag full of material. It was a recent donation of fabric samples from a clothing factory that had closed its doors long ago. I placed the tea next to her and said, 'You found the schmattes. You should be wearing gloves.'

'What? Don't be ridiculous,' said Cookie. 'They're just schmattes.' Cookie pulled one of the pieces of fabric out. It had a pattern of green and white diamonds. Clipped to it was a piece of paper. 'Emma Greenblatt,' she read aloud.

'She was from Łódź,' I said. 'Maybe you know her.'

'Do you know how many people were from Łódź?'

'No.'

'Neither do I. But it was a lot. No. I don't know an Emma Greenblatt. Did she work in the lane?'

Cookie leaned back in Josh's chair, fondling the fabric swatch in a reverie. I needed to sort through the bag and caption each item. It was another job piling up on my desk. I had already begun writing the label for this particular piece of fabric. *Emma Greenblatt was a survivor of the Łódź Ghetto and Auschwitz. She left Poland in 1949 and arrived in Melbourne in 1950. Emma soon found work in the local textile trade in Flinders Lane.* It was the part of the job I revelled in, researching the stories behind the objects, crafting a narrative, giving names to things that had been nameless. Ever since I'd started working at the museum, Josh had delegated almost all of the captioning to me, and I was glad for it.

'She died about twenty years ago,' I said.

'Oh. Poor girl.' Cookie heaved a heavy sigh and handed back the fabric swatch. 'It's funny seeing you here, in among all these old things. It doesn't make sense that you are the keeper of all the old things.'

'I like old things.'

'Even me.'

'Especially you, Cookie.'

'You've always been a strange girl.' Cookie wiped the corners of her mouth with an arthritic finger that bent slightly the wrong way. 'You suddenly seem all grown up.'

'Ha.' I looked at my computer screen, which had gone dark. I tapped the keyboard to refresh it. 'I ... I don't feel very grown up.'

'Well, I don't feel grown up either.' Cookie narrowed her eyes. 'Nu. Show me something on that thing.'

'On the computer?'

She nodded.

I scrolled through the Sephardic object collection. She yawned while I pointed out the intricacies of a havdalah spice box from Yemen. 'Some people fill it with rosemary, cloves, cinnamon ...' It felt oddly disappointing describing the spices to her.

Cookie rubbed her hands together for warmth and looked out the window. I passed her the cup of tea and she sipped it, slurped it until it was gone. She handed me the empty cup. Her gaze shifted back to the window outside, the weeds attached to the drainpipe of the next-door building.

After some time I said, 'Would you like to see something else?'

'Yes!' she said, turning back to me and startling me with her enthusiasm.

I brought up one of Paula's photographs, one of the bathroom shots. Cookie leaned in and studied the photo with a furrowed brow.

'Do you like it?' I asked, feeling my cheeks becoming warm.

Cookie thought about it and shrugged. 'She looks miserable.'

I looked more closely at the picture. 'Does she?'

'Why do you like this sad stuff?'

'Because life is sad?'

Cookie hit the air. 'Not your life.'

'No, I guess not,' I said.

'People want happy things. Like babies. You should make a show about babies. Or puppies.'

'I want to make a show about her.'

'Okay. Sure. What do I know?'

A calendar invite appeared over the top of the image. It was from Josh. It just read *Meeting – 4.30 pm*. 'What does that say?' Cookie leaned forward, trying to read the notification.

I felt a sudden urge for the toilet, put my hand to my stomach and scanned my desk for water. I managed to knock a mug onto the floor, shattering it. It was from the museum shop, and I still hadn't paid for it. 'Shit, shit,' I stuttered, bending down to collect the remains.

'What's wrong with you?'

My eyes started to get hot. 'What do you mean?'

'You've been avoiding me.'

'No, I haven't.'

'You haven't come to visit for two months!' Two months. Was that how long it had been? I looked at the date on the top right-hand corner of my screen. It was almost two months since we'd been to the conference. It had been both the longest and the shortest two months of my life.

'I've been busy. I've seen you at Shabbat.'

'You're skinny.'

'I'm normal.'

'What's he done to you?'

'Who?'

'I don't know who. I just know you're not my Naomi. So is there a he?'

'Kind of.'

'Ha!' Cookie banged her fist on my desk, which startled us both. 'Well, "kind of" doesn't sound like much of anything. "Kind of" sounds like a waste of time. You don't want to be in a "kind of" situation, do you?'

'No.'

'No. You don't. Trust me.'

I took the remaining fabric swatches out of the bag and tried to iron out the wrinkles with my fingers. Cookie grabbed some and started doing the same. For a time we sat in silence, hypnotically tracing diamonds and squares once fit for gowns and party dresses.

'Visitors all gone?' Josh asked, poking his head around the door. It was 4.30 pm on the dot.

Right then, I wanted to leave almost as much as I wanted to stay. If I left, I could continue with the not-knowing, and then find an opportunity to see him in some dark space – a cinema or a car park – and have sex with him and not speak at all. It would just be about feeling him on me and in me, which is what I felt I needed. But if I stayed, I would have to reckon with what I wanted, which, very plainly, was him, or the version of him I had come to know: a version that revolved around me.

I stayed. Of course I stayed. I was sitting at my desk and he grabbed a manila folder, sat down at his desk and swivelled around to face me. 'I want you to look at this,' he said, wheeling himself in my direction.

I took the folder from him and opened it. Inside there were brochures from the Jewish Museum in Manchester. Josh had just met with their curator who had wanted to discuss an exhibition they were considering bringing on tour to Australia. It occurred to me then that I would have liked to have met the curator. I felt sick with the thought that I may have just, in these past two months, sabotaged my own career in the nook of Josh's armpit. He could have easily included me, but he hadn't. Maybe he didn't really need me, or believe in my abilities. What had this been between us, in the dark, that no one could know, that his wife could never know, that I didn't even know? Maybe I'd just liked the way he looked at me, from his desk. The distance between his chair and mine. Maybe that would have been enough, to let whatever it was flow between us without ever touching. Maybe I had really, well and truly, fucked everything up. And now this was the unravelling, which I had seen coming. And yet it was agony, pulling on me like an unwieldy cuticle, bleeding on the side of a nail. You pull. And you pull. And you wince each time. And then you pull some more.

'Is this what our meeting is about?' I asked.

'Yeah … I want your opinion.'

I let out an inaudible sigh and leafed through the brochures, hoping that, with my head down, he wouldn't make out my expression. The glossy pages appeared wet in my grasp. The Stars of David blurred. I could see maps with wobbly lines leading to nowhere.

Josh wheeled himself closer. I could feel his breath: a gentle breeze nipping at the back of my neck. He pointed at the brochure sitting on top and told me that Adele might raise some funds to send him to England to check it out. 'Imagine if we could both go,' he whispered, looking over at the closed door.

I silently shook my head.

'It would be—'

'What would be the point?' I cut him off.

'Okay,' he said, rolling his chair slightly away from me. 'You're pissed off at me.'

I swallowed hard. 'I don't know.'

'You can tell me. I want you to tell me.'

'I don't know. I guess. I don't know.'

'Tell me,' he pleaded, his hair falling into his eyes.

I said nothing.

Josh stood up. 'I should go home.' He rolled his chair back to his desk and cleared his throat. He looked at his phone and then looked back at me. He was wearing a short-sleeved shirt: the kind of shirt that revealed his arm muscles, which were toned just the right amount. Which bulged beneath the sleeves just the right amount. 'I ... I like you, Nay. So much. I know we've been having fun,' he went on. 'I've never done anything like this. I really didn't expect anything like this to happen. But you made it so hard. You were so ... You. And me— I don't really know what it is I'm doing. And maybe I should.' He sat down again.

'It's been fun,' I strained to say.

'Yep.'

We sat like that for a while. Me looking at my fingernails and Josh staring at the floor. 'I guess I need to sort my shit out with Kimiko, don't I?' I looked up at Josh and a foolish tear escaped my eye and I tried to swipe it away before he saw it, but he saw it, and it was something that couldn't be unseen. 'Maybe we should draw a line. Before we get hurt. And go back to working together without the—'

'Okay.' I nodded my head quickly.

'Come on. Don't make this sad.'

'I'm not. I'm—'

'Your face. Your face is— You will always be so sensitive and I want you to keep that. I do. Shit, I'm telling you. It's not easy for me.' Josh stood up. He seemed taller. He put his bag on his shoulder. 'Can I give you a hug?'

It was too much: the shame for the mess on my desk, for the unanswered emails, for the vanilla yoghurt in the fridge at home that was caked with purple mossy mould that I couldn't bear to open or just throw out. For the sheets on my bed that I hadn't changed since the last time he slept on them – well, not slept, dozed on – before he disappeared into the night of children and laundry and googling pendant lights for that awkward dark corner in his lounge that no one knew what to do with. For Paula Hohenberg. For how little I'd spoken her name aloud. For how little I'd spoken. He walked over to me and I stood up. He put his arms around me and I sank into him. He felt large, father-like. He kissed the part of my hair, that tender bit of exposed scalp. Raw bone, like a knife's edge. The door opened and Marilyn popped her head in. She saw us and mumbled something of an apology and closed the door behind her.

Josh took a big step back. I took a small step. Then he exhaled deeply and said, 'Fuck. Does she know?'

'What?'

'Who have you told?'

'Who have I told?' I was suddenly very cold. I ran my hands up and down my arms. 'No one.'

'Bullshit,' he said, and began clicking his fingers. 'You've said something. To Marilyn.'

'God, no. I would never—'

'Well, she clearly knows.'

'I don't think she knows anything,' I said to the ceiling. 'If she asks, I'll say I was having a bad day and you were comforting me. That's all.'

'I'm fucked,' he said sharply, leaning against his desk.

'Can you lower your voice?'

'This has all been so easy for you. You've got nothing to lose.'

I felt my stomach hollow out.

'What?' he said. He must have felt it too. 'Say something.'

'Put your bag down,' I said, quietly.

'What?'

'Stay.'

'I can't hear you. Speak properly, Naomi.'

'Just stay,' I said, louder. 'We can talk this through.' I reached my arms out to him.

He readjusted the shoulder strap on his bag and shook his head. 'We— I— I have to go.'

He opened the door and left. I followed after him but stopped at the threshold of the office.

*

Derek turned off the light switch, said, 'Oh, shit,' and then turned it back on. I was on the ground with my back against the wall, clutching my knees, feeling the carpet on my bottom like stinging nettle. I could see that he wanted to touch me but wasn't confident to so left and returned moments later with Adele, who upon seeing me there swiftly told him he could leave.

She handed me a box of tissues and then sat in my chair, watching me blow my nose. 'I'll just sit here,' she said, 'and you get up when you're ready to get up.' I nodded but remained glued to the carpet. She brushed her hands over a catalogue that was sitting on my desk, and I had the feeling she wouldn't leave until I'd peeled myself up off the floor.

'Nobody died,' I said after some time.

'Okay,' she said, looking up at me and closing the catalogue. 'It's something else then. Did something happen here? At work?'

I looked at the swatches of fabric that only hours before had been in the hands of my grandmother, thought about how tenderly she had caressed them, going over their patterns with her bony fingers, feeling for defects, rips, stains, blood. 'No,' I replied. 'It's— It's personal.'

She nodded. 'Okay.'

I took in a deep breath. 'Would it be alright if I took some time off? I think I have some leave owing.'

'That's fine,' she said. And then, 'Shall I let Josh know?'

Suckling

My parents and I sat in their good lounge. I told them what I could, and Mum kept repeating, 'I knew it' until Dad told her that was not useful. They seemed intent on establishing that my pain was emotional and not physical, and that reassured them that there was nothing they could do in the short term, like call a doctor friend to take a look at some bruised or broken part of me. When I had used up a handful of tissues, my mother gently offered her lap for my head and I continued to weep onto her jeans, which I apologised for, but she said, 'they're just jeans' and stroked my hair. I couldn't recall the last time I cried like this, and there was a part of me that was thinking about that and not about Josh. Her hands danced over my head and I sank deeper into our unfettered closeness, remembering a time when the world was just the two of us, when Melanie was at school and my father was at work, and all our interactions were low to the ground, barefoot. I fell asleep and woke up when it was dark, and found I'd been covered with a pale green mohair throw.

For a while I stared up at the skylight and counted stars until my brain hurt.

I went to the kitchen and found my parents eating pasta and drinking wine. I pulled up a chair at the table. Dad got me a plate. I ate what I could, picking out the cheesy bits, finishing the glass of wine and asking for another. I left the table again without saying much, went to my old bedroom, which was now full of artworks kept from my mother's gallery yet to be hung, shut the door and climbed into bed. I called Josh three times, and three times he didn't answer. I thought about going to his house. There were still things I wanted to say, not that I knew what they were. I could hear the television blaring in the other room and thought it would be quite easy to sneak out. I would carry my shoes so as to not make noise on the parquetry floor. As I lay there like this, plotting, the door opened. Mum shuffled inside and closed it behind her. She had brought three things: whiskey, a sleeping pill and a Ferrero Rocher. I considered only eating the chocolate, saving the rest for later and following through with my plan, but I chose sleep instead and consumed everything while Mum watched on, rolling the metallic chocolate wrapper between her thumb and index finger until it resembled the shape of a pea.

'Do you want to sleep in our room tonight?'

I thought about it, only for a moment, then shook my head. I half wished to ask her to tell me a story, so I could lie back and listen to the sound of her voice, while feeling the effects of the pill and the alcohol. But I said nothing, too afraid of what else I might say.

There was something exceedingly familiar and comforting about this whole scenario. I slept in my parents' bed until I was thirteen. Over the years they attempted multiple strategies to get me back to my own bed. At age two, when I began climbing out of my cot, they took turns sitting with their backs to the door while I screamed and pounded on the other side, until one of them (usually Dad) would relent and take me to their bed. At age five, when my nightmares began in earnest, they would allow me to stay up with them, watching TV till I fell asleep (though perhaps the content wasn't entirely appropriate – Dad always had a penchant for British crime shows). At age nine they bought a sleeping bag and put it on the floor next to Mum's side of the bed and instructed me that if I wanted to sleep with them I would need to sleep on the floor, and I wasn't to disturb them whatsoever. I utilised the sleeping bag almost nightly, would creep inside it quietly as if entering the womb, fall asleep and grind my teeth. At age thirteen, just after my bat mitzvah, I got braces and my first period and slept through the night in my own bed. I still suffered from nightmares, but sometimes all it took was standing in their doorway, listening for signs of life to soothe me.

After Mum left I took the last sip of whiskey. I winced as it went down and decided to call Josh again. He didn't answer. I texted him: *You could at least answer the phone.*

Around ten minutes later he wrote back: *I can't speak tonight. I will call you.*

I wrote back: *When? I need to speak to you.*

In the morning Mum said to me, 'What did you think was going to happen?' I was waiting for this line of questioning. I just hadn't realised it would come so soon.

'I don't know,' I said. I was now lying in her bed. When I woke up I'd moved from my room to hers. The paintings in my old bedroom unsettled me, and in the night I'd had to turn one of them around to face the wall.

I watched her clip a black meshed bra under her shoulder blades, sharp sugar lumps. When she turned to face me I couldn't take my eyes off her breasts; small and dark, her areolae seemingly unweathered by time.

She slipped on a black shirt dress that tied in at the waist with a gold clasp. 'Did you love him? Do you love him?' She came and sat on the bed and rested her hand on my leg. 'Did you think he was going to leave his wife? Did you talk about that?'

'No,' I said, feeling foolish. 'Just—'

'Tell me.'

'There was so much that worked. A level of understanding. I don't think he has that. With his wife.'

Mum shook her head, opened her mouth to say something, and then closed it again. 'I knew it,' she said finally. 'I knew there was something going on. I wish you would have come to me.' I didn't know what to say to that because if I had told her about it, she'd have told me to stop. So I cried. Then Mum cried a little too, which made me stop crying. Then she hiccupped and said, 'Naomi, you are perfect. You are beautiful and perfect.' I didn't find this overly comforting. As if sensing that, Mum offered, 'Would you like me to call him?'

'No!' I gasped.

'Maybe it would make you feel better. I mean, he probably hasn't told anyone about any of it. Men often don't.'

'I don't want you to talk to him. I don't want to talk to him.'

'No. Good. That's right. You will get over this. And so will he. He needs to go and be who he is meant to be. A husband. A father. We want you to be happy. This relationship will not bring you happiness.' After that, Mum offered to leave me in her bed and bring breakfast on a tray. I tried to conceal myself deeper under the heavy quilt, hot and sweaty with defeat. Mum returned ten minutes later with some black coffee and a piece of wholegrain toast with butter and vegemite. 'You know,' she continued as if she'd never left, placing the tray on the bedside table, 'you think this is the hardest thing you'll ever go through. And I hope it is.'

'Are you about to tell me that people have it much worse off? Because of course I know that. This is so trivial. It's all so stupid.' I reached for the coffee.

'Sit up properly to drink,' she said, taking the coffee from me while I readjusted. 'It's not stupid. Your pain is your pain. But listen to me now. It will pass. It will all pass. And you will find love again. Real love.'

'Real love.'

'Yes.'

I took the coffee and sipped it. I had wanted it to be comforting but it tasted sour.

'What is it?' she asked. 'Too hot?'

'Did you like him?'

'I only met him a handful of times!'

'But what did you think of him?'

'Oh, Naomi.'

'Please, Mummy.'

She padded the quilt along my legs until she found my toes and began squeezing them, giving each toe an equal turn of her touch. 'He was charming. He was— It was familiar. I knew his type instantaneously. Nothing like you.'

'What does that mean?'

'Well ... You're layered. Unassuming. Too good for him.'

Nothing my mother told me had been definitive. I was raw, I was being prised open. I needed stitches, but I was being tugged at like a Band-Aid caught on a hair. Josh hadn't been a boyfriend, he'd barely been a friend. He was no one I could tether myself to; no hook nor harness would hold him to me. He was a freefall descent straight back into my parents' bed and, though the landing was soft, it was painful nevertheless.

Mum closed the blinds, and I fell asleep to the sound of her wandering from room to room.

I woke up sometime later, hearing my father looking for his cufflinks. I sat myself up, discombobulated at first. He apologised for waking me. I switched the bedside light on. He was dressed formally, which I wasn't used to seeing since he'd retired a couple of years ago. He was off to lunch with some old workmates. 'You look nice, Daddy.'

He looked momentarily surprised by the remark and then said, 'Here, I'll open the blinds for you.' The sun shone into the room. Before he left, he kissed the top of my head. I heard the vacuum. The cleaner was here doing her weekly rounds. 'Don't worry,' he reassured me. 'I've told her not to come in here.'

Josh didn't call the following day. Or the day after that. When there was a noise outside the window, I went to it thinking I would see him there in a baseball cap, but it was only ever the weather, and the weather was mocking me. The weather was saying, he doesn't even know you're here. The weather was saying, you're an idiot and a slut and when you touch yourself, you don't deserve to think of him.

A week later, Gemma came to take me out (it turned out my mother had called her). Before she arrived, I took a very hot shower and cried because I felt nothing. I had never felt this nothingness. As a teenager, I would sometimes lie awake at night imagining all the people I loved most dying, one by one. And then I would imagine my own death, and it would be this imagining that made me cry, thinking of how all the people I loved most would be mourning me. This nothingness was something like that, but much, much worse. When I got out of the shower, my skin was red and flaring, my eyes swollen.

My jeans were loose around my hips. My lips were cracked and salty. Mum and Gemma stood by the front door and spoke in low tones while they waited for me to emerge from the bedroom. When I did, they both smiled inauthentically. As we went out the door Mum called out, 'But you're coming back here tonight, yes?' I turned back and nodded silently.

We ended up at a queer bar called Stella, and sat on a low leather couch and drank amaretto sours. I stopped weeping after the first one, and by the second drink I had the giggles, and by the third a couple of women were sitting with us. One of them, wearing a pink tie-dyed jumper, had her hand on Gemma's thigh. I watched Gemma chase the pink pattern with her finger, up and down the woman's sleeve. The other woman, sitting next to me, had smooth bleached hair that appeared to glow. I laughed, without knowing why, and drank some more. The woman got up and said she was going to the bathroom. I followed her there, pretending not to stumble. We went into a cubicle and I pressed myself flat against the door while the woman pissed with emphasis into the toilet. She said she was sorry, but that she didn't fuck straight women. She flushed the toilet and pulled her jeans up, and then she watched me piss before holding my hand and leading me back to Gemma.

By the time I returned to my parents' place, only the hallway light was on. I crept into my old bedroom and lay on the bed, pulling clumps of black mascara from my eyelashes. I thought about calling my high-school ex-boyfriend so he could validate some part of me, but he wouldn't answer anyway. He was married and I was sure his wife hated me. My eyes were damp, more from exhaustion than crying. The cocktails percolated in my stomach. I felt my intestines, worm-like and cramping. I took off my clothes and sat by the toilet basin shivering, before vomiting yellow muck into the toilet. I was holding onto the seat with a strong grip as if it were a lover. As if it was the woman who wouldn't fuck me. Or even kiss me. I vomited three more times before I crawled to the shower and sat on the drain, feeling the water snake over and under, under and over.

The next day I woke up with a headache. I stayed in bed until I heard the front door click shut and I was home alone. I pulled on the clothes that were nearest to me, got in the car and drove towards Josh's suburb, and then I found myself around the corner from his street. Then I drove down his street and slowed down in front of the picket fence and the rose bushes, and watched the flywire door slam open and shut in the wind. Then the blinds in the front bedroom began to open upwards, and I saw Kimiko's face framed by the glass. She was smiling. She knew nothing.

Don't tell the rabbi

The weather had turned as had everything in my life and it was raining heavily by the time we got to the synagogue. I entered the driveway and a female security guard dressed in navy and heavy black boots approached us under the cover of a large black umbrella. Her ponytail swished from side to side. She came to my window and peered inside, seeing Cookie in the front passenger seat waving like an innocent and David sitting diligently in the back. I told the guard I knew I couldn't park here, but I had two elderly people with me and asked if I could just drop them off before finding a spot in the street. The guard nodded without moving her face and opened the security gate. Cookie leaned over, put a hand on my shoulder, smiled through her bright pink lipstick and said, 'We promise to be good, darling.'

It was my parents' fortieth wedding anniversary and they were being honoured with a call-up to the Torah. They had saved seats near the front, and after I had dropped off my grandparents and then driven around the block three times to find a parking spot, I entered the shule. Cookie and Mum waved in tandem, and I shuffled down the aisle, avoiding eye contact with the regular congregants and a group of boisterous twelve-year-olds studying for their bar and bat mitzvahs.

I sat down between Mum and Cookie. Mum shuffled away from me and whispered, 'You're wet.' She placed an unopened prayer book on my lap. Cookie poked around in her handbag, and then shoved a butterscotch into my palm and said too loudly, 'This place is awful.' David snored and Dad turned the pages of the prayer book on his lap, humming along to the music. He wasn't on the correct page, but after the recitation of the Shema, the rabbi announced the page number and Dad reoriented, flicking the book at first left to right, and then, remembering, right to left. I looked around for Melanie, who'd failed to show up. I wished I'd stayed in bed like I'd wanted, but I had already agreed to give Cookie and David a lift to shule. Now my car stank vaguely of urine, and I didn't know how long I'd have to leave the windows open for the smell to dissipate.

We all stood as the Torah was removed from the ark, its ornate floral covering sewn by a member of the congregation. Shortly after the rabbi invited my parents to join him. They looked small up there on the bimah. Smaller than usual, or perhaps older. Mum was wearing sheer black stockings, her legs like knotted twigs. My father wore a suit without a tie and he was drowning in his large, creamy tallit, which he'd imported from Israel on the occasion of Melanie's wedding. Mum held on tightly to Dad's arm and they recited the prayers together, reading the transliteration nervously, proudly, overlapping each other and tripping over Hebrew that Rabbi Grossman kindly mouthed along with them with a patience that could only have been handed down from God.

It was a strange feeling to be jealous of your own parents. I couldn't say whether or not they were entirely happy, whether they still had sex, whether they liked each other. But I could say that they were committed to each other, understood each other, that they held hands when they walked down the street, and the other day, when I had been looking for a pair of earrings in my mother's bedside drawer, I had found a bottle of lube. And for the most part it was nice spending time with them. There wasn't an undercurrent of seething resentment or revulsion. It was comfortable. My mother liked to tell me that my father wasn't perfect, and he liked to counter this with 'I *am* perfect, but so is she.' When they met, he was dating someone who wasn't Jewish. Not long after, they broke up, and then he asked my mother out. She liked to tell me this story. She took pride in it. 'Her name was Sally. She had legs for days and hair like hay,' Mum had said. Sally was very sharp and studied law with my father, but there were some things she would never understand about Dad. 'Like what?' I'd asked. My mother paused for a while as if searching for the right answer and said, 'She wanted a Christmas tree.'

After my parents sat back down, the rabbi invited a young couple to join him on the bimah. It was the week before their wedding, and he said the Shehecheyanu: Thank you, God, for bringing us to this moment, this new beginning. While they were up there, baskets of soft kosher lollies were passed around, and when the rabbi said amen congregants began throwing them at the couple and small children who appeared to come from nowhere rushed at the bimah and stuffed the lollies in their mouths and pockets. My mother whispered, 'They look so happy, don't they? Just like your father and I, don't they?' I agreed to placate her, and also felt thankful that she was using that moment to talk about herself, and not me.

Cookie talked through the rest of the service, commenting on everything from the bride-to-be's dress (too short), the rabbi's shoes (too scruffy), the thick mole on the neck of the man sitting in front of us (he should get that removed), the strength of the air conditioning (do they think it's summer), and, of course, the overuse of the word *god*. This was even more pronounced when Rabbi Grossman delivered a sermon about that very subject – God. 'We know, we know,' Cookie said too loudly. I tried to shut out the clacking of her tongue on her butterscotch and listen to his words. He was saying how at Hebrew school he had a teacher who said they believed in evolution six days a week, but on the seventh day: God, Creation, Moses on the top of Mount Sinai receiving the ten commandments. You can be a Jew and hold both things in your heart. You can be a Jew and question all the things in your heart. I looked around me, at all the shule-goers, sitting and then standing and then sitting again, intoning millennia upon millennia of prayer and ritual, a spare seat at every Seder table reserved for the prophet Elijah a stark reminder that the spirits have also reserved their place here. What was in my heart? Tradition? Yes. Ritual? Some. God? As the rain bucketed against the windows, I thought maybe. And then Rabbi Grossman was finished and we stood and recited Kaddish for all the people who had been buried that week, month, at this time in years gone by, victims of terror, victims of war, and the rest of the unnamed souls in our hearts, and as we sat back down my grandmother said, 'Thank God that's over.'

We stayed for the Kiddush. Rabbi Grossman had been at my bat mitzvah and remembered me well. He seemed pleased to see me and came over as I took a thimble of grape juice from a tray. He was a large and soft man with a round, closely shaven face. He wanted to know how I'd been and what I'd been up to. He asked me these questions in a tone that was both gentle and careful, which made me suspect that my parents had said something to him about my situation. I couldn't tell him the truth, which was that I'd been up to nothing. That despite my parents' protestations I'd emailed my resignation through to Adele, and hadn't the courage to return to collect god-knows-what from my desk. That for weeks now I'd been counting the disappearance of time. Observing the regrowth of my pubic hair. I couldn't tell him about overhearing my parents' conversations about whether or not I needed to be medicated, whether they should contact Adele directly, or speak to a friend of theirs about getting me a job, whether they should force me out of the house, dunk me in cold water, push me down a hill … I didn't want to tell the rabbi how I had now been included in their breakfast roster: poached eggs on Mondays, yoghurt and muesli on Tuesdays, cottage cheese and jam on toast on Wednesdays. How I didn't eat much of it. How my parents held their breath when I scraped untouched food into the bin.

Smiling broadly through my teeth, I lied to Rabbi Grossman, telling him that I had been well, because otherwise I would suffer the humiliation of crying in a room full of people, fried fish balls and kosher soft drink.

We went back to Mum and Dad's house for lunch, which was when Melanie turned up, wearing tight black leggings, a crop top and an oversized black puffer jacket. I was stacking the dishwasher when Melanie handed me a dirty plate, disconcertingly gazed directly into my eyes and said, 'Here you go.'

I took the plate. 'Thanks.' She kept staring. 'What?'

'Nothing.' Melanie smiled.

I reached under the sink for a dishwashing tablet. 'Where were you this morning?'

Melanie smacked her lips together. 'Mum knew I wasn't coming,' she said, as if that were an answer. 'What's with Cookie's limp?'

'She's not limping,' I said quickly.

'Uh. Okay. She's pretty limpy.'

'Limpy?'

'Whatever. Do they have any San Pel?'

'I don't know.' I grabbed a wet cloth and started wiping down the bench, even though there wasn't really anything on it to clean.

'You live here, don't you?' Melanie headed for the fridge and pulled out a bottle of supermarket-brand mineral water and scrunched her face. She poured herself a glass, took a sip and put her hand to her mouth to suppress a burp.

'It's temporary. Gemma's away.' Gemma had been away, but it was only for a long weekend, though I told my parents it had been longer so they wouldn't question why, four weeks later, I was still sleeping in my old room.

'Sure.' Melanie nodded, staring into her glass. 'You never liked sleeping alone.'

'It's not like I'm sleeping in their bed.'

'Oh, hon. I don't care if you are,' Melanie said, taking another sip of water. I went to take the glass and Melanie swiftly clutched it with both hands. 'I'm not done.'

'Sorry,' I said. 'How are you, anyway? Mum said you were enrolling in a PhD?' I looked over to my grandmother. I definitely hadn't noticed a limp. But maybe I hadn't been looking.

'Mum and Dad are really worried about you, you know?'

'They're not worried about me.'

'Yes, they are. Mum rang me. She was practically crying.' I suspected that Melanie was exaggerating. 'You quit your job?'

I flinched. Melanie's words felt like an assault. 'It's not that simple.'

'You didn't quit?'

'No I— I guess I did.' I looked down at my hands.

'Don't tell me you got fired.'

'Fuck you,' I said, quietly.

My sister laughed but I couldn't tell if it was a fake laugh. 'Naomi! Language!'

'I didn't get fired. I just didn't want to be there any more.'

'Okay ...' she said, hands in the air. 'Anyway, I think I might know of something going in retail,' Melanie continued. 'Do you remember Beth?'

I shook my head.

'Beth is like the state manager for this store. I can't guarantee anything. But you should put together a resume, okay?'

'What is it?'

'A bedding store.'

'They sell beds?'

'No. Sheets and pillows and shit. It's called Linen Palace.'

'I don't have any experience.'

'Just lie then.' Melanie slid the water glass towards me. 'I'm finished now.' She took her phone out of her pocket and walked towards the lounge.

I thought about how I was still paying all the bills at my house, as it felt easier to just pay them than talk to Gemma about it, and my savings were rapidly depleting. The last thing I wanted to do was ask my parents for money, on top of everything else I was taking from them.

I reluctantly followed Melanie out of the kitchen and sat next to Cookie on the couch. Cookie took my hand.

'Where's your sister? Why aren't you talking to her?'

'I just was,' I said. I couldn't quite figure out how Melanie managed so effortlessly to do everything wrong and yet be forgiven for doing so, whereas I tried to do everything right (well, almost everything) and yet felt that I was perpetually disappointing everyone around me. I was always expected to put in the effort with my sister, because Melanie couldn't be relied upon to do so.

'You like being here, huh?' I was surprised that Cookie knew I'd been staying here. I thought maybe my parents hadn't told her. 'You can move in with me, you know? I'll kick him out,' Cookie said in a low voice, pointing to David. David didn't hear her, but knew she was talking about him and put his arms out as if to say 'what?'. Cookie shook her head as if to say, 'never you mind'. I felt my eyes begin to water. I opened my mouth to say something but couldn't. Cookie looked at me and said, 'Enough of that, now.'

'Sorry.'

'Crying makes you look ugly.'

'I'm sorry.'

'I want you to be beautiful. You want some lipstick?' I shook my head. She licked her finger and rubbed it into my cheeks until they responded with a flush of colour. 'That's better. Now smile.'

I forced a smile, feeling the rise of my cheeks, the smell of her wet finger, until she looked satisfied and then we sat in silence, watching Melanie and my father in conversation, possibly having an argument, though it was hard to tell. I looked down at Cookie's feet and noticed the right foot was bandaged. 'What happened to your foot?'

'Nothing. Old people problems.'

'But you don't have old people problems.'

'Exactly. Now help me up. I need to make pishies.'

I stood up and held out my arm. Cookie grabbed it and heaved herself off the couch, and when fully upright let me go. 'That'll do it,' she said to me. I watched her as she made her way to the bathroom, slowly, off-balance, limping.

I want you back

A week later Melanie texted: *Resume?* I repeated that I had no retail experience, and she wrote back: *Leave it with me.* The next day there was a resume in my inbox that Melanie had fabricated entirely, which I numbly forwarded to the email address Melanie had provided. I wasn't sure why she was being nice to me and would have liked to thank her in some way, but then I figured she wasn't doing it for me. She was doing it for my parents. And so I paid my gratitude forward by agreeing to see Shelley.

Mum mentioned a few times that she'd bumped into Shelley – an old school friend of mine – down the street and she was keen to catch up with me. And then Shelley texted me too, saying that a group was getting together on Saturday night and I should join them. I wondered what my mother had told her, or whether they'd bumped into each other at all and instead Mum had just called her, pleading and desperate. As pleasant as she was towards Gemma, I knew that she lamented the fact that I didn't have more Jewish friends.

'But Shelley's so nice,' Mum had said forcefully after I'd made a face.

'Gemma's nice too.'

'That's not the point. You see Gemma all the time. You need to try harder, Naomi.'

'At what?'

'At friendships. They need to be cultivated. Groomed.'

'That sounds creepy.'

'Don't be ridiculous. Just try.'

A few days later I found myself in Shelley's car, which was tidy and small. She worked at a real estate agency but was considering leaving it to start her own business selling gift hampers online. When she told me about this in the car, I so wished I could be like Shelley. She'd met her boyfriend at uni, though I'd never met him. At a traffic light she showed me photos of their latest weekend escape, all of which looked unreal and I had to stop myself from asking whether it was in fact stock footage of vineyards and waterfalls and chiselled men with good teeth. But I knew it was all real because Shelley didn't lie. She was the worst great person and I detested her and cursed my mother for forcing me out of bed. I gave Shelley the phone back and she wedged it between her legs, which were tanned and hairless and on display, even though it was a cold night. I detested her even more then. I bet Shelley had no hang-ups. I bet all her boyfriend had to do was touch her nipples and she'd come instantly.

Shelley apologised about the bar we were going to. 'Sorry, but it's painfully hipster. Doron wanted to try it. It's so Doron, you know?' I had barely worn any make-up, save for some red lipstick that I felt achieved the minimum required, and wore an oversized long grey dress that my mother said did nothing for me and swallowed me whole, to which my father responded, unconvincingly, 'She looks lovely.' The bar was actually awfully daggy (as I suspected it might be), but that was somewhat comforting. Not having to make an effort was a relief.

While Shelley ordered a bottle of white wine I went and sat next to Doron. He had thick black curly hair, said 'cool beans' more than once, and seemed pleased to see me. We reminisced about sitting on the same school bus and memorising all the words to 'Back for Good' by Take That in year seven. I drank quickly while the rest of them laughed for a long time about something Shelley had done last week. I laughed too and offered up a memory from one speech night when the vice-principal tripped on the stage. They all laughed even harder. Then, by some nineties miracle, 'Back for Good' came on through the bar's speakers and we all sang loudly and off-key. For a moment it felt wonderful.

When the group started to disband, Doron asked if I'd stay and play a round of pool. I drank more wine and agreed. As Shelley left, she gave me an all-embracing hug, and said, 'It is *so* good to see you.' I told her it was good to see her too, and it was. I was still high from the singing and felt a wave of nostalgic affection for Shelley. I then thought, wouldn't life, in general, be easier if you never really had to know anyone?

Doron won at pool, kissed me rather sloppily and confessed that he was drunk, and then I said the same. I went with him to his place, which he shared with two of his workmates, and although I wasn't in the mood for much, found myself sprawled on his bed when he turned off the lights. He told me he didn't have any condoms and I hoped (for that reason) we might talk or reminisce, but he promptly had his hands all over me, found his way through the excess fabric of my dress, removed my underwear and was soon on top of me. He moved himself up to my face, thrust his erection into my mouth, and before I could do anything else I felt the surge of his come in the back of my throat. He passed me some tissues to spit into, rolled off me and fell asleep. I lay next to him for some time, watching shadows on the wall, unsure of where or how to move. When he started to snore I proceeded to fumble for my undies in the dark but couldn't find them. I slunk out of his house feeling the wash of breeze under my dress, called a taxi, realised I was unsure of where I was exactly, and had to search the front fence for a street number in order to provide an address.

I got home at around two am and poked my head in to see my parents sleeping. My mother was making unintelligible noises and I lingered a few moments longer, fighting the urge to decipher the sounds. I shut their door, took a shower and brushed my teeth twice. I couldn't sleep, so went to the kitchen and took two mandarins and a large slice of chocolate cake back to bed with me. I ate the mandarins first, sitting up in bed, and looked at my phone. I plunged my finger into the cake and sucked bits of chocolate off my nail. I'd been so disciplined, not writing to Josh, not calling him, not googling him or driving by his house. I thought fuck it, and using the hand without cake on it sent him a message: *The Budapest files are in the 2008 folder. I just figured you might not be able to find them.* I slid the phone under the pillow and closed my eyes. Moments later it vibrated, and I jolted with the unexpected shock of it: *Thanks for telling me.*

I thought you were dead

I'm not dead

OK then

He rang. He told me that he missed me and that he was sorry, so I said I missed him and was sorry too. Though I wasn't sure that what I was feeling was missing; it was more like an ache. He told me he was looking for work elsewhere. Things weren't the same at the museum. He wanted to know what I was doing. I told him I'd just applied for a job at a bedding store in South Yarra while I was figuring things out. He told me I always looked good in bedding, and then said sorry again. I told him I'd be happy to offer him a discount if I got the job. He wanted to know if I'd been seeing anyone. I told him no, and sunk my finger into the cake again. I wondered where he was sitting. Was he in the lounge? Was he outside? He told me he was in his car. He goes to his car when he can't sleep, turns the heater on and listens to music. I said I could picture that, and he said he could picture me sitting in the car next to him. I asked him what he'd say to me if I were there now. And he said he wouldn't want to say anything. He'd just want to touch me. I said I wanted him to touch me. Then he said he wanted to talk about my tits and asked if that was okay. I said it was. He told me that he couldn't stop thinking about them, that when he jerked off he imagined he was sucking my nipples, sucking them dry, or that his cock was between them. He told me that my tits were everything and asked if I could touch them now. I said yes, and then he went on to tell me more of the things he wanted to do to my tits – my magical fuckable tits – and I closed my eyes and muttered things like 'yeah', 'I like that' and 'mmhmm', trying to stay as quiet as possible in between, so I could hear his breath and the slapping of him jerking off. After he came, he told me he wanted to hear the sound of me coming, but I felt shy and told him so. And he told me not to feel shy and it seemed he wouldn't leave the point alone, so then I told him I was touching myself, but I wasn't. I was touching the cake. I was touching the cake and making my breaths longer and deeper, and then I told him that I came. And then we hung up. And then I finished the cake.

I took my plate to the kitchen and returned to bed. I felt restless and tried to scan my body meditatively for tension. But it kept reminding me of all the parts of my body he had once touched. I snuck into my parents' bathroom, found some sleeping pills and took two, and slept till ten am the following day. When I woke up, there was a message on my phone from Josh: *Meet me at the Westin.*

'You got home late. So it was a good night?' Mum was on the computer at the kitchen table. She looked up at me, and put her reading glasses on top of her head.

I opened the fridge and stood there longer than I needed to. 'Yep.'

'That's wonderful, darling. She's a sweet girl, that Shelley. I always liked her.'

My stomach tightened, trying to quash the memory of Doron's soggy breath. 'Yep.'

'You probably noticed that I picked up all your clothes off the floor and put them in the machine.'

But not my underwear from the night before. 'Thanks,' I said, feeling nauseous at the thought.

'I'd rather you didn't drape your things over the paintings.'

'Well, hang the paintings then.'

'Naomi ...'

'Sorry.'

She sighed. 'Look, I don't know what to do with that room.'

'My room?' I asked, with a slightly panicked inflection.

'Oh,' she said, and turned her head to the blue light of the fridge. 'Don't worry. The room isn't going anywhere.' She smiled, forced, but a smile nevertheless. 'Now, are you going to eat something? Otherwise close the fridge.'

I closed the fridge and began making coffee. Mum said she was having trouble with the website she was on and asked if I could take a look. It was a homewares discount store and Mum had two Le Creuset pans in her cart. 'What are you trying to do, Mum?'

'The email said it was twenty per cent off, but when I go to the shopping cart I can't see the discount.'

I sat in the chair next to her and peered at the screen. 'Maybe it doesn't apply to Le Creuset.'

'Oh. Forget it,' Mum said, closing the computer. 'I'd much rather go in to the shop anyway.' She put a hand on my back. 'Have you heard from Adele?'

I felt the heat of her hand there, fixing me to my spot. I had heard from Adele, who had asked if there was anything she could do to convince me to stay in the role, at least until they found a replacement. I hadn't known how to respond, so I replied politely that I would think about it and thanked her for her support. Marilyn had also made contact on Facebook with a message laden with emoji hearts and flower bouquets. Josh, however, hadn't made contact until last night. I put that detail out of my mind and answered my mother, 'Why would I?'

'You know it's not too late to go back. It won't be easy for them to replace you. It wouldn't hurt to reach out.' She began to rub her hand across my shoulder blades, from each bony knoll to the shallow pastel mess in between. I reached for my coffee, shaking her off.

'Melanie is helping me find something.'

'Oh yes?' Mum was doing a bad job of pretending she didn't already know. 'At least it's something. What are you doing today? We could buy you a new chopping board. I know that other one I bought you is cracked.'

I took a sip of coffee. 'Not today.'

'Why not?' She pulled her glasses from her head and they got caught on a curl, and she spent some time untangling them.

'I have to pop out for a bit.'

'Where?'

'I said I'd meet Gemma for lunch.'

'Oh. She's back, is she?'

'Uh huh.' Gemma had been asking when I was planning on moving back in. I wanted to. I did. And I felt guilty leaving Gemma in the house alone, even though I suspected Gemma didn't care too much, but the thought of leaving my parents made me wobbly in the tummy. I knew I would miss the way they sounded when they slept, or when they bickered in front of me and I'd role-play being the arbiter and then we'd all have something to laugh about. Of course, I couldn't articulate any of these thoughts out loud. It was hard enough admitting them to myself.

'Oh well. Another time then. It's nice to see you being more social. And you look better too. You're less pale, or something.'

*

Josh met me by an elevator in the lobby. He was half in shadow and had grown a beard that made him look like someone else and frightened me momentarily. We mouthed *hello* to each other and he pushed the up button. We stepped inside the elevator and watched each other nervously through mirrored reflections. He reached for my hand. His fingernails were chewed down to the flesh.

'I'm sorry. I can only stay an hour,' he said once we were in the hotel room. He sat on the bed. He patted the empty space next to him. I sat down and looked at our knees, which were touching.

'You got this plush hotel room and you can only stay an hour?'

'Yeah. Sorry. Maybe it was a crazy idea to do this.'

I touched his cheek scruff. 'Maybe.'

'Do I look wild? You look so good.'

Suddenly I became concerned with the thought that I'd lost too much weight, that my breasts were smaller, and that we'd fit differently together. I swallowed and then said, 'What does Kimiko think?'

'Of what?'

'Of the beard.'

'She hates it.' He shook his head. Something about him seemed changed too. Like his eyelashes had grown longer or his hands looked older.

'I don't,' I said quietly. He still hadn't kissed me. I really wanted him to kiss me.

'I didn't think we would be doing this again.'

'Neither. What do you want to do?'

I wondered if we might just hold each other and thought that might be pleasant, but he began undressing and then asked if he could take my clothes off. I nodded. I let him fondle my body all over, only slightly self-conscious of the purple bruise on my left breast from where Doron had kneaded his fingers, but Josh didn't seem to notice. He touched me like he was buttering me, like he was scraping the last of it from the plate – my hungry, salty skin. He licked my lips and kissed me deeply, and then climbed on top of me saying how much he'd missed me. He parted my legs and started fucking me without a condom. His hands moved from my breasts to my stomach and back to my breasts again. He pulled out quickly and came on my stomach, apologising and apologising. He flopped next to me and rolled onto his side and asked me what I wanted. I was conscious of the time and that he only had an hour, so I told him I wanted nothing.

'I can go down on you?'

I shook my head and wiped my tummy with a hand towel. 'I'm fine.' I wondered how many of these hand towels had been used for mopping up sex.

'Sorry. It's been so long and I was a bit excited to see you.'

'It's okay, really.'

'And Kimiko and I don't—'

'I'm fine.' I smiled benevolently and closed my eyes. I heard him get up and turn the shower on and for a moment I wondered if I could somehow wash myself down the drain.

He came back into the room with a towel over his shoulders like a cape. He sat next to me and I put my head in his lap and he stroked my hair a little. His cock was flaccid and I liked lying next to it, the bristle of his pubes against my cheek. I loved him in this moment and wanted to say so. Neither of us had ever mentioned love, and it felt greedy to pronounce it now in this moment of reunion. He turned on the TV and we watched the news and had a little laugh at an innocuous story involving a politician. I thought we might fuck again, that an hour might extend to two or three, but he looked tired and showed no signs of arousal. After a while he offered to run me a bath and left to turn the tap on without waiting for my reply. He dressed to the sound of running water, saying, 'I'll wait for you to get in before I go. Stay the night. It's all paid for.'

I followed him to the bathroom and watched him check the temperature, swirling the water with his hand like he was playing with dough. The assuredness of it. The bleak reminder that he had run many baths for his children.

I steadied myself against him as I stepped in the water, hoping he'd strip off and join me. He didn't. He smiled downwards at the rippling water and chewed at his index finger.

'Okay then.' He sighed.

'Okay.' My breasts bobbed like jelly.

'I wish I could stay.'

'I love you,' I stuttered. I glanced at him momentarily, saw his mouth hang open like a fish, and then submerged my head under the water. Even as the words came out, I wasn't sure I meant them. It just seemed, after all this time, well, what would it all have been for, if there wasn't love between us? I thought back to the conversation with my mother the morning after I moved back in with them. She had asked me if I loved him, and I didn't answer because I didn't know what the answer was. Now, being with him again, I still didn't know. In fact, I'd never before felt that I knew so little.

I opened my eyes and the bath water flooded my irises and stung. Maybe Josh had put soap in it, or an oil of some sort. I could see that he had now squatted down to meet my face. I was scared to come up for air, but breathing was inevitable. It wasn't like I had stones or pockets to weigh myself down. I lifted my head out and asked for a face washer. He nimbly grabbed one and handed it to me. 'You okay?'

I took the cloth and dabbed my eyes. 'Yeah. I feel stupid.'

'I love you too,' he said, quietly.

'You do?'

'Is it so surprising?'

I pulled his face towards me and kissed him. 'You need to go.'

He nodded, shrugged his shoulders and kissed the top of my head, and left.

I called Gemma from the bath, grasping at his and my pubic hairs floating to the surface, and invited her over. Half an hour later Gemma knocked on the door. I opened it in a robe I'd found in the cupboard. We ordered room service and ate hot chips and a cheese platter sprawled out on the bed.

'He's not paying for the room service,' I said.

'He's not?'

'Should I ask him to?' I licked some salt off my fingers.

'I'll pay for it,' Gemma said.

We finished the meal, and then Gemma dropped me back at my parents'. Before I returned the key, Gemma had asked me if I was sure and that she'd stay the night with me in the hotel, if I wanted. I shook my head, too embarrassed to say that all I wanted to do was to sit between my parents on the couch, and watch *Midsomer Murders*.

Parasites

I got the job at Linen Palace, which was situated in a high-end shopping strip in South Yarra, surrounded by overpriced bakeries and Pilates studios. I called Melanie to thank her but she didn't answer her phone, so I sent a text: *Thanks so much for helping with the job. Come by and I'll sort you out with a discount* and two days later she replied with a thumbs-up emoji. I showed it to Dad over dinner and we laughed about it. And then Mum wanted to know what we were laughing about so I showed the exchange to her and she said something along the lines of 'it's the thought that counts', which made Dad and I laugh even harder.

My manager was new to the role and often flustered. I surmised that that's how I might feel if the job meant anything to me. I kind of relished falling into a semi-catatonic state while I was there. Initially, I said I'd only wanted to work part time, but they were forever understaffed so quickly enough it became more of a full-time job. My main duties consisted of folding towels and, when there was no one in the store, taking the towels down from the shelves and refolding them. I spent a lot of time on the towels, but even so they never looked as neat as when the manager did them. The face washers were the worst. They were so small I could never figure out how to make them look good.

I had to wear an apron, and during my initial training session I was told that phones were to be kept in the storeroom, but as soon as I saw another staff member conceal their phone in the apron's big front pocket I followed suit. Josh had begun messaging me on a regular basis, asking when my break was. Sometimes he would come and meet me, and we would walk around the corner to a little playground where there was a park bench. If there was no one around, occasionally we would kiss and he would snake his hand up my skirt, or down my back, or encourage my hand to his hard cock.

After one such day, I was taking a walk around Caulfield Park with my mother and she asked me – point blank – whether I'd met someone. When I told her I hadn't, she asked me whether I was seeing Josh again, and I said no to that too.

'Well, you just seem better,' Mum said.

'I am.'

'Good. Your father and I are doing something right then,' Mum said, triumphantly. I'd only just noticed that, having borrowed her leggings, she was wearing another pair exactly the same so we looked like we were matching.

'Uh huh.'

'Why don't you just call the museum?'

'No,' I said. She was walking fast and I struggled to maintain the pace.

'Why?'

'It's been three months. I'm sure they've found someone by now.'

'I saw an ad in the *Jewish News* just last week!' She swung her arms back and forth.

'I can't. It's too humiliating.' I looked around and sensed that everyone in the park was eavesdropping.

'You loved that job, Naomi. Now, I know you're working and feeling better. So you need to be courageous. It's not easy. I know all about "not easy". I ran my own business for thirty years, and that wasn't easy.'

'I like the shop,' I said, swatting a bug. 'And I thought you liked the thirty per cent discount.'

Mum stopped walking abruptly and I almost tripped over myself. 'Naomi. Can we be serious here?'

'I am being serious.'

'Bullshit. Look, we all like the discount but that's not the point, is it?'

'What is the point?'

Mum raised her eyebrows to the trees and began briskly walking again. 'I think you should call the museum. It doesn't hurt to check in with them. Let them know you're still alive.'

'They know.'

'But you're not still seeing him, are you?'

'I've already told you I'm not.' I licked some sweat off my top lip.

'Because men like that—'

'Mum. Can we leave it? Actually, can you slow down a bit?'

'Slow down?' She cackled. 'You are the laziest girl in the world. Move, child!'

'It's my fortieth on Saturday and I don't know how I feel about it.' Josh had turned up with freshly squeezed juice the colour of grass, and we shared it on my lunch break, sitting side by side on a park bench. He had a plaster on the left side of his chin. He told me that he'd had something removed. This was the sort of thing my parents would say. They were always getting things removed.

I bit down on something gritty, either celery or kale, and resisted the urge to spit on the ground. I didn't know what I was supposed to say. 'Happy birthday.'

'I feel old.'

'Forty's not so old.'

'I think it is, isn't it?' He pushed his hair back with his hand. 'Kimiko's organising a party.' Her name lingered between us and the air and the birds. 'I'm not really in the mood,' he continued.

'Wow,' I said, letting some moments pass. 'A party.'

'Sorry. I shouldn't be telling you this shit.' He looked at his watch. 'Your place isn't too far from here, is it?'

'Why?'

'Maybe we could go there now, if you have time left on your break?'

'I don't know,' I said, looking at my hands. 'It would be weird. I'm not living there at the moment.' This hadn't come up before, which was unsurprising. Our relationship lived in a liminal space, where neither of us discussed life outside of the cheaper hotels we had now met at a handful of times. I much preferred the Westin, but as I wasn't paying for it I couldn't say anything. He'd always leave quickly after and I would be left in the room, contemplating whether housekeeping had sanitised the TV remote, analysing the blotches on the walls. He never asked me if I ended up staying the night. I never did, but he never asked. 'I'm living with my parents,' I continued.

He looked confused and touched his plaster. We stared at each other without speaking. I knew then that he wasn't going to ask me why I had moved. It occurred to me also that he'd never even asked me about leaving the museum, and he never would either. All these things he never asked. Gemma had raised this point with me more than once. And I had shrugged it off, because it wasn't like I'd wanted to talk about it anyway.

He stood up and took his keys out of his pocket and jingled them. 'Okay, well. I should go.'

'Really?' I swallowed. I wanted him to stay. I always wanted him to stay. I wanted to not go back to work and for him to stay. I wanted to tell him that I loved him again, if that would make him stay. I would unzip him and blow him here in the park in front of the playground if that would make him stay. I'd let him fuck me in the arse in broad daylight if it would make him stay. 'Why do you need to go?'

'Naomi …' He touched his plaster again.

'Is it sore?'

'No. It's just a bit itchy.' He blew out through his lips. 'I'm sorry. I feel bad. And I thought this would make me feel good. Sorry.'

'You're always saying sorry,' I said, quietly.

He took the juice cup from me and jiggled it. 'All finished?'

I nodded, and he kissed me on the head and walked off, dumping our two juice cups in the rubbish bin on the way to his car.

I called him on Saturday to wish him a happy birthday but he didn't answer. I texted him: *Happy birthday. I wish we could celebrate.* He didn't reply. Later that evening I texted him again: *How's the party?* He didn't reply. At midnight I sent him another message, a picture of me naked in the bathroom mirror, my super-fuckable tits on display. He didn't reply.

Days later, Gemma couldn't believe that he still hadn't replied, and my mortification was growing thick and ugly. I started to believe that Kimiko had found the phone, found my messages. All the messages. Had he not deleted the messages? I stood over the sink, retching at the thought.

'She hasn't seen it,' Gemma said, wiping herself on the toilet seat at my parents' house. I was standing in front of her, whipping half of my hair on top of my head in a scrunchie. I let my hair down again and scratched my scalp furiously.

'Like, he's been using his phone to text and call you this whole time and she's clearly had no idea, otherwise he'd have a burner or something, right?' Gemma said.

'We don't know that she's never seen the texts.'

'Come on. If she had, he would disappear.'

'He has disappeared!'

We crossed paths with my father in the hallway. 'Gemma, darling. How are you?' She kissed him on both cheeks. 'Taking this one back home with you?' He was joking, but not joking.

After Gemma left, I took a long hot shower. My scalp felt tender and I soaked it in a hair mask and sat on my bed in my towel, brushing out the knots. I pulled the matted hair from the base of my brush only to discover a copper-coloured bug nestled there. On closer inspection of the brush I found more lice; some smaller, some darker, juicier. I heard myself laugh outside of myself. I put my fingers to my head and thought for a moment about finding the sharpest blade in the house and performing a dramatic chop.

How old had I been the last time I'd had them? A time closer to my mother's womb, to the rough and tumble of my dress-up drawer, playing like a puppy on springy floors with girls like Shelley. How long had the lice been there for, devouring, feasting? Days? Weeks? Months? It was an infestation. Had they infested my brain? Maybe? For a moment I'd hoped so. For a moment I wished that I wasn't solely responsible for my own corrosion. That I was being worn down by some hungry and malevolent creature, other than myself.

I stripped the bed and piled all my sheets, towels and unwashed clothes and kicked them out the door of my bedroom. I stood there, in the nude, itchy. I thought of stories of women in concentration camps making meals of the living: vermin, insects. My toes sank into the plush carpet. I am those women and I am not those women. Those women are laughing at me. So they should.

My phone buzzed and I grabbed it. A message from Josh appeared. *Are you naked?*

The lice shampoo reeked of poison, my hair stank of metal. No matter how much I washed it with regular shampoo, the stink remained. I hadn't been able to reply to Josh. What could I say to him? Yes, I am naked. I am always naked. By the way, do you have lice?

I was at work a couple of days later, faced with the near impossible task of stuffing a fitted sheet back into its packet after pulling it out to show to a customer who promptly changed their mind. It looked terrible. The plastic crackled as I slid my fingers in and out, trying to smooth it. I heard someone call my name and looked up. I saw Kimiko standing there with a child on her hip. It was Ava, sliding her fingers in and out of her mother's hoop earrings. I looked at the child, daring to make eye contact with her, thinking, oh God, do you remember me? What do you remember about me?

'Oh, hi,' I said, clutching the packet close like it was one of the fluffy cushions on display. I could feel my palms gathering heat against the plastic. I could feel the urge to retch returning.

'Josh mentioned you worked here,' Kimiko said. Her mouth was turned upwards. It was almost a smile.

'Oh, he did?' I swallowed, focusing on the child, her fat fingers.

'A bit of a career change?'

I set the fitted sheet down in between some toilet brushes and wiped my palms on my apron in a casual manner although it was anything but. 'Not really. Just a bit of time out while I figure out what I want to do.'

'Fair enough. I thought,' she said, glancing around the store, 'that you were invaluable to the museum. They still haven't found a replacement for you.'

'Oh. Really?' I shuffled my feet, left and right.

'I've always loved this store, actually.'

'I'll give you a discount,' I blurted.

'Oh,' Kimiko said, blinking her eyes a few times. 'You don't have to do that.' She shuffled Ava awkwardly on her hip.

'Do you need help with something?'

'Can you show me some quilt covers?' Ava pulled hard on her mother's earring and Kimiko's face contorted for a moment. She grabbed the child's hand firmly and said, 'Stop it,' in a low voice. The girl's bottom lip crinkled and then straightened. She released herself from her mother's grasp, put her fat fingers into her hair and began to scratch. Again, Kimiko grabbed Ava's hand and said, 'Stop scratching.' Then Kimiko looked up at me, blank and expectant. Her nose twitched. Was she smelling me?

The quilt covers were at the front of the store and I was aware Kimiko could have easily shown herself. I pointed to some light grey stonewashed linen, telling Kimiko these were my favourite, not because they were but because I'd heard the manager say the same thing a couple of hours before and I was finding it hard to think of things to say. Kimiko paused for a moment and then asked me if I had these. I wasn't sure how to answer. Everything I'd told her was a lie, so my answer didn't matter. I said that I didn't have them, yet, but I really wanted them. And she said 'okay' and that she'd take them, along with a high thread-count sheet set, a couch throw and some new pillowcases for the kids. It was more than enough to get me to my selling target for my shift, even with the thirty per cent discount. Kimiko's hands were clearly full with the child and some other shopping, so I reluctantly offered to take the things to the car, again, not because I wanted to, but because I'd seen my manager do the same earlier in the day.

I numbly followed Kimiko outside to a red SUV parked around the corner in a side street. Kimiko opened the boot and then proceeded to put Ava in the car. There was a dog leash and a muddy tennis ball on one side, and on the other Josh's crumpled jumper. I inhaled deeply as if I could smell him, but my nostrils filled with wet grass and the smell of dog.

Kimiko returned to the back of the car. 'Thanks for the discount.'

'No worries.' I dared myself to look Kimiko in the eye. 'Did you get a dog?'

'A few months ago. A border collie. The kids love it, but Josh especially.' He'd never mentioned a dog.

'You don't like dogs?'

'I don't like fleas. Or bugs.' She grimaced. 'Or lice,' she added in a hushed tone. 'We've just recovered from a bout of that.' Kimiko shuddered and then stared at me, a little too long. 'And the car reeks. I don't like that.' Kimiko lingered a moment, and then shut the boot. She patted herself down with the intensity of a person who had lost everything. 'My keys,' she said.

'Are they in the car?'

'Oh. Yes,' she said, looking very tired. 'Goodbye, Naomi. Take care.'

That night I doused myself again with the lice shampoo. When I was done I called Gemma. She came over to help me pack while Mum watched from the doorway, open-mouthed. Mum kept looking like she was about to say something, but she couldn't, or wouldn't. I was pretty sure my parents never actually believed that I would ever move out. Not the first time, at twenty-four, and not now.

Back home, Gemma had changed the sheets on my bed and filled the fridge with fresh fruit and vegetables. We ordered Thai and sat on my floor slurping green curry and listening to indie bands on the radio. After dinner, Gemma went through my phone, deleted all the text messages from Josh and blocked his number.

Repressed grief

A month had passed and I wasn't sleeping. It had been Gemma's idea to go to a therapist. Even my mother, who when speaking on the subject of mental health would do so in a whisper, concurred it was a good idea. Especially after she'd confronted me again about rekindling whatever dwindling fire was left between Josh and I, and I had finally admitted it because I knew it was over.

'You say it's over,' she'd said. 'But it's not over until it's over.'

'Trust me,' I'd said. 'It's over.'

She nodded, and then started crying.

'Mummy, what is it?'

She shook her head. 'I could have done more.'

I took her hand. 'I'm okay, you know?'

She pulled away from me and retrieved a tissue from somewhere on her person and blew her nose. 'But are you?'

I visited a new GP to get a mental health assessment. It wasn't that I didn't trust the doctor who I had shared with my mother since I'd got my first period, it was more that she was the kind of doctor who – and this happened numerous times – would want to chitchat with me if we were standing in a line to buy movie tickets, or stop by my table if we were at the same restaurant.

To curtail this, I found a GP a couple of suburbs away. He was a young man and could have been a fraction older or younger than me. He appeared nervous in my presence, had trouble using the printer and required the matronly receptionist to come and assist with a paper jam.

I filled in the mental health assessment form with a grey lead pencil, and after typing my answers into his computer he told me that my score was 'moderate'. I wondered whether this was a good or bad thing as I watched him go on the internet and search for therapists in the area.

Eventually, he gave me a referral to a woman who he said 'specialises in stress, anxiety, relationship issues and family conflict, as well as alternative medicine'. I asked him if he thought the therapist was any good. He said, 'I can't see why not.' And then he pivoted the computer screen to face me, scrolled down the therapist's page and showed me that they had been given multiple four- and five-star reviews.

The therapist was a tiny woman with a pixie haircut. I immediately felt gigantic in her presence.

One of the first things I did was tell her I was Jewish, expecting it to inform the counselling session somehow. She responded by telling me not to worry, that she'd had many Jewish clients in the past. I shifted in my seat.

'I've made you uncomfortable,' she said.

'No.' I sighed.

'Would you say that you sigh often, or deeply?'

'I don't know. I can't say I've ever noticed.'

'You've sighed a lot since you've arrived. Maybe six, seven times. It is actually a sign of repressed grief, which many of you are holding on to.'

'Many of us?'

'Jews,' she said, looking me squarely in the eye.

'Because of … the Holocaust?'

'Well.' She smiled. 'It goes back much further than that, doesn't it? How many times have your people had to flee? How many times have you not been able to bury your dead? Listen. Don't worry. It is a starting point but not the end point. We're getting to know each other. This is just context.'

I sat with that for a moment, was about to sigh and then stopped myself.

'What's been going on?' she asked me.

'I can't sleep.'

She nodded and made a note. 'You can't get to sleep, stay asleep, or you're not sleeping at all?'

'Mostly the first two. I mean I sleep, but—'

'Do you dream?'

'Yes.' Nightmares. Worse than they'd ever been. My bed was full of them. Josh, Kimiko, soldiers, my breasts in their mouths, my breasts on the floor, cut away, a boot on my neck, flesh caught in zippers. 'A lot of— Unpleasant dreams, I would say.'

'Is this just recently?'

'I've never slept well.'

'And what do you do for that? Have you tried meditation?'

'Some breathing.' A lie. 'But sometimes sleeping pills, or antihistamine. The drowsy one.'

'You need to be careful medicating.'

'I am.' As a child my mother would sit with me in the kitchen, a light left on for these sort of midnight adventures, and give me a sip of port. I loved it and would always ask for more. 'But yeah. I suppose it's been worse, recently. I had a bad— It wasn't really a relationship. But there was an ending. I guess.'

'Tell me about that.'

I spoke at length without her saying anything. The silence she offered made way for the most gruesome and humiliating of details, which I delivered while staring at a terracotta mandala on the wall. When I got to the lice, I stopped, because that was the ending. The feasting was over, eggs and all.

'I'm sorry, Naomi. That all sounds very hard.'

Her kindness startled me. I wanted to cry, but was sure I didn't deserve to. 'Well, it wasn't a real relationship so—'

'It was a real relationship,' she said, and with that I let out one wretched sob and reached for the strategically placed box of tissues, blew my nose and swallowed until my mouth was dry. 'But it was also harassment in the workplace. You do realise that, right?'

'Oh,' I said, shaking my head.

'You're shaking your head.'

'Well, it wasn't like—'

'You were very vulnerable in that situation. He had an incredible amount of power over you. And you essentially lost your job because of it.'

I didn't know what to say, because I'd never thought of it in those terms, not in any meaningful way. I was thinking about Josh and all the places we'd fucked. How I'd acclimated to being screwed on tiles and benches and couches and up against walls. The thought made my lips tingle. 'I— I wouldn't say I was powerless.'

'Why did the museum think you left? Did you ever tell anyone?'

'Of course not,' I whispered. 'It was an affair.'

She wrote something down. 'There's a lot to process here. There's the relationship, there's work, there's family. Your parents? You're close.'

'Yes.' I knew my father took his morning shit in the powder room, leaving my mother to shit in the ensuite. 'They're very supportive.'

'You moved in with them during the break-up.'

'Yes. They wanted me to.' Her smile widened. I had excited her in some way.

'So there's a lot of co-dependency there, I'm sensing. And are you dating?'

I shook my head.

'When you meet someone you're interested in, and you will, I want you to try not to sleep with them immediately. Get to know them first. Have a friendship and see what happens.'

She then asked if she could touch me. I said yes, and she placed two cold child-sized fingers on my wrist. 'Your energy is off.' Then she asked about my diet and said that if I wasn't prepared to eat meat, I was to go and have breakfast with a hearty dose of greens – spinach, kale, whatever's available – and that should help with the sleeping. But being here, talking, unburdening, that was going to be most helpful of all.

I looked at the time. There were five minutes left of the session. I said, 'Sorry. That thing you said about meeting someone I like … well … how do I know if I like someone?'

She said, 'That's exactly why you shouldn't be having sex with people before you know if you like them or not.' She closed her notebook. 'Everything is achievable. But it takes time. You will get there, Naomi. I have no doubt. Whether you do it here, or you do it in your own way.'

'Thanks,' I said, and told her I would book my next appointment online.

'Sure,' she said, and I hated that she knew that I had no intention of returning.

Yenta

It was lunchtime and David and Cookie were in the dining room. Cookie was dressed from head to toe in animal print, with a large seashell necklace draped over her bosom. She always liked to dress well for lunch, as dinner wasn't usually much to speak of – an egg sandwich, a tuna salad. David, on the other hand, was noticeably dishevelled. He was unshaven and his jumper was inside out with the label protruding under his chin. They shared their table with two women, who smiled at me as if they'd never seen a young person before. One of them was wearing a large plastic bib that resembled a poncho I'd worn to a music festival Gemma had once dragged me to. (I missed the festival entirely – she'd taken ecstasy and I spent half the night inside a chill-out tent refilling her water bottle and wiping her forehead.)

I pulled up a chair next to Cookie. She patted my arm and then clutched it tightly, looking at the women, and said, 'My granddaughter.'

They nodded as if they'd never seen a granddaughter before. The woman with the bib leaned forward and said in a thick accent, 'Beautiful.'

Cookie clucked her tongue and swirled some watery soup with her spoon. 'You want some?' she asked me.

I shook my head. 'You have it.'

'Do I have to?' Cookie winked and then took a white sachet of salt from the middle of the table. 'Would it kill them to add some flavour to this mush?'

I looked around. 'David is eating it.'

'David can't taste.'

Cookie began slurping her soup in earnest, while the bibbed lady kept staring at me. I smiled at her and said, 'I'm Naomi. What's your name?'

'Frida.'

'Don't talk to her,' Cookie said, in a tone that was discreet but a volume that was not. 'She's crazy.'

I ignored Cookie and said, 'Where are you from, Frida?'

Frida smiled broadly and said, 'Poland. We're all from Poland here.'

'I'm not,' said the lady sitting next to her.

'I was sixteen when they took me,' Frida continued.

'Oh, here we go,' said Cookie.

'Sixteen when they shot my brother. Right next to me. Right next to me. I had his guts on me for the whole ride in the cattle car.'

'Frida, darling,' Cookie said. 'We're trying to eat.'

David started coughing and Cookie, seemingly unfazed, slapped him on the back so hard that he lurched forward in his seat. A nurse came over, gave him some water and wiped his mouth, and they all continued eating in silence. After Cookie had eaten some apple compote she sneered and announced, 'And that was lunch.' I walked with her back to her room, leaving David, who had told us to go, behind. He still hadn't finished his fish.

As Cookie opened the door the smell hit me hard. It was my grandmother's perfume, which had been sprayed vigorously, masking another scent – urine. The plants on the windowsill were thriving in the humidity of this room. But in the corner a succulent was weeping green jellybean leaves and a swarm of fruit flies were gathering on a saucer below: a mutinous army sensing decay. Weren't those plants almost impossible to kill?

I found this whole scene terribly unsettling, and I told her I had to get going to work, but Cookie pleaded with me to stay for another five minutes and I agreed. I'd started turning up five or ten minutes late to Linen Palace anyway, as no one in the shop seemed to care.

Cookie told me to sit down, so I did. Then she told me that Mum had been worried about me, and now she was worried too.

'You don't need to worry about me.'

'Of course I do,' she said.

Cookie turned her gaze to the wall of photographs. Weddings, bat mitzvahs, reunions. And there was also a photo of a young Cookie, standing next to her father, in front of her mother and baby Marta on her father's lap. 'Do you like my photos?' Cookie closed her eyes for a moment and then opened them, like with each blink her thoughts refreshed anew.

'Very nice,' I said. 'I like looking at photos of you as a little girl.'

'Oh, yes?'

'Do you remember having that photograph taken?'

'Are you crazy?' She squinted at the photo and let out a chuckle. 'Look at Marta's pudgy thighs.'

'How did you bring the photo with you to Australia?' I had a vision of the photograph secreted somehow on Cookie's body, maybe in her underwear, hot against her skin.

Cookie turned to me and scrunched her face. 'I carried it.'

'But how? Surely you couldn't take very much with you.'

Cookie picked a scrap from lunch off her jumper. She looked up at the photo again and shrugged her shoulders. 'I don't remember. Anyway, what does it matter?'

'It doesn't,' I said, feeling guilty for trying to stoke her memory. 'I like that photo most of all.'

'Yes. I like it too.'

A fruit fly flitted past my face. I clapped my hands forcefully and opened them again checking for a black smudge. A little life so easily demolished. There was nothing there but my pale and pink skin, and the familiar lines of my palms going every which way. 'Please don't worry about me,' I said, looking up.

'Have you thought about ... romance?'

I laughed. 'Sure.'

'But are you interested?'

'Why? Do you know someone?'

'Ha. What do you want? A geriatric?'

'Or a geriatric's grandson, maybe?'

'Anything for you, my darling.'

I remembered I had a pair of decorative face washers in my bag that I'd picked up for Cookie at Linen Palace. I pulled them out and handed them to her.

'What's this for?' she said, thumbing an embroidered rose on the towel.

'They were on sale at the shop.'

'Forget about that place already,' she said, indiscriminately turfing the face washers, which landed on the floor by her feet.

She told me to water the plants. I nodded and did as I was told. As I filled up the water jug I felt shame. And as I poured the water into the thirsty palm lily I felt longing. I missed my museum work. It was something: to hold an object in your palms and watch a story unravel from fingernail down to wrist, palm to knuckle. The story was always different but the context remained the same – Jews and our ways. Birthrights, naming rights, blood rights. Death, feasting, renewal.

David pushed his walker through the door. 'Naomi, dear! What a nice surprise.'

'David, she was just at lunch with us,' Cookie said.

'She was? Oh. Yes. That's right,' he said, and continued on through to the bathroom, shutting the door behind him.

*

That evening at my parents' house, I noticed a friend request on Facebook from a guy called Julian Blume. I didn't recognise him, but we had a handful of friends in common. Without thinking I mentioned it to my parents. Dad looked up from the show they were watching and said, 'Is that Mina and Russell Blume's son?'

'Why do you ask?' Mum said.

'He's added me as a friend on Facebook.'

They shared a quiet smile. Their glee was eerily disquieting.

'What else?' Dad said.

'What do you mean what else?'

'What else does he say?' Mum now. They were chiming in in tandem.

'He doesn't say anything. It's just a friend request.'

'Show me the picture,' Dad said. He took reading glasses from his pocket and squinted at the phone. 'Looks familiar. Handsome boy. What does he want?'

'He wants to be her friend. Isn't that sweet?' Mum said.

'It's not the same as—'

'That is lovely,' Dad said.

'Facebook friends are not real friends. Like, I could add the post office lady as a friend.'

'Why would you do that?' Mum asked.

'No, you're not getting it. I don't usually accept people as friends unless I know them.'

'Well, we know him. Sort of,' Dad said.

'Accept! Accept!' Mum beamed. 'I don't know about this Julian, but his parents are very lovely people.'

'Very,' Dad agreed. 'And I'm sure he is too.'

'Okay. Everyone needs to calm down. He's not asking me out. It's a friend request.'

'We all have to start somewhere, don't we? Keep an open mind,' Mum said, and turned up the volume on the TV. Dad patted the couch, inviting me to come and sit next to him. His aftershave had almost worn off for the day, and there was just the faint smell of alcohol and jasmine.

'Did you get the money I sent you?' he asked.

'Yes, thanks.'

'I gave you a bit extra this month.'

'You did?' I hadn't checked my bank balance.

'Well, I don't know what you're making at that shop. Are you still paying your bills?'

'Of course I am.'

'Good girl,' he said, directing his attention back to the show. The lady detective was about to go to bed with a good-looking guy she'd met at a bar. 'Don't look, Naomi,' Dad said, and the three of us had a laugh.

Later, at home, I wondered whether or not I should accept Julian Blume's friend request. On reflection, I had enjoyed my parents' reaction to the idea of it. It had felt like we'd spent the last few months avoiding any topic related to my relationship status, and now their excitement was palpable. I accepted the request and went to bed.

The Red Sea

Gemma arranged for us to go to visit Liv in Launceston. She brought along her new girlfriend, Ash, who was tall and slender with a shaved head. She was handsome in a way that made me lose my words around her. They held hands the whole way on the plane while I sat by the window, contemplating the cerulean breadth between Tasmania and the mainland and wondering if it would be possible to swim back home again.

I felt happy for Gemma, but whenever she started seeing someone it made me anxious that she would no longer be available for me in the same way. I liked imagining that it would always be the two of us. Except, perhaps at some point in the future, we would both be partnered, and there would be more limbs in the picture. I would give my children biblical names, or the names of great-grandparents who went up in smoke, and Gemma's children would be fashionably feral, with bare feet, amber necklaces and Steiner school enrolments.

I tried not to look at my phone and the most recent slate of texts from an unknown number. The last one was: *Hey. Been thinking about you. I think about you all the time. Sorry to dump this on you. I know you can't do much with it. Anyway. I just thought you should know. Take care. Josh.* I told Gemma I'd deleted it, but I hadn't and it sat there like an in-grown hair.

It was dark and freezing when Liv met us out the front of a house that sat on the border of dense bushland, and the smell of wet eucalypts was omnipresent. Gemma and Liv hugged for ages, swaying back and forth and giggling, while Ash and I stood back and waited for it to end. I figured there was probably something wrong with me for not wanting to give Liv the same kind of hug. I often marvelled at how Gemma was able to pursue so many friendships so convincingly, and felt a little jealous.

There were a lot of people milling around, including Liv's brother, Moses, and her boyfriend, Luke. In the kitchen I landed myself on a wonky chair and tried to make conversation with a woman who was telling me about her cat who'd been hit by a car the previous week but had miraculously survived. I didn't like cats and struggled to appear sympathetic. When she turned to someone else, I promptly took my wine and wandered outside to the large creaking deck.

Not long afterwards Moses appeared, looked at me and said, 'Oh,' as if he'd been expecting to see someone else. He was wearing a well-worn grey cable-knit jumper and black skinny jeans. His hair was longer than I remembered, shaggy down to his ears, with a few wayward curls falling in front of his eyes.

'Hi,' I said.

'Hey. Sorry, I thought Liv was out here.' He looked around and muttered something under his breath, was about to turn back into the house and then paused. 'I'm Moses.'

'I know. I saw your play.'

'Oh, yeah.' He started laughing. I couldn't tell if he was laughing at the play or at me. I smiled at him dumbly. 'Oh well,' he said and turned back into the house. I watched him go and was struck by a pain beneath my hips and an aching in my legs. I was getting my period and wondered if the blood had already started to seep.

I went to the toilet and stuck a finger inside myself and wiped it on the roll of toilet paper. I was reminded of a conversation I'd had at the museum with Josh and Adele. We were creating an exhibition about Jewish ritual and had discussed whether or not to include a bedikah cloth, that Orthodox women used to check themselves internally to see whether they had finished menstruating. I had argued that it should be included, seeing as there was an entire section dedicated to circumcision. Josh privately told me he agreed with me but said nothing in a subsequent meeting where it had been deleted from the proposed exhibition catalogue. I blinked away the thought and checked the toilet paper. There was no blood.

After dinner, large bulbous candles flickered and the music was wrenched to almost-too-loud. Fairy lights waved about the place like low-hanging glinting stars. An outdoor fire pit burned orange and angry, and I sat around it with Gemma and Ash who passed me a joint. I was just starting to stop thinking about leaving when Moses came and sat next to me. I passed the joint to him and he took it and smiled. Then a spark from the fire flew into my lap and I jolted, letting out a yelp. He asked if I was alright. I started giggling, unsure of why. I must have been stoned. He giggled too. Then I laughed a little too loudly. It went quiet between us and I felt exceedingly self-conscious. The feeling that I wasn't supposed to be there rose up inside me again. Then he slapped his legs, looked around and said, 'Well, I'm off to bed.' He gave an indefinite wave to the group and walked steadily into the house.

About half an hour later I also went inside, slightly disoriented. I walked through the kitchen and opened a door, thinking it was the room where I'd dumped my stuff. It wasn't. It was Moses's room, and it was sparse, without decoration or embellishment. There was a trestle table in one corner and a bike in the other, with clothes draped over it. At the foot of the bed there was a small electric heater and the room was warm like toast. He was sitting up in bed with a computer on his lap. I mumbled an apology and backed out of the room and wasn't sure which direction to go in. He called out, 'You lost?'

I stuck my head back through the doorway. 'Um. I think so?'

He offered to show me to my room and got out of bed, just in his T-shirt and boxer briefs. I turned around, embarrassed, though he didn't seem to be. I suddenly couldn't stop thinking of him kissing the man in the play, how tenderly he had held the other actor around the ears and pulled him close.

I followed him, back down the hallway to the kitchen, out another door to another hallway that I had totally forgotten about. And there was the room with my bag open on the bed and my phone charger on the floor. 'This is you, right?'

I nodded. He nodded too, and looked as though he was about to leave, so I blurted out, 'Moses is such a name.'

He was amused by this. 'Yeah. It's a name.'

'Very Jewish. I can say that. Because I'm a Jew.'

'Liv said that.'

'Really? She did?'

'Sorry. Was that the wrong thing to say?'

I thought about it for a moment. 'Not really. I guess. I mean, I am Jewish.' And then I said, 'Naomi was in the Bible too.'

He nodded and then stretched his arms over his head, black tassels of armpit hair poking out of his T-shirt. Neither of us spoke and then he said, 'Cool. Goodnight,' and he walked away.

I checked my phone, half expecting there to be a message from Josh. Now I was always half expecting there to be a message from him that I wouldn't respond to but I wouldn't delete either. Instead, there were two missed calls from Cookie and one fifty-three-second voicemail that contained the distinctive laboured crackle of her heavy breathing.

*

I woke early and went out to the kitchen to make coffee. Moses was also awake and standing at the kitchen bench. He'd already filled a coffee plunger and poured me a cup. He said that the weather looked clear for now, and if I was keen for a walk he'd be heading out soon. I said okay, and then Luke appeared in the doorway and told us to wait for him.

We drove to a walking track in the national park. Luke and Moses walked ahead of me up a path that got incrementally steeper. They spoke a little to each other and not much to me at all. They were both agile and made me feel sluggish. I had the passing thought that I barely knew either of them, and how simple it would be for one or both of them to attack me. I wondered whether I'd try to fight them off, or just let them do what they wanted.

As we wandered through some more dense bush, Moses held ferny branches back for me, releasing them like rubber bands once I'd passed under them. We stopped at a waterfall on the way down and Luke wandered off to find a tree to piss on. Moses started to peel an orange, and he ripped it in half and offered it to me. I took it, sat on a jagged rock and kicked some mud off the soles of my white sneakers. I looked at his shoes. They were boots with thick treads.

'Do you work as an actor full time?'

He laughed. 'I'm a carpenter by trade. Joiner. You know. Bookshelves. Kitchens. Toilets. Trapdoors. What about you?'

'I work in a palace.'

*

We returned to the house and left our shoes by the back door. Everyone was still asleep and everything was quiet, except for a radio that had been left on. A news reporter was announcing the weather, and Moses turned the dial until he found some obscure music he seemed satisfied with. Luke snuck off back to bed and I was tempted to do the same, but Moses offered to make more coffee and so I stayed and washed some dishes that had been abandoned by the sink. I was unsure of where everything went, and we ended up passing cutlery and crockery between us in a sort of domestic dance. When the coffee was ready, we sat at the kitchen table.

'So, have you always worked in a palace?' he asked.

By this stage it had been established that I did not work in a literal palace. 'It's a long story. Six months ago I was working as a curator at the Museum of Jewish Heritage.' I put a grape in my mouth and heard it split. 'Long story.'

'You said that,' he said, picking a grape and rolling it between his fingers. I noticed his thumbnail was blackened. It looked like an injury that had been there for a while and I'd almost mistaken his thumb for the grape. 'You must have a good eye for things.'

'Yeah, well. I'm also quite good at folding towels.' I felt worried that not having talked about the museum for some time, I no longer had the authority to discuss it.

He wrapped his hands around the arm of a chair, and I noticed there was a long scar across his forearm. His body and mine clearly had a different relationship to the earth. 'I've never been to a Jewish museum. But I'd really like to go.' I worried he expected me to offer to take him there, but instead he asked, 'This might be a dumb question but do you pray there?'

'At the museum?'

'No,' he said, answering his own question. 'You don't pray there. Sorry, that was dumb.'

'It's okay,' I said, wanting to make sure he knew I didn't think he was dumb. 'I mean, some people might pray there. You can pray anywhere. At home. In the car. In synagogue.'

'Of course, of course.' He shook his head. 'Sorry. It was a really dumb question.'

'Not all Jews pray. Or believe in God.'

'But they're still Jews. Even if they don't believe?'

'Somehow. Yes. For some people, it's cultural.'

'Because I wouldn't call myself a Christian.'

'Sure. I get it.'

He leaned forward. 'Do you believe in God?'

I leaned forward too, finding myself wanting to be closer to him, to the whirl of his hair. 'I don't know. But I know that I have envy for people who do. Their lives seem more resolved. Their destiny is bound up in it. For non-believers, destiny is in their own hands. And sometimes that feels like too much.' Moses looked at me and his eyes were kind and I felt at once embarrassed by what I'd said and galvanised to keep talking. I cleared my throat. 'My favourite thing about the museum is the family histories.' Paula Hohenberg's face flashed into my mind. A smile. A half smile. I looked to see whether he was still listening. When I felt his eyes on me, I continued. 'The things that define us as a community.'

'The things that define us as a community. I like that. I don't think I have one.'

'One what?'

'A community.'

'Sure you do. You have your sister. And the theatre. Right?'

'Hm. Not sure it's the same.' Then he looked at me like he wanted something but I wasn't sure what. That word, community, was one that got so freely bandied about in my world. I'd never before thought of it as something to be coveted.

That night Liv, Luke, Gemma, Ash and I had planned to go to the pub for dinner. Before we left, Liv had shouted out to Moses to ask if he was coming. He had poked his head around a corner, taken a look at me in the hallway and said, 'Okay,' and grabbed a denim jacket that was hanging on a hook by the front door. On the way he sidled up next to me and said, 'There's a much better pub two streets away. Liv likes this one because they put umbrellas in the cocktails.'

'That sounds like a legitimate reason,' I said, and rubbed my hands together for warmth. Mum had warned me that it would be ice-cold here, and even cautioned me against coming, asking why we weren't going to Queensland instead. Sometimes I wondered if my mother's aversion to the cold was some entrenched genetic memory of a Polish winter.

Gemma paid me little attention at the pub, apart from following me to the bathroom and apologising for not paying me attention. I told her I was happy for her and Ash and that I was fine, and she said, 'I can see that.'

'What do you mean?' I was looking at myself in the mirror, worrying that I'd put too much foundation on and that it was masking my freckles.

'You look beautiful,' she said. 'And he's a nice guy.'

'Who?'

'Moses, dummy.'

I looked at Gemma. 'Isn't he gay?'

Gemma looked confused. 'Who?'

'Moses.'

'No. I don't think so. Why? Because he kissed the guy in that play we saw?'

I shrugged.

'That's just actors, darling,' she said, and kissed my cheek.

Moses asked me if I wanted to walk back to the house with him. I said yes, realising that up until that point I had presumed he wasn't interested in me at all and had unwittingly had my guard down and been more myself. I wasn't sure if it was a good thing or a bad thing. He opened the front door to the house without a key and I said, 'You don't lock it?' He just shrugged.

I followed him to his room and he turned the little heater on. There was a script on the bed with highlighter all through it. He moved it to one side. We sat side by side and took our coats off.

'Where is the scar from on your arm?' I asked.

'Mountain biking accident.'

'So that's not just a clothes rack?' I said, pointing to the bike in the corner. Moses laughed and then asked if he could kiss me. I nodded and he leaned in and kissed me on the mouth. I kissed him back. And then I said, 'So you're not gay,' and he said, 'I'm not gay.' I slowly snaked my hand up his back beneath his clothes. His skin felt warm and smooth. He took hold of my hair, but tenderly, not pulling it, just holding the weight of it, kissing my neck, my ears and my mouth again. The ridge of his nose was hard up against my cheek. I traced the left side of his face where there was a pockmarked area of acne scarring the size of a twenty-cent coin. We got under his covers and he gingerly removed his clothes. His body was taut and muscular, dark ribbons of hair lining his chest. I undid my pants. He slipped his fingers inside me and moaned when he felt how wet I was. I wrapped my hands around his bum and we rocked back and forth, me biting his shoulder.

I found it hard not to think about what the therapist had said to me, especially the advice about getting to know someone before fucking them. I was tempted to tell him about it but didn't. But I started giggling at the thought of it.

'What's so funny?' he asked, rolling onto his side so we were face to face.

'Nothing,' I said.

After some time, he said, 'I like your laugh,' and kissed my nose.

'I like your nose,' I said, pressing it with the tip of my finger. Outside the door I heard the others come back and enter the kitchen. 'Should we go out there?' I asked quietly.

Moses turned his head to the sliver of light under the door. 'What for?'

'Just in case Gemma worries about where I am.'

'Sure. If you want.' He put his hands behind his head and stretched out like a sunbather. I felt annoyed with myself. It was as though regardless of what I was doing I was only ever half doing it. I was always torn between here and there. This world and some other realm. Someone who wanted me and someone who had rejected me. Between what I thought others wanted of me and what I wanted for myself. The problem was I didn't know what I wanted for myself. I wanted to see Gemma but only because I thought Gemma might want to see me.

In the end I stayed.

We talked a lot between the suggestion of sleep. I asked him why he liked acting, and he said he didn't really know but that he'd accidentally been in someone's short film and then one thing led to another. Now he liked inhabiting other people's lives and he supposed it was a sort of escape. I said, 'Escape from what?' somewhat warily, and somewhat flirtatiously. And then he laughed and told me his mother had died from breast cancer when he was twenty and that his father remarried not long after and moved away, 'probably because Liv and I reminded him too much of our mother, and probably because he's an arsehole'. I wasn't sure if this was an answer to my question or another tangent completely, and we continued to squirm around each other like two little fishes.

He told me he hated hospitals, and I stroked the middle of his back and asked him whether anyone actually liked hospitals, and he kissed my elbow and said, 'I guess not' and laughed a little. Moses confessed to speaking to his mother in his dreams and how he would tell her things like 'I bought a new pair of shoes' or 'I made really delicious toast this morning'. I said I didn't know death in its immediate form, I only knew it as a shadow (Marta's ghost, the cold press of a filing cabinet in the museum collection storeroom). I told him about one of my recurring nightmares, in which Hitler was my boyfriend and he was kind enough to accompany me on my walk to the gas chambers, and I kissed him goodbye as he pushed me inside. As I said this I had a sudden flash of memory: Josh pushing me into the storeroom, teeth on my breasts, steel trays rattling, the threat of an unlocked door. I stiffened and Moses asked me if I was okay. Of course I was, I said, and then he tickled my armpit and said, 'Oh, you're ticklish, aren't you?' I cackled loudly and harshly as he ventured to find all the most vulnerable dints on my body.

In between these snippets we drew back into each other, kissing and stroking and working each other up again. At times, he'd close his eyes and begin breathing deeply and I'd think he was sleeping, but then I'd shuffle around and he'd reach out to me again.

By the middle of the next morning there was an unspoken agreement between us that one wouldn't leave the other, even to use the toilet. He brushed his teeth and I watched him, sitting on the edge of the bathtub. He asked me if I wanted to use his toothbrush and I nodded as if it was nothing, as if my toothbrush wasn't only at the other end of the house. The bristles were warm and I liked the way they felt in my mouth. We took a shower together, bumping naked bodies and laughing, and I asked him about the tattoo of a fire pit on his lower back, and he said that he was young and drunk when he got it and often forgets it's there until someone asks about it. Then I asked him if every girl he fucked enquired about the tattoo, and he told me he didn't fuck many girls. I didn't believe him. Someone banged on the bathroom door. We ignored it and sat on the bathtub edge and kissed each other deeply. Kissing him was so good. It was like plunging my mouth into snow.

We went into town to have breakfast before Gemma, Ash and I were due to leave. We held hands at the cafe counter and he bought us coffees and toast and eggs. We sat at a four-seater table so we could sit side by side, my head resting on his shoulder. He told me he was about to fly to Canberra to tour an adaptation of Moliere's *That Scoundrel Scapin*. He would have to wear pancake-thick white make-up, which he detested, but the gig was well paid and he couldn't say no. All up he would be gone for three weeks. As he told me this, I wondered if other people were watching, and if the other people would presume that he was my boyfriend. I was suddenly overcome with the feeling that I wanted to make them all jealous. I wanted them all to hate me.

Out the front of the house, Liv gave me an extra-long hug, similar to the one she'd given Gemma when we had arrived. I hugged her back. Maybe it was from the lack of sleep, the headiness of the sex and touching or all of those things, but I felt looser in Liv's arms. It was almost sisterly. Then she walked away. I saw the cloudy vapour of my breath in the distance between us, but my body was warm.

Gemma and Ash were already in the taxi. I leaned against the car door and Moses came and gave me a hug and said, 'It was great to meet you. Again.'

I felt a surge of emotion, quashed the urge to cry and felt stupid for it.

At the airport, I hadn't wanted to sit directly on the toilet, but all of a sudden my legs felt weak and I collapsed onto the seat. Blood was pooling in the bottom of the toilet like red velvet.

'I got my period,' I said to Gemma, who was in the next cubicle.

'Lucky you got all that fucking out of your system first,' Gemma snorted. I looked at the skin between my legs, reddened from chafing and friction. I felt a pang of delight.

I was thankful to be taking this abrasion home with me, a little souvenir.

Gemma thrust a tampon under the door. I took it and unwrapped it. I peered into the toilet, saw the clot of blood and thought, isn't my blood a beautiful thing, ruby and sparkling? And as the pain surged from my hips to my thighs I thought, isn't my pain a beautiful thing, anchoring me to the ground? And for the first time in a long time, I felt truly glad.

That night, in my own bed, I fell into a deep, satiating sleep, thinking about the stillness of the Launceston streets, clumps of rotting leaves and the metallic fragrance of Moses's bodywash.

Let's look him up

I don't know what I had been expecting, but I was surprised to discover that the museum was exactly the same as it had been before I'd left.

Upon my return from Launceston I had received an email from Adele. *Hi Naomi. Are you able to meet with me this week? I'm not sure if you are aware, but Josh has moved on, and I'd like to discuss an opportunity with you.* I only told Gemma about it, who grabbed me by the shoulders and insisted I meet with her.

I stood by the reception desk and waited for Adele. I was relieved to have Derek's chitchat to calm me. He spoke about the football and I reacted like I knew what he was talking about, which propelled him to keep going with more of a recount of the weekend action, which I found comforting. I looked to the walls, the floor, the ceiling. I looked for signs of Josh, whispers of his hair, his smell. It was odd to be here knowing that he wasn't.

I was already trying to perform a completely unfazed version of myself with regard to my weekend in Launceston.

It was challenging, because I couldn't shift the feeling that something had been released; part of me was opening, making way for something new. And as much as I tried to suppress these thoughts I couldn't help but picture Moses in my little courtyard, or in my bedroom, watching me dress. After I arrived home he messaged and reiterated that he'd enjoyed being with me, so I'd written back the same, and he said he'd see me soon, which I interpreted as neither true nor false and reposed all emotion somewhere between my rib cage and my lower intestine.

'You can go up to see her now, Naomi,' the receptionist told me. I nodded. She was new, and I hoped she didn't know who I was. I gave an unconvincing wave to Derek, who responded by giving me a thumbs up.

Adele and I sat at the small circular table in her office and she tucked her silver hair behind her ears. She poured water from a carafe and her large-gemmed rings made chiming sounds against the glass.

'So, I'll just jump in. As I mentioned in the email Josh resigned last month. It's been a real blow. He was, as you know, a huge asset to the museum.'

I nodded and smiled, both relieved and irritated that he had been so adept at concealing what had transpired between us. 'Where has he gone?' I asked.

'He's at the National Gallery now,' Adele said. 'He'll do well for himself there.' I nodded, unsurprised.

'We've been trying to recruit for your position since you left,' she continued, 'but haven't had much luck finding a replacement. Now with Josh having left, we're in a bit of a pickle, so to speak. It turns out good curators, and, quietly, Jewish curators – I've been told I'm not allowed to say that – are not in high supply.' I delicately took a sip of water. 'I'm unaware of your current situation. Are you working?'

I thought of towels, sheets, toilet brushes. I swallowed. 'Kind of.'

'Right, right, right. Well, I would like to see if I can encourage you to return here. I was never quite clear on why you left but, to be frank, up until that point I was very impressed with you. You and Josh made a very good team, and from what I observed you also had a terrific grasp on the work itself. I'd like to see if you'd be interested in taking up the role of curator again. It would be a larger role, incorporating some of the more senior responsibilities. We would compensate you for additional duties performed, as well as an increase in your previous salary package. So. Thoughts?'

The thick spines on her bookshelf gaped at me, authoritative, meaty. 'Would you continue looking for someone more senior, to replace Josh?'

'That would depend on you. Ideally, I'd like to see you graduate to that senior position. And I'd be happy to work closely with you to ensure that you get there.'

'Wow,' I said. 'Yes. Okay. I am interested.' And then added, my throat catching on the last word, 'Thank you for thinking of me.'

'No thank yous necessary. We would treat it as a new appointment, so you would be on a three-month probation period,' she added.

'I understand,' I said. And I understood that this three-month period was insurance in case I suffered from another bout of 'personal issues'.

She pushed an envelope towards me. 'Have a read over this, and, I'd appreciate if you could get back to me by the end of the week.'

The first thing Cookie said when I opened her door was, 'Where were you? I tried to call. I think your phone is broken.'

I swallowed sharply. 'I went to Tasmania, remember?'

'Tasmania? What for?'

'For fun,' I said.

'Don't be ridiculous. Come. Sit.'

I sat by Cookie's side on the couch, opposite David, who was asleep in the armchair, his chin resting on his chest. He let out a purr from between his lips. 'Is David okay?'

'Who? Him?' Over the weekend, David had been found wandering out the front of the home trying to catch a tram. Someone from maintenance spotted him there and had been kind enough to steer him back inside. David had insisted he'd had an appointment, but there was no appointment, and he'd forgotten his shoes. 'Never been better,' Cookie said.

I tried to take her hand but she crossed her arms. 'Dead,' she continued. 'This place is completely dead.' She stared forlornly at the oversized digital clock.

I remembered the activities timetable stuck up on the wall of the elevator. 'Isn't there a lecture later today?' At that, Cookie slumped further into the couch, making herself appear smaller, teenager-like. Next to her there was a little white vase holding a bouquet of plastic flowers, the synthetic leaves gathering a furry layer of dust. 'The flowers are pretty,' I said, trying again. 'Are they new?'

Cookie curled her lip. 'Aren't they hideous?'

I looked around the room and clocked the absence of Cookie's plants. The fruit flies had turned into an infestation, and a few weeks ago, while Cookie and David were attending a concert performed by the local primary school, Mum had had the unit fumigated and all of the plants removed. When they got back, Mum had been there to greet them with the plastic replacements. Cookie had called Mum a murderer and a thief and refused to speak to her for a whole week.

In opposition to the lack of living things, a hair was sprouting from Cookie's chin – so taut and stiff I couldn't help fantasising about tweezing it off between my thumb and forefinger.

My phone pinged. It was Moses. I smiled without meaning to.

'So, your phone does work,' Cookie said, shifting her body to face me. 'Show me.'

'What?'

'Show me what it says.'

The message on my phone from Moses read: *Thinking about the shape of you. Can't stop smiling.* I obviously couldn't show her that message, but the guilt I was feeling for not having done the thing I was supposed to do (unclear as I was to what that thing was) was quickening, and the smallness of her and the beigeness of everything in her room was somehow my fault. 'I met someone,' I said, hoping this would pacify her.

Cookie grinned with delight. All was forgiven. My eyes flitted to a framed photograph on the shelf of Cookie at age twenty-one. She had her arm around a friend's shoulder and was standing next to a sign that read *St Kilda Foreshore*. The sea salt had crisped their hair, the squinting sun had turned their cheeks freckled and glossy. She and her friend looked ecstatic, like this was their first time being by the ocean. It probably was. 'Please don't tell Mum. It's not serious. Really.'

Cookie smirked and pawed at the edge of her mouth, satisfied with the secret now wedged between us. Cookie wanted to know what he looked like. Did he have a good head of hair? How were his teeth? She reached under the table and heaved the fat White Pages into her lap. It was from 2006, and I wondered if Cookie had refused to part with it when she'd been moved out from her house. 'What's his surname?'

'Why?'

'Let's look him up.' The White Pages was now splayed open on her lap to the letter C. A little grey spider the same colour as the text crawled across the page. Chester. Chesterfield. Chesterman. Chesterton. Cookie didn't notice the eight-legged creature, or, if she did, wasn't bothered by it.

'Look him up? I know where he lives.'

'But what about his people?'

'He won't be in there. He lives in Tasmania.'

'Go on.' She sat forward. This news made her seem like a limp balloon that had just taken a hit of helium. I couldn't help but be lifted by her enthusiasm as well.

I looked at David, who now appeared to be drooling slightly. 'Do you think it would matter if I was with someone not Jewish?' I was suddenly unsure of what her answer might be. Her attitude towards religion had always been one of disdain, and yet she had married a Jewish man and so had my mother. So regardless of what her attitude was or wasn't, the outcomes had remained the same and this scared me.

'Matter to who?' she asked.

'You?' I reached over to touch the synthetic flowers. I wanted to see if they would feel real. They felt impermeable, like a raincoat.

'Forget about me,' she said. 'Does it matter to you?'

I realised in this moment that I'd never really thought about whether it did matter to me or not. I'd only thought about what mattered to other people. I looked at Cookie and thought: your blood is in my blood and therefore your blood will be in my children's blood and so on and so forth, but we are all going to die. You will die. Mum will die. I will die. My children and my grandchildren and my great-grandchildren will die. So all there is is blood and death and the stories we tell ourselves and each other. 'I don't think so,' I said, finally.

'Bah,' she said, shaking her head. 'He's in Tasmania. That's what I'd be worried about.'

I graciously accepted Adele's offer. It would be more money, and responsibility, than I'd ever had before. On my last day at Linen Palace my manager gave me a card and a scented candle and asked if I'd like to go for a drink sometime. I was touched, especially since the shop didn't sell candles and the woman had clearly gone out of her way to get it. I told her I'd like that, even though I knew I was never going to see her again.

My parents made no attempt to conceal their excitement and Mum insisted on taking me shopping for new workwear. We settled on a black jacket and a couple of tops that she confirmed 'didn't wash me out'. Then we browsed through David Jones looking for bras on sale. I tried on a couple of lacy ones. Mum said the bras were very flattering and bought them for me, along with matching briefs.

'Are you still using that laundry bag I got for you?' she asked, stirring her coffee. We were sitting at the in-store cafe.

I couldn't think where that laundry bag had got to but smiled and nodded anyway.

'It's good to see you smiling.' She took a breath and then said, 'We're just so pleased that you're getting back to the museum. You'll really thrive there.'

'On probation.'

'Please,' she said and squeezed my thigh a little too tightly. Then she cleared her throat to allow space for what she said next. 'Are you worried about going back without him being there?'

The mention of Josh made us both nervous. I was glad to be in the department store, where we were unlikely to see anyone we knew.

'I'm not worried about him not being there,' I said. 'I just— I don't know how it will work.'

'You'll be in charge. And so you should be.' Mum put her hand on my back and rubbed it up and down a few times. 'He's moved on and up in the world, and so should you. That's what I think.' I nodded, and we smiled at each other. 'Fuck him,' she said.

'I was trying not to.'

'Oh ha ha. Honestly, Naomi. You can't let this schmuck keep shitting on your life.'

I considered telling Mum about Moses then. I would present the information in a gossipy tone, like girl-talk, like: 'you'll never believe what I got up to on the weekend'. A holiday romance. A bit of fun. And she might lean in on her elbow, clasp her chin in her hands and say something along the lines of: 'Go on. Tell me more.'

'Anyway,' she said in a low voice, curtailing my fantasy. 'Did Dad tell you we bumped into the parents?'

'Whose parents?'

'Julian Blume's. I don't know why we haven't seen more of them over the years.'

'Oh.' I took the bra out of its tissue paper wrapping and pulled the tag off with my teeth. I'd almost forgotten all about Julian Blume.

'You should really do that with scissors. Yes. We saw them at the theatre. Isn't that funny? After all this time?'

I spat a T-shaped plastic twig into my hand. 'What were you seeing?'

'*Death of a Salesman*. It's very good. You should get tickets if you can. Anyway. I wonder if he'll get in touch.'

'Probably not.'

'Why not?' Her brown eyes narrowed in on me and darkened.

'Because that's how the youth of today operate. We all stalk each other online without any intention of meeting in person.'

'The youth of today.' Mum rolled her eyes. 'Bullshit.'

'Mum, it's really not a big deal. I shouldn't have said anything.'

'I'm not saying it's a big deal, darling.' She tinkered with her spoon. 'But you do want to meet someone, don't you?'

I could see Moses, naked, outstretched, the large gum outside his window rapping melodiously on the glass. 'I do.'

'He runs a dental practice in Richmond. Very trendy.'

'Dentistry is trendy?'

'Why not? Don't be so judgemental, Naomi. It's not cute. Anyway, I meant Richmond. Richmond is trendy.'

201

'Is it now?'

'You need to find someone on your level.' And then under her breath, 'And preferably ours too.'

'Oh God. What did you say to Julian's parents?'

'Nothing much. We don't only talk about you, you know?' Mum received a message on her phone and reached into her handbag to get her glasses. 'Someone from the home. They want to have a meeting.'

'What about? Is Cookie okay?'

'It's not about Cookie. It's about David.' It was then she told me that David had stolen someone's walker and when they tried to take it back he'd thrown a vase at them. He had missed them completely but the intention was clear. His brain was failing him and it was all terribly unjust. 'They want me to move him into the dementia ward.'

'What does Cookie say about that?' I asked.

'Cookie doesn't know.' She put her phone away and signalled to a staff member that she wanted to pay for the coffees. She looked at me, undeterred. 'Maybe you could send Julian Blume a message.'

'No, Mum.'

'It would be very modern of you,' she said, taking a twenty-dollar note from her purse and leaving it on a saucer.

Europe, darling

Moses and I were now messaging each other once, twice, three times in a day. Yesterday he'd sent me a photo of himself. It was surprising to see his face again. He wasn't on social media so all I had was what I had conjured, and it was very pleasing to see him as I'd remembered him: handsome, gentle, real.

I decided to visit some other museums and art galleries in preparation for my return to work, and was about to step into the Italian Museum when he called me. It was as though years had passed since I'd heard his voice, though it had only been a few weeks. We were nervous at first, then like puppies, tripping over each other's tails. I told him where I was and he asked if he could stay on the phone while I visited the museum. I explained that phones and museums don't generally go together, but he said he'd promise to be quiet, which made me laugh, and I couldn't bring myself to end the call.

I spoke quietly with my hand over my mouth and described what I was seeing: a film clip of a family's annual ritual of making passata – three generations of women sorting the tomatoes, discarding the damaged ones, removing the seeds, sterilising and collating glass jars, all the while laughing and shifting between Italian and English without disruption. He asked if that was what it was like with me and my mother and grandmother. I said, 'What do you mean? Do we all speak to each other in Polish while making pierogi?'

'I don't know,' he said. 'Or challah.' He made a point of pronouncing the guttural 'ch' sound, and I laughed and said, 'You're such an actor.'

I stepped out of the museum and headed towards the city. I explained that neither my mother nor Melanie nor I could speak Polish or Yiddish, apart from a choice selection of words of Cookie's choosing: dobry (good), na zdrowie (bless you), zupa (soup); and commonplace Yiddish: spiel (story), shtup (fuck), shluf (sleep).

We didn't speak Yiddish because David didn't speak Yiddish. His family were too 'la-di-da' – her words – to speak the language of the shtetl. And we didn't speak Polish because, well, I could only provide the answer my mother had given me: Cookie didn't want us to understand.

I told him how when I went on a school trip to Poland, Cookie had armed me with the one phrase she thought I'd need: ile to kosztuje (how much does it cost). When I was there I befriended a girl named Margosia and I'd gone back to her apartment. I repeated this phrase to Margosia's family and they all laughed. Then we watched an episode of *Beverly*

Hills 90210 dubbed in Polish. On the phone to my parents I told them how much Margosia and I had in common, and I couldn't wait to show them the photos I'd taken on the Olympus camera I'd gotten for my birthday. Then my father said I should look out for swastikas on the streets of Warsaw and if I saw them I should photograph them. I had been confused by this instruction but nevertheless did as I was told. Eighteen of my seventy-two photographs were of antisemitic graffiti, and I'd felt a deep sense of embarrassment when I'd collected the prints from the local pharmacy.

I went to the National Gallery next and Moses said he would stay on the call, if I didn't mind. I felt bold going there, knowing that somewhere in the depths of office space Josh was likely smoothing his hair from side to side.

When I approached the glass wall of water at the front of the building, Moses asked me to touch it and I did. I pressed my index finger to the window and described the feeling of the water cascading past it. Is it a trickle or a gush, he wanted to know. 'Gush,' I whispered, shutting out the security guards and the children who were being scolded by their parents for rushing at the wall and getting too wet.

I wandered through to the red carpeted Great Hall, where there were large red velvet cushions. I lay down on one of them, stared at the stained glass ceiling. He looked it up on the internet and read aloud to me, '224 triangles of diamond-cut primary colours weighing 300 kilos each. The colours are very dramatic, aren't they?'

'I think it looks like hard lollies that have been smashed with a hammer,' I said.

'I wish I could see you right now.'

My mouth pooled with saliva. 'Where to next? The gardens?'

'Sure.'

I came to a little mound of grass, sat down with the purple wildflowers. 'I think this is my favourite part of the whole gallery. Are you bored yet?'

He stayed on the phone on the tram ride home and then it wasn't long before I was in bed with my phone and the quilt pulled over my head. It was hot under there and I had to breathe extra hard. From here I took some photos and sent them and he did the same. The camera picked up parts of my face and left the other parts in shadow. I took off my clothes and moved the phone up and down my body taking pictures at each juncture and he had to guess what he was seeing. Half a chin, an outline of an areola, the small hump under the knee, the memory of a scar. We played this game till we got tired of it, and then we just talked, the phone pressed hot and sweaty against my ear. He told me he'd never seen *The Prince of Egypt* and I'd asked how this was possible, the hero being his namesake. I explained it was the story we told every year at Passover. How over and over again we would speak his name, Moses, the liberator of our enslaved ancestors. I felt shy saying all of this, revealing I had been uttering his name at the Passover Seder since the time I could talk, like I had somehow cast a spell and conjured him into existence. But he seemed to enjoy it, and kept asking more questions until his speech got quieter and I could sense him drifting off, and I knew that he probably wouldn't want to be the first to hang up the phone, because by now I understood him to be a kind and sensitive person, and that it would be up to me to do so, so eventually, after straining to hear his heavy breathing, I did.

I tried to use my buzzer to get into the museum car park but it didn't work, so I parked on the street. 'I think I've lost my security clearance,' I told Derek as I walked by his post at the front door.

'Nah,' he said, and gave the buzzer a light bashing on the counter. 'Let's try it again.'

I followed him outside and asked after his wife and children. He showed me a family photo of them on his phone, and I realised I'd never seen him out of his uniform. He pressed the buzzer again and the gates opened, a slow and protracted parting of the Red Sea.

'Told ya it'd work,' he said. 'They do need to upgrade the system. I've mentioned it I don't know how many times. Do you want to move your car inside?'

'No. I'll just leave it on the street.'

'Are you sure?'

'Yeah.'

'There've been a few break-ins around here lately. I think you'd better move your car in.'

'Oh. Okay then.'

Derek watched me with intent as I fumbled for my car keys in the pocket of my coat. 'Did you have a good holiday?' he asked. 'You were in Europe, yeah?'

I felt embarrassed. Was that what he thought? That I'd been to Europe? 'No. That would have been nice though.' I squinted at the sky, unsure why he was still there. 'I'll go get my car then.' I walked away from him and the car park. My black jacket flapped in the wind. Derek watched me get in the car and bring it around to the car park, waving me through the gates like he was marshalling in a plane.

I walked upstairs to find my office. I passed an elderly lady with skunk-streaked hair and a volunteer badge pinned to her shirt who, sensing my unease, stopped to ask if I was lost.

Most of the things that had been on my desk before I left were still on it, pushed to a pile in the corner, including my shawl and a half-eaten packet of corn chips. I had 586 unopened emails. The receptionist had been trying to sort them, but seemed to have stopped a month or so ago. At least a hundred of these emails were from my father, who had continued sending me jokes in my absence.

Josh's desk had nothing of him left on it, apart from a lone strand of hair. I was reluctant to sweep it off, but then rationalised that it could have belonged to anyone, and what would I do with the hair if it was his in any case? Tape it to my diary? Scrounge on the floor for more scraps of him and fashion a voodoo doll out of it? There was just the computer and phone, and a manila folder with 'handover notes' scrawled across the front of it, written in a hurry. Even the pinboard was bare: silver thumbtacks only just holding on to the corner edges of A4 sheets of paper that had been ripped off. I expected there to be more of him left behind. His presence had loomed so large I figured so would his spirit, but all I felt was emptiness, departure.

I sat in his chair and found it to be far more comfortable than the one at my desk, so I swapped them over. His chair, unlike mine, had armrests. I dug my elbows into the back of them and spread my legs for a moment, inhaling deeply, trying to inhabit the memory of him. I laughed out loud – not a real laugh, more like a 'ha'. I wasn't used to having this office all to myself, and so I repeated the sound, 'ha', more forcefully this time.

Adele told me to take this week slowly and catch up at my own pace, but wasted no time in telling me that we needed to get together some fresh exhibition ideas to present at the next board meeting. 'Anything that springs to mind?' Adele cocked her head to the side and rested her palm under her chin. Her silvery hair sat perfectly still like a helmet.

'What about that Modigliani exhibition Josh was pitching?'

'Seriously?' she asked. 'Pipe dreams. You clearly haven't seen the budget yet. We are going to need to work with what we have in the existing collection.'

'The second-generation Holocaust survivor exhibition?'

'God no. Our last three exhibitions have had Holocaust-related content. I think we all need a break, don't you?'

'There are over twenty thousand pieces in the collection.' My cheeks flushed at the thought.

'Exactly. So?'

Since Josh had left, they'd made the decision to extend the dates of the current exhibition, Jewish Poetry Across the Ages, until I returned to manage the de-installation. I was certain they would be relieved to see that exhibition depart. Josh had wanted to fill the space with moving projections, but ultimately the museum could only afford one projector so the text was laid flat on the walls. The words of the poets from the Bible through to the Warsaw Ghetto through to Ginsberg sat languorous, motionless. My mother had described it as being as dull as its title promised, and I felt quietly validated that Josh had taken the lead on that one. I quickly tried to think about the things I'd loved about the job before I'd started up with Josh. I thought about how badly I'd wanted to get the job when I initially applied for it and how badly my parents had wanted the job for me. How I'd begged them not to mention anything to their good friend who was on the board. I'd wanted to get by on my own merits. I thought about Cookie and the family photo she'd smuggled out of Poland. And the fact that it would be up to me to interpret what my great-grandparents had known and what they hadn't known when they put Cookie on the train out of there with some rye bread and tomatoes wrapped in an embroidered handkerchief. I thought about how when I'd enquired after a detailed family tree, I was told simply that because of the war, everything had been destroyed: the roots, the stem, the leaves, the entire vascular system. I thought of my Paula Hohenberg proposal, likely still sitting on my desktop. I wasn't confident to present this idea to Adele. It was hard enough getting people through the doors, let alone trying to showcase an artist who was all but a footnote in the photographic canon.

'I think the museum's strength is telling stories,' I said finally, conscious of the fact that I had been staring out the window for too long, likely with a stupid look on my face, hoping the wind might rush at me with a lightbulb of an idea.

'Uh huh.'

'And I think,' I continued, struggling not to interpret Adele's encouragement as pity, 'that we need to be doing more of that. Featuring different objects and treating them like characters, with real personalities. There is such a rich history of innovation and design, architecture, fashion and style, in this community in particular, in this very building, in fact. Something along those lines, maybe?'

Adele sat back in her chair. 'Okay. Write me a proposal. Formulate it into an exhibition idea and we'll talk.'

Back in my office, I'd missed two calls from Mum. I called her back and she answered urgently. 'How is it?'

'It's okay.'

'Good to be back?'

'Yes. I think so.'

'I'm sure they're over the moon.'

'I don't know about that.'

'You want me to bring you something to eat?'

'No. It's okay.'

'Your father and I are so pleased. Now we just need to find you a husband. Ha. I'm kidding.'

I smiled into the phone, thinking about a spin class I'd once attended, the instructor yelling at me to smile, saying it would make it easier. 'Okay, Mum. I have a lot to catch up on here, so …'

Later on in the day, Derek brought a bouquet of flowers up to the office. It was from my parents and the note read, *So proud of you. Mum and Dad.*

Marilyn came up to say hello and admire the flowers. She was keen to fill me in on the staff news and had brought with her an oversized card for me to sign for the new accountant who was going on leave to get married. I hadn't met the accountant yet but thought better of saying anything and signed the card. I did my best to appear enthusiastic around Marilyn, who seemed to be fishing for clues, hoping I might reveal something intimate about my leaving and returning, but of course I didn't. Before Marilyn left she showed me pictures of her grandchildren eating, with sauce-covered faces and large bulging eyes. The pictures turned my stomach but I smiled appreciatively, telling Marilyn how cute they were and how lucky they were to have her as a grandmother.

'We've missed you around here. We were all so worried about you when you left. It was so sudden.' I looked her directly in the eyes and smiled. She saw this as an invitation and leaned in closely. 'You know, I think Josh was completely bereft without you. He just adored you, didn't he?' She lingered, waiting for my response.

'Uh huh,' was all I could muster.

'Now he's gone too. But here I am, old bugalugs still on the job. Can't get rid of me.'

'The museum's lucky to have you,' I said. This seemed to satisfy her, and she left.

I didn't have time to make you a cake

David had been married once before, however this marriage produced no children. I may have been told his wife's name though I couldn't remember it, which indicates how little she was spoken about. They had fled Poland together and, within the first week of arriving in Australia, were employed by a wealthy household in Armadale where David was to look after the garden and his wife was to do the cooking and cleaning. David would take any opportunity to lean under the shade of the chestnut tree and smoke cigarettes, pocketing the chestnuts for roasting later on. His wife, however, was barely off her feet. It was there in the kitchen, polishing the silver candle holders, that she felt a debilitating pain in her left hip, which turned out to be an incurable cancer. She was only twenty-five, and twenty-six when she died. It was as if she had brought the destruction of the war with her in a coat pocket, unleashed it upon their arrival, and it had ravaged her to just skin and bone. David never smoked again after that. He never stood still really, which is why he worked so well with Cookie. Together they were thrust into a forward motion, powered by grief, aware that nothing good ever came from looking back, lest you be turned into a pillar of salt.

It was now evident that David's mental deficiencies had progressed well beyond forgetting birthdays and recalling the name of the current prime minister. His English was starting to disappear altogether and a Polish carer who roamed among the residents was often called upon to interpret his mutterings.

The wellbeing manager urged my parents to move him to the dementia ward, where the doors locked behind you and the internal courtyards resembled something of the outside world, birds flying in and out with flagrant abandon.

The decision had been awful for my mother. We spoke about it in her kitchen.

'I can't separate the two of them,' Mum said in a stricken whisper. She looked aged. 'I can't hurt them.'

'It's not hurting them. It's helping them.' I pressed my fingers into her bony shoulders.

'Cookie? She'll never forgive me.'

'She—'

'No. She won't. I can't. I can't do it. I can't. But I have to do it. I just have to. He's a danger to himself. He's a danger to her. She'd have to know that we don't have a choice,' Mum said, wiping her eyes.

Over the next few days, my parents quietly moved David from his and Cookie's room, telling him it needed to be fumigated again, which he accepted without protest.

This put a bit of a dampener on my upcoming birthday celebrations but Mum assured me she wouldn't cry at all over Shabbat dinner, especially since Cookie would be there. The move to the dementia ward had actually gone smoothly, in the sense that David accepted his new surroundings very well. It had gone less smoothly in the sense that Cookie was refusing to speak to Mum. She had told Mum that putting him in there was unforgiveable, and Mum had replied that it was no longer safe, for either of them. Deep down Cookie knew that, because when given the opportunity to join him there, she laughed and said she'd rather walk in front of a bus.

Gemma and I picked up Cookie from outside the home. Gemma moved into the back seat and Cookie sat up front. She was out of breath from fumbling with the seat belt and I reached across her and slotted it in. I thought she might wish me a happy birthday, but instead she looked at me and said very sternly, 'David should be here,' and let out an exasperated puff so forceful I thought she might break a rib.

'I know, Cookie.' The new medications he was on made him incredibly sleepy, and we were advised not to take him out at night. I put my hands on the steering wheel and said in a loud voice, 'Right, we good to go?'

'Yep, all good back here,' Gemma said cheerfully.

'The stars look dead,' Cookie said to no one and stared forlornly out the window.

I found Mum in the kitchen, chatting to Melanie, who I hadn't expected to turn up.

'Here she is, the birthday girl!' Mum exclaimed a little too forcefully.

'Happy birthday,' Melanie said.

There was a paper bag on the counter. 'What's in here?' I asked.

'Birthday cake. I didn't have time to make you one. Sorry.' Mum rubbed her two front teeth with her finger, removing a lipstick stain that wasn't there. I opened up the bag to see a moist chocolate babka wrapped in tight plastic. I looked at my sister, who was chewing gum. 'Have you finished your interview yet?'

Melanie paused her chewing momentarily and the gum stretched out like a white sports sock between her top and bottom teeth. 'What interview?'

'Weren't you interviewing Mum?'

'About what?'

'Oh, that,' intervened Mum. 'That never really got off the ground.' She turned on the hot water tap and squirted lime-green detergent into the sink. The scent reminded me of a body spray I used to wear as a teenager. It was called Desire, and I'd spray it over my pubescent chest urging my breasts to grow.

'That was for my PhD,' Melanie said.

'How's that going?' I asked, my voice monotone.

'I'm not doing that any more. I don't think now is the right time.' Melanie tapped Mum's hip so she'd move aside, opened the cupboard under the sink and spat out her gum. 'What about you?'

'What about me?'

'You're back at the museum?'

'Yes, she is,' Mum said, placing a soapy chopping board in the drying rack. 'She's back.'

'And what about the guy? What was his name? Josh?' Melanie smiled performatively.

Mum dropped a large silver serving spoon into the water and it clanged at the bottom of the sink. 'We're going to start dinner in five minutes.' She left the kitchen and headed for the lounge, where she indulged Gemma with extra attention, considering Cookie's refusal to speak to her.

The table had been set in the formal dining room. There was a centrepiece of flowers and candles and cloth serviettes that smelled like the bottom of a drawer. We said the blessings over the candles and the wine and the bread, and then as everyone sat down Dad rose to make a speech of sorts as he tore the challah with his hands and passed it around the table. 'To our darling daughter, Naomi. Happy birthday. You are as sweet as this challah, as sweet as the wine.'

Cookie kicked me under the table and whispered, 'What is he on about?' I could tell that there was more he wanted to say. He probably wanted to acknowledge David's absence, knowing that David would be eating his own challah in the home, probably rather enjoying it. But between Cookie's disdainful looks and Mum aggressively asking who wanted soup, he knew better so cleared his throat and sat down.

Gemma, who was sitting on the other side of me, bit into the challah and rolled her eyes back into her head with an expression of delirium. 'Why don't you ever bring this shit home?' I laughed. My phone pinged and it was Moses.

'Who are you texting now?' enquired Mum.

I looked up from my phone and cleared my throat. 'No one.'

'Who's no one?' Mum asked, smiling. 'It's not Julian, is it?'

'Who's Julian?' Melanie said.

'Julian Blume!' Mum said.

'Seriously?' Melanie laughed. 'I remember him. He was such a geek.'

'He's no geek now, is he, Naomi?' Mum said.

'Enough about Julian, please, Mum.'

'Someone's tetchy,' Melanie said.

'Well, who is texting you then?' Mum asked. 'You know I hate it when you have that thing at the table.'

'Viv, it's her birthday,' Dad said under his breath.

'Alex, please. I just want to know who she is texting at the Shabbat table. Am I not allowed to enquire?'

'A friend,' I said.

'Please tell me it's not Josh.'

'No!' I reached for some hummus and lathered it on the challah, taking a bite so I was momentarily unable to speak.

'It's clearly someone or she would just say,' Melanie said, looking at Gemma who smiled, not wanting to get in anyone's way.

Mum nodded in support of Melanie's accusation. 'Nu? Tell us.'

I took a breath, the kind of breath you take before you go under water. 'It's a friend I met in Tasmania.'

'I knew it,' Mum said, taking Dad's plate.

'I'm not finished, darling,' he said softly.

Mum ignored him and began clearing the rest of the plates. 'You didn't tell me about a friend? A male friend?'

'His name is Moses.'

'What sort of a name is Moses?' Dad chuckled.

'Very biblical. Is he Jewish?' Mum asked.

'Doubt it,' Melanie said.

'If he was Jewish he'd be Moshe. Or Moishe,' Dad said.

Mum hovered next to Cookie's plate, but Cookie held on to it like it was her purse. 'Remember Moishe from the—'

'Of course I do.' Dad looked at me and crunched a pickle between his teeth.

'He's really nice,' Gemma said. Melanie snorted.

'Is he, Gemma?' Mum asked. 'So Gemma has met him?'

'In Tasmania, remember? We went together,' I said.

'Well. Okay. I just thought we were interested in Julian,' Mum said.

'Oh my God, there's nothing happening with Julian!'

'Is he a Tasmanian?' asked Mum.

'Yep.'

'Tasmanians are generally nicer than mainlanders,' Melanie said.

'I don't think that's true,' Mum said.

'Wow, this is so funny,' Gemma muttered almost inaudibly.

'There are no Jews in Tasmania,' Mum said.

'There are actually Jews in Tasmania,' I said. Everyone turned to look at me as if there was something on my face.

'The oldest synagogue in Australia is in Hobart. Remember, we learned that on that course we did last summer?' Dad said to Mum.

'So he is Jewish?' she asked.

'No,' I said.

Mum held the stacked plates tightly against her ribs. 'Right.'

'It's literally a guy I know, texting me happy birthday. Can we stop talking about this now?'

Mum tried to organise her face into a placid expression. 'Well, I think on Shabbat you could at least try not to text at the table.'

Without thinking, I grabbed Cookie's hand and held it tight. Despite the arthritis, despite the wrinkles and weak nails that were prone to splitting down the middle, I knew intrinsically that there was no way I could possibly hurt these hands or hold them too tight. They were indestructible, shatterproof. Cookie gripped my hand in return, and I knew that Cookie could hurt me. She could break my delicate, soft, freckled skin but she chose not to, or did so unwittingly, not knowing her own strength.

'Quiet. All of you,' Cookie said. And everyone did as they were told.

I went to the kitchen to help with the soup. I ladled clear chicken broth into bowls with a couple of carrots floating at the centre. Mum came into the kitchen, opened the oven door and checked on the potatoes that were crisping under the heat.

'You're not having soup,' she said, turning the potatoes over with tongs.

'Because you made chicken soup.'

'It's Shabbat.'

'It's my birthday. And I'm vegetarian.'

'You used to love my chicken soup.'

'It smells delicious,' I said, resting the ladle down, leaving a plump ring of oil on the bench. Gemma came in. No one said anything, and she smiled sweetly and stealthily took some bowls of soup out to the dining room. When she left Mum turned to me.

'So. Who is this guy?'

I plucked some lettuce from the salad bowl and ate it. 'I told you. He's a friend. Do you want me to dress the salad?'

'You didn't tell me you'd met anyone in Launceston.'

'It's not a big deal. I met a lot of people in Launceston.'

'A lot of people? Well. If he's just a friend, I don't know why you're making such a big fuss over it.'

'I didn't think I was.'

Mum looked around the kitchen. 'I wanted to make everything nice for you. And it's not been an easy week.'

'I know, Mum. I know it's been hard.' I wanted to touch my mother then, but found that I couldn't.

'Anyway.' She sighed and smiled quickly and then frowned.

'It's a really lovely dinner,' I said.

'Good.'

I drizzled olive oil over the lettuce and cracked some chunky flakes of salt onto the tomatoes. She kept looking at me as if she knew there was more. And of course there was. Halfway through his stay in Canberra, he'd told me he was going to change his flight and come to Melbourne once the show was done. He insisted (in the kindest possible way) that this had nothing to do with me (I was a bonus), and rather his agent had arranged a handful of auditions for him in Melbourne. I offered for him to stay with me, and he said okay. 'He's coming to Melbourne to visit, for a little bit. He's an actor. He has auditions.' Then I tried to recall all the commercial credits he had in an effort to impress her.

'So it's not romantic,' she said.

'Well … It is, a little, I guess.'

Gemma sashayed in to collect the last bowls of soup. We watched her intently. She wasn't quite sure what to do, winked at us both and left.

'You said you wanted me to meet someone,' I said.

'Of course I do. But you don't have the best judgement on these things.'

'Right. Okay. I see.'

'What? Can you blame me?'

'Can we just not do this maybe? It is my birthday.' My voice shrivelled.

'If you want my honest opinion,' Mum said, 'he sounds completely inappropriate. What do you have in common?'

'We both work in creative fields.'

'And he's not Jewish.'

'Do you honestly really care about that?'

'Actually, if you're asking, I honestly really do.'

'But why? Cookie doesn't care.'

'Doesn't she? And anyway, what's this got to do with her?' My mother pointed to the doorway, sending a bullet out and away. She was gritting her teeth but trying not to, as if remembering in this moment that it was indeed my birthday and that I was her daughter and all of this evening was for me. 'What was the point of it all?'

'The point of what?'

'The thirteen years of Jewish education, the bat mitzvah, the Shabbats, the festivals, the trips to Israel. What is the point of it all if you're going to throw it all away. I already have your sister to worry about.'

'Who says I'm throwing it all away? I am trying very, very hard to not be a disappointment to you, Mum.'

'Yes. Well …' She turned away from me. The ridges of her shoulders two fisted peaks.

'Josh was Jewish,' I said to her back, 'and look where that got me.'

'Oh, Naomi,' she said, and turned back to face me, hard and fast. 'You're not even trying.'

'After that dinner, I need a drink,' Gemma said once we'd left. I agreed. We ended up at a newish bar that Gemma wanted to try, and that you had to descend three flights of stairs to get to. It was ten pm and the venue was already filling up with bodies. We ordered cocktails with lychees and pomegranate syrup and parked ourselves on a pair of stools. After a few sips Gemma said she felt like she was on a beach somewhere where everyone wore the same coconut-scented sunscreen. I tried to smile and when I couldn't she gave me her lychee.

We were on our second cocktail when a Facebook message from Julian Blume appeared on my phone: *Happy birthday! Are you celebrating tonight?*

Before I could say anything, Gemma grabbed my phone and zoomed in on his profile picture. 'Honey, he is cute! Let's invite him out!'

'No way!'

'Listen. Don't put your birthday on Facebook if you don't want people to know it's your birthday.' She began typing back.

'What are you doing?'

'Don't take everything so seriously, Princess.' Gemma squealed. 'Ooh. He wrote back immediately and said he's on his way. This guy has no game, but I like it.'

'What about Moses?'

'Naomi. It's your fucking birthday! You are the worst straight person ever.'

'I don't even know where I know him from,' I said, putting my head in my hands.

'Literally the worst straight person ever,' Gemma repeated, and took me to the middle of the bar where a few people were dancing. Gemma held her arms above her head and swayed her hips and tipped her hair back. I held onto my drink and shuffled from one foot to another, sipping through the straw, half looking around for Julian. I wasn't really sure if I'd know what he looked like.

Then I felt someone tap me on the shoulder and there he was, wearing a slim-fitting polo shirt, jeans and white sneakers that looked as though they'd been kept in a box. My mind went to clear cellophane, a tray of scalpels. A tall woman with a toothy smile was standing next to him.

'Happy birthday, Naomi.' He grinned. 'This is my cousin, Amy.' He was speaking very loudly, trying to overcome the music.

'Hi,' I said, almost shouting.

'We were just at my parents' for Shabbat.'

'Us too,' I said, leaning close to his ear.

Gemma floated over and reached out her hand to Julian. 'I'm Gemma.'

He nodded enthusiastically and said, 'What is that pink thing you're drinking?'

'I don't know. I think it's the special?' I directed this question towards Gemma, who agreed.

He said okay and went with Amy to the bar. Gemma and I found a tall table with stools, which was further away from the dancefloor and less noisy. 'He's handsome,' Gemma said.

I shrugged.

'He seems … very straight.'

'Yeah. He does.'

Julian and Amy returned with more drinks for everyone and sat down. I pieced together that Julian and I had gone to the same school, years apart, and he remembered an article that had been published in the *Jewish News* about the museum just after I'd started there. I'd been interviewed and had made a comment trying to sound smart and thoughtful but was mortified when I saw it in print alongside a photo of me solemnly holding a silver Kiddush cup. I told him I only read the *Jewish News* for the marriage and baby announcements, and my grandmother only read it for the deaths. He laughed with his belly and told me he understood this dynamic well.

I was suddenly awash with relief that in this moment I could pretend that I had never left the museum. I could pretend that none of it ever happened. And here I was, out in the world like a normal person, talking to another normal person. 'You're a dentist?'

'Did you google me?'

'My mother told me.'

'Ha. Of course she did.'

We clinked our pink drinks together. 'So why did you add me as a friend on Facebook?'

'I don't know.'

'Oh.'

'No. I do know. But I'm embarrassed to say.'

'Now you have to say.'

'Well,' he said slowly. 'It's stupid, really. You just came up on my Facebook feed and I remembered you, and I remembered liking you but not knowing you in that very high-school way. But we're not in high school any more.' Then he took a square white envelope out of his pocket and placed it in front of me. I asked him what it was and he told me to open it. Inside there was a fifty-dollar gift voucher to a department store. He leaned in close and said that he was sorry that it was a very impersonal gift and confessed to getting it at the service station on the way over, and I said I didn't expect any gift, and felt genuinely touched by the gesture. I wasn't quite sure what to do, so I hugged him. He smelled like hair product and expensive aftershave. I liked it, and caught whiffs of it in my own hair after.

Julian asked me if I wanted to dance with Gemma and Amy, who were already on the dancefloor, but I said no: not because I didn't want to, I just didn't know how I would look dancing with him, or in front of him, and this worried me. Gemma and Amy returned sometime later, sweaty and glossy, with four more drinks. Julian said that Amy worked at the National Gallery, and we'd probably know some people in common. Gemma lunged forward and said, 'Hey, didn't Josh go to the National Gallery?' and then looked at me apologetically, as if it had just slipped out.

'I know the one,' Amy said. 'Or I know of him. So embarrassing. The only other Jew who works there turns out to be a creep.'

I was momentarily stunned, so Gemma chimed in on my behalf. 'What do you mean?'

'He's being investigated for sexual misconduct with a junior colleague. It's all he-said, she-said so it probably won't go anywhere. It's supposed to be hush-hush but everyone knows. Was he like that when you worked with him?'

I had the sudden urge to vomit. Maybe it was the third cocktail or Julian's aftershave or Amy's large teeth. Maybe it was the memory of cleaning up his daughter's urine, the dead lice in my hairbrush. Maybe it was all the looks, grabs, given and stolen. Maybe it was the therapist's words, rising up in me now like an incantation. I swallowed down whatever was coming up and eventually stammered, 'Sorry, what was the question?'

Gemma grabbed my hand and said, 'Happy birthday, Naomi!' and we all clinked drinks and the conversation quickly morphed into politics, and then holiday destinations, and then coffee orders, and then Julian sat closer until our knees were touching. As the number of cocktails increased we discussed which of us would have survived the concentration camps. Julian believed he was in with a good chance with his scientific knowledge and rigorous workout regimen (I'm not sure whether he added that purely for my benefit), but Amy disagreed and said he was sickly as a child and wouldn't withstand the deprivation. She, on the other hand, was made of stronger stuff. Everyone unanimously agreed I had next to no chance of survival. I didn't protest. Gemma said we were all obsessed with the Holocaust, and Amy slurred and said, 'Oh, Gemma, while you were busy reading *The Hungry Little Caterpillar* we were playing Spot the Number on the Arm.' And then Gemma said, 'What about me? Wouldn't I have also been in the camps for being a queer?' I took her by the shoulders. 'No, oh no. You can conceal that shit. I'm not letting you go down with the rest of us.' By midnight we were all dancing together and were all quite drunk, which I assumed meant that Julian didn't have work the next day. At one point Julian leaned in and told me he thought I was pretty, and I said, 'Thank you.' Then he put his hand around my waist and kissed me. It felt good, so I kissed him back.

As we were leaving, he tried to kiss me again but I pulled away and said, 'I just want to be up-front with you.' I told him that a friend was coming to stay, and he asked me what kind of a friend. It was a good question. Chats after dark. Foodie snaps. Selfies. Trawling the internet for evidence of his existence which amounted to theatre reviews (his current play earned three-and-a-half stars and Moses's performance was said to be 'competent, infused with humour and subtlety'). Eventually I told Julian that I wasn't sure what kind of friend Moses was but I needed to find out, and he said, 'Oh.'

I couldn't sleep. I poked my head out of my bedroom and listened for Gemma, but the hallway was cave black and soundless. I went to the kitchen, made two Saladas with butter and Vegemite, took them back to bed and lay against the headboard crunching on the crackers murderously. Then I brushed as many of the crumbs off the bottom sheet as I could, lay down and began to masturbate. First, I imagined sitting on Moses's lap while he fondled my breasts. And then Julian appeared and I took him in my mouth. My nipples hardened and my clit swelled in my sweaty fingers, and my feet spasmed under the covers so much that a gush of cold air rushed in and out the other side of the quilt.

The new you

After much deliberation between myself, Adele and an external marketing agency, the title of the new exhibition was set to be Kitsch – From Tchotchkes to Treasures. Being my first exhibition it had a small budget but fortunately I had been able to utilise most of the objects from our existing collection. For the rest of it, I had asked the receptionist to post a call-out for Jewish retro pieces.

I arrived at the museum the Monday morning after my birthday to find a large parcel wrapped in brown paper on my desk. I opened it up and inside there was an old Remington typewriter with a Yiddish keyboard. The typewriter was beautiful, with a solid black rectangular frame and faded Yiddish lettering in white. I turned to Charlotte, my newly appointed curatorial assistant, to ask where it had come from. She said she didn't know.

I rang Marilyn, who was usually on top of all things coming in or out of the museum, and said, 'Do you know who left the parcel on my desk?'

'Good morning to you too, Naomi!'

'Sorry. Good morning.'

'Did you have a good birthday? Are we still doing cake at two?'

'Yes, sure.' No doubt she had organised an oversized card.

'Good. So. You got the typewriter. Isn't it lovely?'

'Yes. It is.' I pressed a finger on one of the keys. It was smooth and buttery to the touch.

'Perfect for the new exhibition, don't you think?'

'Yes, though the objects have mostly been finalised.'

'Josh brought it in yesterday after you'd left. Apparently he was clearing out his parents' garage on the weekend, found it, and thought you could use it. He apologised for not showing the usual protocol with donations, but I guess he knows better than anyone the sort of thing we're interested in. I'm assuming you'll know what to do with it.'

I hung up the phone and picked up the typewriter, which was heavier than I was expecting. A card floated from beneath it. Written in Josh's handwriting was a description of the object, as per the museum's style guide: *Remington Yiddish typewriter, Melbourne circa 1940s, metal 360 x 360 x 170 mm.*

I took the typewriter over to Charlotte's desk and placed it there without saying anything. She looked up at me, all eyelashes, and said, 'Would you like me to catalogue it for you?' She was in her final year of art curatorship, which was the same course Josh and I had completed. I liked her and tried to show it by offering to make her tea or coffee, which she mostly declined, but regardless of what I did she was still genuinely nervous around me. I recognised in her the same feeling I had when I started at the museum – that maybe I shouldn't be here at all.

'Naomi?' she prompted.

'Sorry,' I said. I couldn't get out of my head what Julian Blume's cousin had told me. The morning after, hungover and nauseous, Gemma had said, 'But of course that was bound to happen. He'd gotten away with it with you, so I guess he thought he'd give it another crack.' I'd turned pale as the moon by then, and she said, 'Aww, not that you're not special.'

The phone on my desk started ringing. I was immediately stricken with the thought that it might be him, so I told Charlotte to answer it. She pointed to herself and said, 'Me?' somewhat confused. She diligently walked over and picked up the phone and said, 'Naomi's phone. Charlotte speaking.' I dumbly nodded as she said, 'Uh huh,' and then, 'Who, sorry?'

I leaned in closely to her so I could smell her breakfast and whispered, 'Who is it? Who is it?'

She pulled away from me slightly, put her hand over the mouthpiece and said, 'I think your grandmother's here?'

'What?' I took the phone from her and spoke to the receptionist who repeated that my grandmother was indeed downstairs and waiting for me.

When I got her back to my office, I asked her how she'd got there, knowing she scorned taxis (too expensive) and the last time she'd taken public transport Bob Hawke was prime minister. She winked and said, 'Oh, I have my ways.' It turned out she'd convinced one of the carers to drop her off at the museum and expected me to drop her back.

'Are you okay?'

'Am I okay? What a question!' Cookie hadn't been herself since David had moved, and Mum had confessed to me that she was worried she'd made the wrong decision. Who cared if David got confused from time to time? Who cared if their room smelled or if the tap was left running? That was what air fresheners and drains were for. It was a circular conversation that always ended the same. The danger was too high. The risk was too great.

'Should I call Mum?' I asked Cookie, who was noticeably out of breath from the journey.

'Darling,' she said, unsmiling, 'I am not a child. Who is she?' Cookie said, pointing at Charlotte.

'Charlotte, my assistant.'

'Where's the other chap?' The other chap. My face must have betrayed some grey emotion because Charlotte interjected, 'He doesn't work here any more.'

'Oh,' Cookie said, suddenly brimming with confidence. 'So you're the new him, and she's the new you.' She swivelled in the chair to face both Charlotte and I. Her eyes glimmered.

I mouthed an apology to Charlotte but she just grinned.

I drove Cookie back to the home. In the driveway, I opened the car door, placed her walker in front of her and rested her handbag on its soft leather seat. On one side of the walker, written on a white label in thick black texta was *Cookie Radowski*. Two pink love heart stickers floated above her name. 'Who gave you the stickers?' I asked.

'They made me do it,' she said. 'Arts and crafts. And they think *I'm* the imbecile.'

When I returned to the museum I went to Josh's profile on Facebook. We were still friends. There was a photo of him and Kimiko sipping cocktails in the city and the caption read, *Date night with my girl*. Then my finger slipped and I accidentally liked the photo, and then promptly unliked it.

I went to Charlotte's desk. She looked up at me and said, 'Your grandmother seems like a lovely lady.'

I smiled, picked up the typewriter and took it into the collection storeroom, letting the door slam shut behind me. I held the typewriter against me, feeling the weight of it, sweat gathering on my top lip, its sharp metal bottom sticking into the folds of my middle. I placed it on the floor next to a filing cabinet. A fly promptly whizzed past me and landed on the letter X. It struck me how strange it was to see a living thing in here. I went to the door. I turned the fluorescent lights off. It was forest dark and cold in the blackness, among the unburied, and then I heard the fly buzz right past my head.

Your potatoes are dry

On Friday I took the day off work in preparation for Moses's arrival, which was a stupid thing to do as his plane wasn't landing until two pm and I had nothing to distract me from my own nerves and spent the morning on the toilet with diarrhoea. I told Mum that I wouldn't be coming to Shabbat that evening and she didn't ask why. She just said, 'No comment.'

I waited in my car at the train station nearest to my house and watched him walk from the platform to the street, looking for me. He was wearing a black T-shirt and a grey backpack and pushing an enormous bike bag. I'd forgotten how handsome I'd found him. His large nose and blue eyes. He came over to my window. 'Sorry, I forgot to mention I was bringing my bike. Do your back seats fold down?'

Once he was in the car we kissed on the cheek and then I didn't know what to say to him, so for the five-minute drive I spoke in a semi-formal tone, asking him questions about the play, Canberra, the flight, the train, his pending auditions, whether or not he needed to learn lines, did he get nervous, and then I pulled into my driveway and parked the car and said, 'Here we are.'

'Wow. It looks like a really nice house.'

'Oh, thanks,' I said, suddenly self-conscious.

'Who lives here again?'

'Just me and Gemma.'

Inside, I asked him if he wanted anything: a drink of water, a snack; had he had something on the plane? He shook his head, and I asked him if he wanted to see my room. He nodded.

We sat on the edge of my bed and he reached for my hand. I wiggled my fingers in his and he squeezed them in return. Then he kissed me on the mouth, a long and deep kiss on the lips. And then I opened my mouth, and we kissed with our tongues and our teeth and all the parts of our mouths that were pink and white and dark. He began kissing my neck and removed his T-shirt and I ran my hands along his thick and ripe biceps and kissed the top of his chest. I removed my top and he touched the straps of the new bra that my mother had bought for me. He pulled the bra cup down and my breasts spilled out and over. We shuffled further up the bed and undressed completely, and when he was inside me I felt myself closing in around him, wanting to swallow him with my legs or my teeth. We didn't speak much, except a few times when he said 'hang on' and pulled out, panting and closing his eyes, waiting a few moments, and then saying 'okay' and nodding before entering me again. We were sweating so much we felt stuck together. He pressed his penis against my clit and rubbed it over and over again until I bit into his shoulder and said, 'I'm coming,' at which point he exhaled and came into the condom. After that, we spoke in little whispers and eventually with our voices, at first a little wobbly, but then strong like heavy rain.

That night, we cooked together. He held the knives as if he had always held them and found the glasses in the cupboard without asking. He intuited the placement of things in my home as if he had placed them there himself. He spent a long time looking at a photo of my parents and I, which sat next to a pair of ornate silver candlesticks I'd been given for my bat mitzvah. 'Your family looks nice.'

I immediately replied with, 'Sorry.'

'Why?'

'Because I have this house.'

'So?'

'But I own it.'

'That's amazing.'

'Do you think I'm rich?'

He laughed and said, 'I don't know. But does it matter if you are?'

In the morning we took a walk and bought takeaway coffees. It had just turned to spring and it was warm outside and we were in short sleeves. We circled the perimeter of the cemetery, passing ultra-orthodox families with a multitude of children who were on their way to or from synagogue and

Shabbat lunches. Moses said hi to a heavily bearded man, dressed in a long black coat and large black hat, but the man appeared deep in thought or didn't hear him and kept walking.

We returned home and sat on the small patch of grass in the front garden, drinking coffees with my legs crossed over his and his crossed over mine.

An elderly neighbour strolled by. He was a small man with greying hair wearing a navy blue tracksuit, and he moved with difficulty. He paused and looked over at the two of us and smiled.

'G'day,' Moses said.

The man nodded and smiled. He pointed to the small lemon tree and said in a thick accent, 'You need to cut.'

Moses looked at the tree. 'Do we need to prune it?'

The man shook his head and said, 'Gall wasp. It everywhere round here. You need to cut. See? I show you.' We nodded and followed the man to the tree. He scanned the trunk and the branches and pulled down on a section of it, running his fingers along a swollen part of the limb. 'You see?'

'Right,' Moses nodded. 'So this part is diseased?'

The man shook his head. 'It is the wasp. It hurt the tree. Then fly to my tree. And hurt my tree.'

Moses asked me if I had any secateurs. I said I didn't think so. 'Ah well. We'll get this sorted. Thanks, mate.'

'Good. Good. Have a good day,' and he ambled off.

We went back to bed until lunchtime. In the afternoon, Moses suggested we go to the hardware store. We went and bought cutters and a saw, and then he asked me if I had a screwdriver. I didn't, but he said, 'That's okay. I could bring one with me next time.' I slipped my hand into the back pocket of his jeans and clenched his bum, and we walked like that out of the hardware store and all the way home.

Moses borrowed my car to go to an audition for the role of the uncle in a new children's show. Before he left he paced in the courtyard repeating the words, 'But Patsy, you're my number one,' shifting from word to word until he settled on the word 'my' to place the most emphasis on.

When he came to pick me up from work in the late afternoon I led him through the permanent gallery. He paused in front of every artefact, reading the captions, occasionally asking me something about it. He insisted on watching the ten-minute documentary detailing the Jewish historical timeline. He placed the heavy black headphones over his ears and stared intently at the small display screen, shuffling from side to side on his sneakers. I went to the bathroom and when I returned he looked at me, stupefied, and said, 'Please tell me it gets better from here?'

I felt bad for him then. 'Oh yeah,' I said, enthusiastically. 'Much better.'

Upstairs in my office I asked him about his audition.

'It wasn't great,' he said. 'They kept asking if I could be more goofy.' He forced a grin and then let it go. And then he said, 'Actually, I met your mum today.'

'Oh. Shit. Really?' I said in a rushed voice. My palms immediately began to moisten and I ran them up and down my jeans.

He noticed the stack of black and white photographs on my desk. I'd had a handful of Paula's photos professionally printed. I was trying to make sense of them, hoping to see if I could incorporate them somehow into the latest exhibition, maybe without anyone noticing. He picked up one of the photos. 'This is cool.' It was an ornate inner stairwell of an apartment building, and she had captured a mother and child, hand in hand. The boy's socks were up over his knees. The mother was caught in a moment of anger and looked as though she was about to say something, maybe to Paula, maybe to the boy. 'It reminds me of that photo in your room.'

'Which photo?'

'The Diane Arbus twins.'

'Oh,' I said. 'Yeah.' I studied his face, relaxed and contemplative. 'Maybe. Anyway.' I took a breath. 'What happened? With my mum?'

'Oh, right,' he said, very casually. 'It was weird. At first, I thought she hated me.'

'Oh, no!' My breath left me a little. 'Of course she doesn't hate you.'

He told me that after his audition he'd met a friend for coffee and then went back to my house. When he parked in the drive, my mother was shutting the front door. As he spoke I began laying the photos out on the desk in an attempt to both calm myself and convey that calmness to him. He said he got out of the car and she literally jumped at the sight of him. It had frightened her to see him get out of my car, when she had expected to see me. Immediately he introduced himself, offering as much context as possible in an effort to reassure her. 'And then ...' He cleared his throat.

'What? What?'

'Okay, relax. And then ... she invited me to Shabbat dinner.'

'She did what?'

'Sorry. Should I have said no? It would have been weird to say no.'

'No. Yes. Okay. So. Sorry about that. I guess you're meeting my parents.'

'Cool,' he said, and then he grabbed me and kissed me.

As we were leaving the office, I glanced back at the photos and saw that I'd arranged them in a way that made the subjects look as though they were gliding from one image to the next. I hadn't intended it, but I hadn't intended any of it: Moses, what happened before Moses, what happened before me.

I rang my mother while he was in the shower.

'So. You met Moses?'

'I did.'

'And you invited him for Shabbat?'

'Well, he is staying with you, isn't he?'

'Uh ... Yeah.'

'And you do like him, don't you?'

'Um. Yes.'

'So what's the problem?'

'It's just a bit soon for him to be … meeting my parents.'

'If someone is staying in my daughter's house, I want to know who they are.'

We collected Cookie on the way. She was waiting alone by the entrance, with an expression on her face suggesting she had been there a while. I checked the time and we were punctual to the minute, but Cookie's watch ran fast, which meant that everyone was always running after it, and her. I was still unused to seeing Cookie without David. He was slowly morphing into shadow, like the rest of Cookie's ghosts.

Moses collapsed her walker into the boot, we set off and Cookie's mood lightened. She told Moses that she and her friends had been to Tasmania once on the ferry and that she remembered the whole place being very beautiful and quaint, and he chuckled at that. 'Did your friends like it too?' he asked.

'Friends? I have no friends. All my friends are dead.'

Moses laughed awkwardly. 'You're from Poland, Cookie?' he ploughed on.

'What? That place? Nah.' She thrust her arm into the air then looked back at him and winked flirtatiously. 'A long time ago, darling. And the rest, as they say, is history! What did you say your name was?'

'Um. Moses.'

'Moses?' She looked at me to see whether or not he was joking.

'I know, I know,' he said. And then he straightened his back. 'My mum liked the Bible story.'

'A good story is a good story.'

He nodded enthusiastically.

'And your people? Come closer, darling. It hurts to turn my neck.'

'Um …'

'Where do your people come from? Where are you from?' She was in the front and he was in the back, and he moved over to the middle seat and leaned in.

'I think everyone is from around Launceston,' he said with an upward inflection, as though it might be the wrong answer.

'No!' she said firmly. 'Where are you from?' she repeated again.

Moses scrunched his face and looked at me for help.

'I think Cookie's asking about your background,' I said through the rear-vision mirror.

'Oh,' he said, and looked in his lap as if it might offer him an answer.

'What did he say?' Cookie asked me.

'He didn't say anything.'

'Irish? Scottish?' Cookie went on. 'Are you a convict? Are you a royal? Trash or treasure.'

'Definitely trash,' Moses said.

'What did he say?'

'He's descended from royalty,' I said.

'Ha. Aren't we all?' Cookie held out her hand to me and I took it, quickly, before releasing it to change gear.

'I'm sorry, Cookie,' Moses said, very loudly now. 'I'm not really good with family history. My mother was kind of the keeper of all that.'

'What happened to your mother?'

'She died, Cookie. She had cancer.'

'Oh,' Cookie said quietly. 'Oh,' she repeated. 'I'm sorry, darling.'

'Thanks, Cookie,' he said.

My parents were having a lie-down. I'm not sure what I was expecting. Certainly not fanfare. Potentially a communal gathering to watch the six o'clock news or the headlines at least. A welcome drink on arrival – unlikely but still a possibility. I was not expecting Melanie to be the one to greet us all, scoop Cookie's arm in hers and tell us all that my parents would be out soon.

'This is Moses,' I said.

'I figured. Welcome,' she said and took Cookie into the lounge, who said very loudly, 'Good-looking boy, isn't he?'

'If you like that sort of thing,' I heard Melanie counter.

Moses and I stood for a moment in the hallway.

'Is that a Brett Whiteley?' He was staring at a framed picture on the wall.

'It's only a lithograph,' I told him. 'The real one's down the hall.'

'Uh. Really?'

'Just kidding,' I said, and directed him to some lesser-known artists that my mother had collected over her years at the gallery.

When my parents finally emerged from their room, Mum headed straight to the kitchen to check on the oven and my father turned the television on. This meant I had to escort Moses first to the kitchen, where my mother kept her head in the fridge as we said hello, and then to greet my father in the study, where the volume was turned up loud and my father inexplicably did not turn it down.

As we were sitting around the table it dawned on me that it had been at least two years since I'd brought someone (besides Gemma) to Shabbat dinner. It also occurred to me that it hadn't been long before that that my ex and I broke up. He'd left to study in the UK and I didn't want to go with him. We shared a dramatic scene at the airport where I cried so much that a baggage handler had offered me his hankie, but then a week later we exchanged an email where we both agreed it would be for the best if we stopped communicating with each other and I hadn't heard from him since.

I hadn't told Moses much about the Shabbat dinner. I figured he'd seen enough movies set in New York to have a sense of what he was heading into. And it's not as if my family were religious. Prayers were said, with a perfunctory nod to some higher power, either God or food, it didn't really matter. I only learned later that when Dad had handed Moses a kippah he'd been taken completely by surprise, not entirely sure what to do with it, whether it was offensive to wear it or not wear it, or how long to keep it on his head.

My mother was chatty and charming. I was sure she found him handsome because she said he had a good face for television, to which Cookie agreed with a mouth full of chopped liver. My father, however, was demonstrably silent throughout the evening. He'd always been awkward around my boyfriends and used to follow them around the house, if not physically trailing them then with his eyes. When I was seventeen, my period was late. Despite being a virgin who was on the pill that the GP had prescribed to dull the persistent tenderness in my breasts, I was convinced I was pregnant. I was convinced that my high-school boyfriend's sperm had travelled from the palm of my hand to the inner walls of my vagina. Mum was away that weekend and Melanie had already moved out of home, so it was just Dad and I, pottering around in the large house. Over breakfast he had asked if anything was wrong and I'd begun to cry and apologise. Dad knew the boyfriend well. He was at the house a lot. He'd come to many Shabbat dinners. He'd helped himself to the pantry and the fruit bowl and knew where all the remote controls lived. Dad had even driven us to get our learner's permits, had taken us for ice cream after, and had offered my boyfriend advice on the best law undergraduate program. Dad knew that I was crying about the boyfriend. About which aspect, he wasn't sure. I assume he'd quietly hoped it was over our break-up, but when I told him that I was a virgin but that my period was late, he'd laughed. Then he took me across town to see a movie in Carlton followed by spaghetti and tiramisu. The next morning there was blood on my pyjamas. I'd been so relieved that I woke him up to tell him, and he'd rolled over in bed and said, 'That's wonderful, darling.'

Now it wasn't as though Dad was being rude to Moses, rather just ignoring him completely. Meanwhile Melanie was busy telling Moses that she'd always thought about going to drama school, however she wasn't prepared to live with that degree of uncertainty. I interjected with the tidbit that Moses had been on *Neighbours*, hoping my parents might find that amusing, but neither of them reacted and I'd inadvertently brought the conversation to a complete halt, only to be resuscitated by the news that Melanie was getting a dog. I expected this to be met with disdain by my mother, who never liked dogs, but she seemed thrilled with this new talking point. 'What will we call it?'

'We?' Melanie grunted. 'Meet your great-grandchild, Cookie.' Melanie held her phone beneath Cookie's nose to show her the photo of the dog.

'You know,' Dad said, 'dogs need food and water, and regular walks. Can you pass the salad?' The salad was in front of Moses. Moses stood and took it over to my father, who accepted it with a garbled thank you and avoided eye contact completely.

Moses sat back down and said, 'This is such a delicious meal, thank you for having me.'

'Good,' Mum said and took a sip of wine.

'Is this a rat?' Cookie said, still squinting at the phone.

'It's only three weeks old,' Melanie said.

Cookie gave the phone to me, and I looked at the dog and showed it to Moses.

'Is that a bulldog?' Moses asked.

'God, no. It's a pug.'

'It's a rat,' Cookie repeated.

'Whatever it is, make sure you get pet insurance,' Dad said. 'Remember Marlene's diabetic dog?'

'That dog was feral. Should have been put down from the get-go,' Mum said.

'Vivienne,' Cookie said. 'I hope there's something decent for dessert. Your potatoes are dry.'

Cookie burped without covering her mouth, and Dad stood up and announced he was going to watch the footy. I followed Mum into the kitchen with a stack of dishes. I felt bad leaving Moses, but as I did I could hear Cookie repeating the story of going to Tasmania with her friends and him laughing as if it was the first time he'd heard it.

My mother took the plates without looking at me.

'Mum—'

'Naomi. He seems nice. But I can't talk about this now.'

'Okay, but—'

'Cookie said she wanted tea, didn't she?' I watched her put on the kettle and then grasp the stainless-steel bench with her hands and lean forward with her eyes closed. 'I had a two-hour meeting with the home. They can't just let her roam about willy-nilly. If a resident leaves, everyone should know about it.'

'I took her straight back home.'

'It wasn't the first time.'

'Mum. I. Uh—'

'What? Spit it out, Naomi.'

I said nothing. The kettle boiled, she poured the tea and took it back to the dining room.

I wanted to get back to Moses, but found myself glued to the warm oven, which my mother had left on even though there was nothing in it. The dinner was done save for dessert, which Melanie came searching for moments later.

'Apparently there's cake?' She opened the fridge and took out a lemon sponge bound in cling film.

I wanted her to say something to me about Moses but knew she wouldn't. 'Are you seeing anyone?' I asked, hoping to inspire a dialogue.

'No. But I wouldn't bring them here in any case. That's for sure.' She grabbed a knife, took the cake and walked out.

As soon as we dropped Cookie home I said, 'Well, my dad has major trust issues, so don't take it personally.' The Josh saga had left a space between my father and I. Maybe the space had been there a while. I hadn't studied law like he wanted me to, even though I had tried. My father had pioneered the pro bono program at his law firm, and he came and gave a speech about it at my school. I remember being so proud of him. Of wanting to be like him. I had gone into his office and helped the receptionist make photocopies and I watered the plants in the communal areas. When I dropped law he said he'd understood, but I wasn't sure I'd believed him, and in this past year I was scared of who he thought I'd since become. I felt the overcooked potatoes repeating in my mouth and then said, 'I think in my parents' fantasy, they'd want me to be with a Jewish person.'

He nodded. 'Makes sense.'

'But I'm sure they'd find a reason to disapprove of them too.' I stopped at the traffic lights and we looked at each other. And then I waited for him to say something about my family – how my father was rude and dismissive, my mother was self-involved and my sister exponentially more so – but he didn't. He just said that they have an impressive art collection, and that I was lucky to grow up in a home like that, and that my grandmother was delightful. 'Well, she definitely likes you,' I said. 'I know that.'

'And I really like you,' he said.

'Oh,' I said, feeling awful and wonderful. 'I really like you too.'

I was still hungry so we stopped at a place that sold churros, drove to the beach and sat in the car dipping the doughnuts in warm Nutella.

'Shabbat every week. That's like, really nice,' he said.

'It is?'

'Yeah.' He wound down his window and the dank whiff of seaweed and brine filled the car. 'Liv and I would have loved that.'

I leaned across the gearstick and kissed him and kissed him, until I was full of saliva, chocolate, sugar and salt.

Antarctica

Since Shabbat I was avoiding speaking to my parents altogether, and I suspected they were avoiding speaking to me. A couple of weeks later I turned up to Shabbat dinner alone, and they didn't ask after Moses, and I didn't mention him either. Subsequently each interaction with Moses felt more clandestine, each time I rolled over and saw him lying there another transgression. He'd started calling me 'babe', which felt at once entirely pedestrian and specific to me. One morning he left and then returned with coffee from the local cafe, and as he placed it next to me he told me he was in love with me, and so I said it back. I called in sick that day and we stayed in bed for hours.

We hadn't intended to move in together so quickly, nor had I wanted Gemma to move out so rapidly. But Gemma had been offered a job in Sydney and her girlfriend Ash was going with her, and now her room had nothing in it except for a sheepskin rug that Moses and I had already managed to stain with red wine and bodily fluids. Before she left we had dinner together, just the two of us, and I wept over two saucy plates of spaghetti, cheese and soft white bread. 'Oh, Princess,' she'd said. 'You're still my favourite.' I didn't believe her, but I loved her for saying it anyway.

When a room for rent came up through a friend of his, Moses asked me if he should take it and I said I didn't know. We arranged to go and see the room, but we slept through the alarm and missed the appointment. Neither of us urged the other to follow it up, and so we hadn't. And then he was cast as an overly empathetic teacher in a limited series that was shooting locally. We celebrated by hiking in the Dandenongs and spending the night in a bed and breakfast that he paid for.

A few weeks later my mother called me on the weekend and when I answered she said, 'Oh, you're still alive, are you?' I told her I'd been very busy at work, which was true. The exhibition opening was just over a month away, and there was still so much to do. I hadn't told her all the other things I'd be busy with (Moses), though of course she knew.

She was on her way to visit Cookie and asked if I would like to come. I wondered if it was a kind of peace offering, a moving forward. It wasn't, but then something in her voice suggested she needed the moral support so, reluctantly, I told her yes, I would like to come.

When she arrived, Moses was cleaning his bike with a soapy bucket and sponge out the front. I had hoped he'd already gone for his ride, because I couldn't bring myself to ask him to leave.

'He's still here,' Mum said once we were in the car on our way to see Cookie.

'He got a part in a TV show.'

'And? What's that got to do with you?'

I fiddled with the lock on the door until my mother asked me to stop. Eventually I said, 'He's going to stay with me.'

'Stay with you? For how long?'

'I don't know.' And then I added, 'Gemma's moved out.'

'And you're only telling me this now?'

'It's my house, isn't it?' I mumbled, only half believing what I was saying.

Cookie's room was overheated and smelled bad. Even the plastic flowers appeared to be drooping. Mum pushed open the windows and said, 'Mum, do you need to go to the toilet?'

Cookie ignored Mum and wiggled her fingers at me. I sat on the couch next to her. Cookie placed her hand at the back of my head and tugged on my hair. I put my hand on Cookie's thigh, which felt bony under my palm.

'You want something?' Cookie said in a low voice, as if she didn't want Mum to hear. There was skin-coloured cream on Cookie's nose that hadn't been rubbed in. I touched my fingers to my own nose, hoping it would prompt Cookie to do the same. 'I have something in that drawer over there. Go on. Go have a look.' I went to the drawer next to the television. Inside were piles of paper serviettes, some stained with lipstick, and one-and-a-half biscuits in a plastic packet that had already been opened. It was the kind of packet that sits next to the tea and coffee and pods of long-life milk in a motel.

I looked at my mother, who was now wiping down the table, with nervy eyes. Mum said, 'She's not hungry, Mum.'

'Who said she has to be hungry?'

I closed the drawer without taking anything and sat back down with Cookie. We watched Mum shuffle around the room before she breathlessly sat in an armchair and said, 'How often are they coming to clean, Mum?'

Cookie shrugged her shoulders. 'I tell them to go.'

'Mum!' My mother looked around the room. 'And do they go?'

'If they know what's good for them.' Cookie winked at me. Her hairdresser had stopped coming too. The woman had shown up at Cookie's door with her suitcase and scissors, but Cookie had screamed at her and said in no uncertain terms don't come back. Mum had pleaded with the hairdresser to try again, but the hairdresser had said she was now fully booked and maybe they should try someone else.

'Mum, you need to let them clean in here.'

'Why? What mess do I make?'

'It smells.'

'Pfft.' Cookie turned to me. 'And how's my granddaughter?'

'Good,' I said, smiling sweetly.

Mum huffed. She hated one-word answers.

'And how is work?' Cookie asked, crossing one swollen foot over the other.

'It's good. I just started work on a new exhibition.'

'Naomi's been very busy,' my mother said, looking at her watch.

'And what about ...' Cookie winked at me.

Mum huffed again and went into the bedroom. I leaned into Cookie's ear as closely as possible and said, 'He's good.'

Mum re-emerged with a pile of Cookie's cream underwear. Cookie scowled with a disgusted look on her face. 'What are you doing?'

'I'm going to fold these and put them away.'

'Don't!'

'Mum—'

'Don't!' Cookie repeated, spitting a little. She shifted on the couch, threatening to get up, and Mum tightly pursed her lips together and silently took the underwear back to the bedroom, returned, and sat down.

Cookie looked at me. 'So? Has he got a job yet?'

I looked at my mother, who looked out the window. 'Yes. He has a job. And he just got a part in a TV show.'

'And then what?' Cookie asked.

'God help us all,' my mother said. The light from the window hit my mother's face harshly, as if she were being cut in two.

'He'll get another job,' I said.

Cookie nodded and closed her eyes. Her mouth moved like she was sucking a lolly, but there was nothing in there but a tongue and dentures.

Before we left, I was going to ask Mum if she wanted to see David, but then I didn't say anything because I didn't want to. The last time I had been to see him, a black feathered miner bird had got in through the courtyard door and had darted from wall to wall, discarding little feathers and shitting every time it landed. Most of the dementia ward residents slept through the whole thing, including David, who sat in a chair on wheels, slack-jawed and drooling, while *The Sound of Music* played on the giant TV. His cheeks were hollow and his chin unshaven. At one point he opened his eyes and looked at me. It seemed he was nodding with his eyes, though I couldn't be sure. I had tried to sing along to the movie, but his face reported nothing back and he'd closed his eyes again.

On the way home, Mum looked tired and sallow. I didn't know what to say, so eventually said, 'Are you okay?'

She nodded without saying anything.

'You're very good to her, Mum.'

'No.' She tipped her head this way and that, as if there was water in her ears. 'I'm not. I don't want to be there, Naomi.'

'It's hard.'

'It's more than that. She— she's not my mother any more. She's not mothering me. I'm mothering her. And you think you'll be ready but— I must be selfish.'

And then I knew that whatever discomfort I experienced seeing my grandmother alone in her small room was exponentially more profound for my mother, and this only made all the difficult feelings between us even more pronounced, and the road home stretched on and on. 'You're being too tough on yourself. You—'

'Other daughters,' she interrupted me, 'they want to be there for their mothers.' Her eyes grew wide and glossy. 'Mother–daughter relationships are complicated. You'll learn that when you have your own.' She said this plainly, as if it didn't apply to our own lifelong communion; a lifetime of car trips, buttoning of cardigans, peeling of oranges, kisses on the back of the neck.

A volume of cars before us came to a halt and so did we. Mum's car did that thing where the engine stopped and it was suddenly dead quiet. She stared straight ahead and asked if I could come over that evening, alone. My parents wanted to talk to me.

'Am I in trouble?'

She said nothing.

I bit the inside of my cheek and said, 'Okay. So what do you want to talk about?'

'We just want to talk.'

'Is it about Moses? Because you don't need to worry—'

'It's about you.'

Mum pulled up at the house, and Moses's bike was chained up to the front fence.

'Okay,' I said.

'Good. Come around eight.' She drove off without looking back.

When I arrived, Dad was having trouble with his computer and asked me if I could try to figure it out. I followed him into his study. His desk was meticulously tidy, with nothing on it except a laptop and a white stationery caddy filled with free hotel pens, a miniature stapler and a fat eraser still wrapped in plastic. Above the desk were three framed university degrees and a photo of my mother not looking at the camera and laughing. She looked beautiful in the photo, though I remember her saying once that there were too many lines on her forehead and who did she have to pay to photoshop them out.

I opened his computer and typed in his password without thinking. He put his hand on my shoulder and said, 'Oh. I hope you don't share that with anyone else.'

'Who am I going to share it with?'

Mum had made tea and we sat in the lounge, my parents on the couch and me in an armchair facing them. The tea was too hot to sip. I sat on my hands and stuck out my chin. I was showing them my face, as if maybe they'd forgotten it.

'Well.' Dad cleared his throat.

'Why am I here?' I had desperately hoped for this conversation to be about anything other than what it was about.

'I think you know why,' my mother answered.

My eyes darted around the room. I was searching for something to tether myself to, but there was only a large abstract oil painting and an even larger abstract tapestry. 'Can I speak first?' I asked. They looked at each other again and nodded. 'I know it seems fast. And it is fast. I know that.' I was now rocking back and forth on my hands at increasing speed, trying to get a rhythm going in order to find the right words to say. 'He's kind. He's decent. He's talented.'

'You're talented,' Mum said in a corrective tone.

'You shouldn't underestimate yourself,' Dad said.

'We know you like to do things that make you feel good,' Mum said.

'We all like to do things that make us feel good, don't we?' I asked.

'Lust can be very powerful,' Mum said.

'This isn't that,' I said.

'Isn't what?' Mum asked. 'Isn't Josh?'

'This is completely different!'

'Well, this guy—' Mum said.

'You know his name.'

'But is it really his name?' she asked, crossing her arms. 'It sounds made up.'

'Vivienne,' my father warned.

'Moses, ahem, may not be unavailable but he certainly is unsuitable, right?' She chuckled, looking between my father and I.

'Dad?' I turned to him.

'As you get older,' Dad said, scratching his chin, 'you learn to be less impulsive.'

'I don't think I—'

'You learn to …' My mother fluttered her hands.

'Let her speak, darling,' my father interjected.

'Sorry,' Mum said with a clenched smile. 'I interrupted you.'

'I was going to say …' I tried to maintain eye contact with both of them. 'I'm in a different space now,' I went on. 'Totally different. You know that, right? I'm doing well with my job—'

'And we're very proud of you for that,' Dad said, eyes on the floor.

'Sorry. Can I just—' Mum put one hand up. 'You say you're in a different space. And yes, you're doing well with work. But from a relationship point of view …'

'We're concerned about you,' Dad said, finally looking directly at me and rushing his words.

'We know you won't want to hear this,' Mum said. 'No one ever wants to hear what their parents have to say. I certainly didn't.'

'Nor me,' Dad said.

'Your mother hated me,' Mum said to Dad.

'And you've had a successful marriage,' I urged. Despite my father disappearing, for that month in 1994.

'It's completely different,' Mum said.

'Your mother says he's living with you. Is that true?' Dad said.

I nodded, and then said, just above a whisper, 'We're in love.'

'Oh my God,' my mother said, putting her head in her hands.

'Naomi,' my father leaned forward, 'he has no car. No home. No assets or discernible income.'

'He has savings,' I said, clamping my thighs tighter around my hands. 'He has a house.'

'That he owns?'

'Well, it's his father's but—'

'Oh, darling, please,' Mum said, flapping her cardigan.

'Neither of you had any money growing up.'

'Yes, and we worked very hard,' Dad said. 'We did long slogs at university. Worked jobs that were less than desirable.'

'Did he even finish high school?' Mum asked.

'I can't see how this is relevant,' I said, knowing that Moses left school in year ten. 'Drama school is extremely hard to get into. He was one of twenty in the country.'

'We're just trying to understand,' Dad said.

'Does he pay you rent?' asked Mum.

I swallowed so loudly I was certain they could hear the saliva rolling down my oesophagus. 'Yes.' This was a half-truth. I'd suggested he should pay half of the bills and buy half of the groceries and he hadn't said no.

'With what?' Mum said.

'With money.'

'What money?' Dad said.

'I told you, he's just been cast in a TV show.'

'But has he been paid?' Dad said.

'In a couple of months. But he just booked an ad as well.'

'For how much?' Mum said.

'It was for ten thousand dollars.' Another half-truth. It was for five thousand. 'And he just started another carpentry gig. He could probably fix the shelf in the powder room.'

'What's wrong with the shelf in the powder room?' Mum asked.

'It's wonky,' Dad said.

'Not that I've noticed,' she said.

I took a sip of tea. It was still too hot, but I sipped it anyway and felt the sting of it on my tongue. 'You wouldn't be saying any of this if he was Jewish.' I suddenly felt like I was harnessing a burning sensation under my legs. It was rage, and I realised I had been trying to contain it by sitting on my hands, digging my nails into my thighs, but the burning was spreading. I felt it on my chest and neck and cheeks. Some parents might say that they wanted their daughters to be able to fend for themselves, to never be reliant on a spouse, but it was dawning on me that perhaps they never had faith in me in the first place to take care of myself, and all they wanted, ultimately, was someone for me they could pass the torch on to, someone who – once they were no more – could pay for the nice things as well as the essential things. 'You know, Melanie married an arsehole, and you never said a thing. Because he was Jewish. And because you wanted to believe that that was all that mattered.'

'I didn't think he was an arsehole,' my mother said.

'Yes, you did!'

'Well, we didn't buy Melanie a house,' Dad said.

'But she has access to the same money. I mean, you divide everything equally between us, right?'

'Of course we do.'

'Look, I don't think we need to discuss Melanie right now.' Mum directed this to Dad.

Dad slapped his legs and then looked at his watch and said, 'Well—'

'Cookie likes him.'

'Cookie doesn't have a clue!' my mother shouted and then sat back, and we all looked at each other. 'And you're not helping.'

'Viv …' Dad said, flashing a pitiful smile in my direction. He cleared his throat, and then asked Mum if she had anything sweet to go with the tea, and she said she didn't think so but she'd go look. My father and I sat there in silence. I focused on his fingernails, which were well manicured. They were a similar shape to my own, yet my nails were narrower and my fingers more freckled. I was hopeful for a moment of camaraderie, but he said nothing so neither did I. Mum returned with chocolate-covered rice cakes, and he scrunched his nose and said, 'This is all you've got?'

She looked as though she might throw the packet at him but instead sat down, placing it between them. 'Oh for God's sake, Alex. You do the shopping, if you don't like it.' And then she looked at me. 'Listen, we knew Melanie's husband's parents. We knew where he was from. I mean, what on earth would we have in common with Moses's parents? I'm sure they're lovely people but—'

'His mother is dead.'

'I'm sorry,' my mother said, then looked at my father with an exasperated *I give up* look, and covered her eyes with her hand. Seeing me was too much.

I scanned my mind for everything I knew about Moses: his sister, his home that I'd only been to the one time, his showreel that was on YouTube, his father who lived in Canada but he never spoke to, his mother whose photo I'd seen when he'd clicked the thumbnail on his desktop. I thought about the shape of him. His sharp nose in my armpit. His groin against my arse. 'I do know him,' I said after a time. 'You don't know him well.'

'But you're rushing. You're rushing, darling. And—' Dad clasped his hands together tightly.

'He won't understand anything about us, I can tell you that much,' Mum said.

'He wants to understand.'

'Fetishise, you mean?' she said. 'Oh. The Jewish girl with big tits and hair and money.'

'Jesus, Mum.' I looked to my father, expecting him to laugh, but his face was still as stone.

My mother sighed. 'We're sorry this is hard for you. We hate seeing you upset. But as we said, we worked very hard to get where we are today. We worked very hard to provide for you and Melanie. You know, we didn't have the childhoods you both had. We grew up knowing that at any point, any point, it could all be taken away.'

I watched my father take her hand.

'Do you understand that?' she continued. 'How could you ever expect Moses to understand any of that?'

I let some time pass. Eventually I said, 'It's different for my generation.' I knew how pathetic I sounded. I knew there was nothing I could say that could make me feel less lonely in this moment, that my sadness was pitted against all the sadness of my ancestors.

'Your generation is complacent,' she said. 'Lazy.'

'You don't see things coming,' my father said.

'And you clearly don't read the news, Naomi,' Mum said.

'Shocking,' my dad said, shaking his head. I couldn't tell if he was referring to me or the news.

'He's not antisemitic, you know.' I was so tired of my own voice.

'Ha,' Mum said. 'How do you know?'

'There's one in every family,' Dad said, brushing a crumb off his jumper.

'You two are beyond paranoid.'

'Don't be ridiculous,' my mother said.

'Am I being ridiculous? I think you're being ridiculous.'

'We're not paranoid, Naomi,' my father said. 'We've just lived in this world a lot longer than you.'

'This isn't about you. This is about me.'

'No, Naomi,' my mother said. 'You're wrong. This is about all of us.'

I called Melanie from the car. She answered right before I resolved to hang up.

'What is it?' Melanie said, impatient. We so rarely called each other that I wasn't the least bit offended. It sounded as though she was moving away from a crowd.

'Hi. Sorry.' Now that I had my sister on the phone, I was bereft of things to say.

'Listen, I'm having a dinner thing … Hello?'

'Okay. I won't keep you. I just wanted to run something by you.'

'Hurry up, then. Hello? Naomi?'

I heard a dog bark. 'Is that your new dog?'

'Jasper.'

'Is he cute?'

'Yes.'

'You can bring him by, if you want to.'

'Naomi.'

'I'm just in this really awkward situation with Mum and Dad and I don't know how to deal with it.'

'With the guy? What's his name? Abraham?'

'Moses.'

'Jesus. Okay. Yeah. So they don't like him.'

'No. They've just made all these assumptions about him. And now I feel like I can't talk to them at all.'

'Well, I mean … from the sound of things he is, like, bumming off you. And that's kind of weird. Like he should at least have his own place. You just let him move in.'

'It wasn't like that.'

'Listen. I don't know the whole story, but A, you really should get to know someone properly before they move in with you, and B, you don't have any boundaries with Mum and Dad so of course anything they say or do is going to fuck you up. And C, is that all, because I'm kind of being rude here?'

'That's all.'

'Okay. Well. It will be okay, Naomi.'

'Really?' It was the kindest thing she'd ever said to me.

'I've gotta go. Sort your shit out.' She ended the call.

I had the sudden urge to turf my phone out of the car window and then suggest to Moses that we move to Sydney or Antarctica or take a walk into the bush and dig a very, very, very large hole.

The front door to my house was wide open. Moses said he liked to circulate air and I liked to trap it. I closed the door behind me. I could hear him on the phone in Gemma's room (we still called it that). 'It's Liv,' he mouthed. His voice was easy and light. I nodded and sat on a chair and studied the shadows on the floorboards where Gemma's bed had been. I missed Gemma terribly then and thought she was probably having a good time somewhere in Sydney, at bars and clubs with her hot girlfriend and new friends who liked that sort of thing. I looked down at my phone and it revealed nothing. Social media depressed me and so did my emails.

Moses started laughing and said he'd better go, fixing his gaze upon me. I was afraid to look him in the eye.

It was late and we still hadn't eaten dinner. We went to the kitchen and I sat at the table while he had his head in the fridge saying, 'I could do eggs, pasta, or do you want takeaway?'

I said I didn't know and that I really wanted him to make the decision for me. In the end he made toast with lashings of butter, sliced tomatoes and sea salt. We crunched on the toast for a while and then I gave him the skinny version of my conversation with my parents but all he said was, 'It doesn't matter to me. They're just trying to protect you.' This made me start to cry, which was embarrassing because I had never really cried in front of him before, not properly anyway.

'Do you hate them though?' I said eventually, in my quietest, most bird-like voice.

'No. I don't. Do you?'

'Will you be doing more work soon?'

He shuffled back slightly in his chair and it made a scraping sound on the floor. 'Yeah. Of course, babe. Are you worried about it?'

I looked at his T-shirt. The top of the neckline was frayed and worn and yet it complimented him. I reached out to touch it and slip my finger into one of the holes. 'Dunno.'

'I can call that guy tomorrow and hook something up.'

'That was digging holes.'

'I can dig holes.'

'You hate digging holes.'

'I can dig holes,' he repeated, softly and into my shoulder.

Then I watched him drink two glasses of red wine, and then go outside into the courtyard and roll a joint. I stayed inside, watching him, smoke encircling him like steaming potatoes.

Later, I asked him to show me the photo of his mother on his computer. It was of the two of them sitting side by side. Moses was mid-conversation and had something white in his mouth, and she was turned to face him, smiling. I wanted to know what he'd been eating in the picture and he said he couldn't remember. I imagined that it was soft white bread, and that she had baked it for him. Her skin was sun-weathered, her hair was in a long plait. He said she was outdoorsy and taught him to ride bikes.

'Were you close?'

He hesitated and then said, 'Yeah. Sometimes when I'm on the bike, I can't help but look for her in the distance. Like I expect her to be up ahead of me on the track. I know it's silly.'

'No, it isn't.' My mother was always just up ahead of me on the track.

The earth beneath her

Mum called the following day. I wasn't going to answer, but then I couldn't shake the feeling that someone had died or was dying, and that answering the phone took on the gravitas of holding someone's life or death in my hands.

'I've just been at the home,' she said. 'She hasn't eaten since we were there yesterday.'

'That's okay, isn't it?'

'Naomi, you don't understand. She's refusing to eat. It's very dangerous at her age. They want to put her on antidepressants.'

'I think antidepressants would be good for her.'

Mum snorted. 'Well, you refused to take them.'

'I didn't refuse. I just didn't need them in the end.'

'Alright. Well. I think they would actually have helped a lot.'

'Why are we talking about me?' I held onto the minor hope that she might apologise and take back everything that was said last night.

'By the way, I saw a two-for-one sale at Country Road on those linen T-shirts we've bought before. I've already bought one in black in your size.' She wasn't apologising. She was shopping.

'Okay. Thanks.'

'I can return it if you don't want it.'

I said nothing.

'Do you want it?'

How could I possibly tell my mother what I wanted? 'Sure,' I said, knowing that was what she wanted to hear. 'I'll visit Cookie soon,' I said.

'Good. You should.'

I had meant what I'd said but I kept putting off seeing Cookie. Each time I thought of it, I decided I was too busy preparing for the upcoming exhibition, or Moses. Sometimes I would drive past the home and tell myself I would pop in, but there was no such thing as popping in. There was only being there completely, every sense accosted.

I expressed this to Moses, knowing that he would offer to come. I wasn't sure if I wanted him there, if it would add or detract from my guilt, but he offered to drive and at least if I could be a passenger then that was one less decision I had to make. Turn left or right. Go straight or round and round and around.

Cookie sat against her tan couch in polyester animal print, her arms sticking out like bird legs. She had lost a lot of weight since I'd last seen her. She wasn't wearing jewellery, and I had the sense she hadn't chosen her outfit or dressed herself that

day. Her shock of white hair, set loose from the perm she had
had as long as I could remember, hung limply over her ears.

We sat on either side of her and I felt profoundly relieved
Moses had come with me. Cookie enjoyed him, perhaps
because she couldn't really remember him, or place him, or
because he was handsome and much bigger than she was. She
took his hand and told me to get some of the photos down
from the shelf so she could tell him who all the people in them
were. She'd done this the last time he had come, but Moses
acted as though this was all new to him.

I asked her if she wanted me to cut an apple for her, and a
dark and angry look came over her. After that we sat in silence,
and I wondered what she knew and what she didn't know. She
wouldn't have known that it had been two weeks since I'd
spoken to my parents. That it was the longest we'd gone in
our whole lives without speaking to each other. After our last
conversation, Mum dropped the shirt she'd bought for me at
my front door, followed by a text: *There's a lot to think about.*
Let's speak when you're ready. In the five minutes that followed,
my father sent the same exact message word for word. A couple
of days after that I thought about calling Mum, but couldn't
bring myself to. It was as if a part of me had been bolted down,
and each time I thought about her phone number the bolt
tightened and I was fixed in my spot. It was the first time I ever
thought about the loose floorboard in the kitchen, what was
beneath there – another room, or just dirt and cobwebs and
shadows? *When you're ready.* When would that be? I thought

to myself, this must be what it's like for most people, because most people don't speak to their parents multiple times a day or even every day. Other people were used to being left alone.

There were two knocks at the door and then it opened. A small, young woman whose badge read *Tanisha* entered on tiptoes and smiled fully at me.

'Good morning, sweetie,' she said, and crouched before Cookie with two paper cups. One was full of water, the other held two round white pills, a rectangular blue pill and an orange tablet that looked like an overgrown smartie. 'Here we go.'

'Sweetie,' Cookie said mockingly, looking at Tanisha. 'I've had these already.'

'No, sweetie. You haven't. It's not in the chart.'

Cookie scrunched her nose. 'What did she say?' She looked at me.

'She says you haven't had these ones yet.'

Tanisha looked at her watch and then looked back up at Cookie. 'Come on, Mrs. Radowski. We need to have our medicine so we can be healthy and strong.'

'Ha,' said Cookie. 'Whatever you say, sweetie. You're the boss.' She aggressively grabbed the two cups and consumed them both.

'She's on an empty stomach,' I said. 'Is that okay? She hasn't eaten.'

Tanisha smiled at me and said quietly, 'They do that, sometimes.'

'Do what?'

Tanisha didn't answer me and took a tissue from her pocket and went to wipe Cookie's mouth. Cookie flinched and then farted very loudly, at which point Moses very politely took a phone call and left the room, and Tanisha followed shortly after.

I had hoped (naively) that by visiting Cookie I would make myself feel better, but the visit was making me feel profoundly worse. I wanted to chat, to tell her about my progress at the museum and wait for the inevitable disparaging remarks. I wanted her corroboration of my parents' idiocy and selfishness. I had wanted her to touch Moses, see what I see, feel what I feel. To remember being twenty-seven, but then at twenty-seven she was a single mother, an orphan to a giant pit of an unmarked grave. I wanted her to tell me it was all going to be okay. But Cookie only wanted to tell me how the nurses had refused her entry into the dementia ward to see David. And that someone was taking her things and her doors didn't lock and they wouldn't let her keep a knife in the room.

I went to take Cookie's hand but she brushed it away and said her feet were cold. I found some black socks in a drawer and held them up to her. She nodded and pointed to the floor. I crouched down and took in her swollen feet, toenails thick and slightly curled, dry polka-dot patches on the skin. I had seen a nurse rubbing her feet before, explaining it was good for the circulation. I offered to do the same and she nodded and

277

closed her eyes as I squirted lotion onto my hands. At first I was revolted by the coldness of her heels, her toes, each part more jagged than the last. But as I reached the ridge of her ankles, found the bone beneath the swelling, my revulsion turned to awe. What a thing of beauty, to have traversed the earth on these soles that have borne her weight. Each step taken away from her homeland brought her closer to a life, ripped her away from a death. She released a quiet moan and told me that was enough now, and I slid the black socks over her feet, stretching them upwards and over her calves, and fetched a blanket for her legs that she accepted without protest. Now, sitting next to her again, she took my hand in hers. I wanted her to tell me that I was brave for rubbing her feet, or that she was proud of me, or that I was a good girl. She said nothing but her grip on me was firm, and then her eyes were closed, and again she was dreaming. Then I thought to myself, I do feel better for having seen her, and for having rubbed her feet, and I closed my eyes and dreamed with her a little.

'You're so nice to her,' I said to Moses as we were leaving. He was driving and we were waiting for the gate to open at the car-park exit.

'I never really knew my grandparents. I like being around her.'

'But you only see the old crusty bits. You never got to see the good bits.'

'There are still good bits,' he said, squeezing my hand.

As we were about to pull out, Mum's BMW turned into the drive. We paused inside the gate and Moses wound down his window. Mum did the same. She was wearing large sunglasses that seemed to obscure most of her face.

'Naomi,' she said, peering past Moses. 'I didn't know you were coming.' She put her glasses on top of her head. 'Hello, Moses.'

'Hi. How are ya?'

I looked at his wide hands on the steering wheel of my car. He had purple scabs on his knuckles from a bike accident.

'Sorry. Should I have told you I was coming?' I asked. Moses stared straight ahead, as if by doing so he was allowing us to speak privately.

'You could have told me, yes. She's easily overwhelmed. How is she today?'

'The same,' I said, stopping myself from unbuckling my seatbelt and flinging myself through the windows and into my mother's lap.

'And how are you?' Mum coughed into her hand. 'We haven't seen you.'

'I know. Work's been crazy. The new exhibition. Are you coming to the opening?'

'What opening?'

'Didn't you get an invite?' I shut my eyes sharply as if shielding myself from myself. My exhibition was now two weeks away from opening and I'd been so distracted I had forgotten to send out the invites. I was falling behind on most things, including the catalogue, which still required an introduction from Adele and one from me, both of which I'd need to write. Charlotte was assisting with attributions and installation, though training her had proved to be more work than just doing the whole lot myself.

Another car pulled up behind us, wanting to leave.

'You need to move,' urged Mum.

'What?'

'There's a car behind us,' Moses said.

'Okay, then. Good to see you,' Mum said, wound up her window and descended quietly into the underground garage.

I urgently told Moses to drive straight to the museum, but when we got there it was after six pm, empty, and I couldn't get access. I'd been meaning to ask Adele for Josh's old key but kept forgetting.

'Fuck,' I said, leaning against the black iron door.

'It can wait till the morning, can't it?' Moses asked.

'I was supposed to send the invites weeks ago. No one's going to come.'

'Two weeks is a lot of notice.'

'For us, yeah. Not for all the old people on the list. Fuck.'

'It's really not a big deal.'

'It's actually a big fucking deal,' I said, getting louder. 'Adele is going to be so upset. She trusted me to take the lead on this whole thing. My job is on the line here, literally.'

'I'm sure she'll be fine.'

I shot him a look that was so full of anguish he seemed to step back without stepping back. I'd frightened him. I took a breath and then asked for the car keys, and we got in and I drove home.

Moses had been given tickets to the opening of a play. It was on a Friday night, and so when Mum had texted me to see if I was coming to Shabbat I had replied that I couldn't, and Mum had sent back: *Fine*. That was on Wednesday and there had been no more between us. The *fine* had begun to torment me and terrorise my sleep. I would see it, or dream it, or say to Moses, 'Do you think I should call them?' and he'd nod and say I should do whatever felt right. But nothing felt right.

Moses was wearing his black skinny jeans and black T-shirt. I wore a dusty pink T-shirt dress with sneakers and when I asked him if I looked okay he clutched my waist and told me I looked like sherbet.

As soon as we walked in, Moses was greeted by a woman dressed from head to toe in gold, and she kissed him on both cheeks and congratulated him on his new TV gig. He spoke to her with ease while clasping my hand and smoothing my palm with his fingers. On the way to the box office and then to the bar he kept bumping into people who were familiar to him and who were also congratulating him, and by the time he'd got to the third person I left to go to the toilet, and checked my phone as I pissed, half expecting there to be a missed call from Mum, or Dad, or Cookie, forgetting that I wasn't picking her up tonight. But there was nothing. I sent Gemma a message but didn't receive an instant reply so put my phone away.

When I emerged, Moses was in deep conversation with someone else. I went and collected my wine, which he'd been holding for me, and brushed elbows with the person next to me who nearly made me spill the wine all over myself. I said sorry instantly, as if it had been my fault, and looked up and saw that the man was Josh. I almost didn't recognise him. He was scruffy, pale and unshaven, and his hair was shorn crisp to the ball of his head.

'Naomi,' he said, smiling. He looked so large compared to Moses. I'd completely forgotten the breadth of him. He took a swig of beer and I noticed the absence of his wedding ring.

I felt my hands moisten around the plastic wine cup, my stomach pulling, my mouth dry. I felt like the child lost in the supermarket all over again. I scrambled for something to say, an insult to yell, a fist to punch. Hope you're well. Hope you die. You gave me lice. And then a dark wave of dread: the last picture I sent him, naked in the bathroom mirror, pleading eyes, skin pink like my dress was now. 'Hi, Josh,' I said finally. 'How are you?'

'I'm doing great.' And then he leaned in and said softly, 'It's so good to see you.'

We left not long after that. I dragged Moses across the foyer, told him we couldn't stay, and he looked at Josh from the exit and said, 'Because of that guy?' I knew he really wanted to watch the play but I didn't care.

*

I couldn't sleep at all, and at around two am Moses woke up to go to the toilet and found me with the light on with my computer on my lap when he returned. I was booking a courier to come to the museum first thing Monday morning to collect Josh's typewriter. In the notes section to the recipient I had written *I know who you are.* And then deleted it and left it blank.

Moses got into bed, rubbed his eyes. 'You okay?'

'Not really,' I said. 'It was very strange to see Josh.' On the way home I had expanded on what – up until that point – I had characterised as a 'dumb fling'.

'No, yeah. I'm sure. Well, he sounds like a bit of a loser, to be honest.'

'I didn't think he was at the time, but now ... well. It just makes me feel gross. His wife must hate me. I hate me.'

'Shush. Don't say that.'

'Don't tell me what to say.'

'Okay, okay. I just mean it wasn't your fault. Trust me. Guys are arseholes.'

'You're not like that.'

'I'm one of the good ones,' he said with a smile. But I couldn't smile back.

'I should have stopped it before it began, said something, done something.'

'It's hard to love and hate someone at the same time.'

I closed my computer and sighed.

'You sigh a lot,' he said.

I smiled briefly, thinking of what the therapist had said about Jews and sighing. I wondered what she would make of all of this. But then I remembered that the car needed petrol, so I said that to Moses and he said he'd fill it up the next day. And then I said I'd filled up the last three times, and I'd do it because it seemed as though he wasn't going to do it. And he repeated that he would do it and asked if there was anything else. And I said that there was. And then he asked me if I'd like to list the rest of the things.

'First thing,' he prompted.

I held my pillow tightly in front of my chest. 'I feel like I'm failing.'

'At what?'

'At life.' I clutched the pillow tighter.

'You're amazing. You have an amazing life. An amazing job.'

'Which I'm fucking failing at! I can't believe this is happening to me again.'

'What is happening again?'

'Everything is slipping and I can't get a fucking grip. Fucking fuck.' I tore through my hair, knots upon knots.

'You don't swear very often.'

'Sorry.'

'No. I like it.' He yawned and lay his head on the pillow.

'I don't want you to sleep,' I said.

He propped himself up on his elbow. 'Okay. I'm not sleeping. Second thing?'

I pulled at a knot in my hair till it snapped. 'You'll think I'm silly. Or a brat.'

'No, I won't.'

'I've never not spoken to my parents before.'

'That's not silly. Most people would envy the relationship you have with your parents.'

'I don't know how to be around them at the moment.'

'They probably don't know how to be around you. They still love you.'

I nodded to the window.

'Third thing?'

I bent forward over the pillow on my lap and when I lifted my head up again there were tears streaming down my cheeks. 'I'm scared that they're right.'

He sat up fully and said, 'About me?'

I cried harder then, and for the first time Moses looked as though he didn't know what to do or say. And I waited for him to say the thing to make it all better, but he just ran his hand through his thick dark hair like he was searching for something.

'I don't know, Naomi. Maybe they are right.' I cried harder still. Then I climbed on top of him, pinned his arms above his head and he kept saying are you sure and I kept nodding my head and then I fucked him till he came, my tears and snot falling onto his neck. And then I lay on my back and he used his thigh to press my vibrator into my clit and did that until I came. And then I got off him, had a shower and came back. He said he needed to go to Launceston to sort some things out. He said that when he got back, if I wanted him to, he could move in with a friend until he found his own place. The way he said it felt rehearsed, like he'd been waiting for this moment and there was nothing he could do about it. And then I cried harder at that, and harder again at the thought that I couldn't see Gemma, and I couldn't see my mother, and I couldn't see my grandmother, and I'd never felt so completely alone.

One day we're all
going to die

Rabbi Grossman said it was not unusual. In fact, we would be surprised to hear how often it happened – couples dying together. And by together, the rabbi was meaning months, weeks, days, hours, seconds, side by side, on top, in the next room, country, constellation. First David, who had been checked on at seven pm, and then again at nine pm, and then Cookie, who hadn't emerged for breakfast that morning. They were both in their pyjamas. They had both eaten a good dinner, a last meal, their last rite – to eat, to sleep, to die.

That day Mum had been with the two of them, bringing Cookie to eat lunch with David. When they left him there, Mum said she saw a smile on David's face, as if he still knew them, or Cookie at least. Of course he knew Cookie: by her smell, the shape of her hands, the rhythm of her chest. He knew her by her creaking hips and her firm legs. He knew her by the length of time it took for her to stand in front of a mirror, fetch a newspaper, butter toast. He knew her by the call of her voice, the way her fingers poached buttons from the sewing chest and the droop of her earlobe. Mum said she liked to think he knew all of that when his mouth twitched towards a smile as they left the dining room that day.

I had been getting ready for work when she rang. And I knew from my mother's not speaking and heavy breathing what had happened. I had also known it would not be one death, but two. One would not make sense without the other. One egg without a shell. One jumper without a sleeve. One memory without a shadow. How one knows the things one knows.

I drove straight to the home. I hadn't known what to expect, what I would see. My father was waiting for me outside Cookie's room. He held his arms out and I sobbed into his shirt, inhaling his cologne, feeling the bristles on his chin scrape the top of my head. Then the door to Cookie's room opened and there was my mother, looking for me, and I thought we might fall to the floor, the weight of the grief and the weight of not having touched each other for so long. But there we stood, solid.

They said I could go in to see her, and so I did. She was in bed, the covers under her arms, a rolled up towel under her chin (to stop her head from falling? But where could it go?), her eyes closed, asleep. The smallness of her, the peacefulness of her, was almost too frightening. My mother took me to her and stroked her cheek, and so I copied and stroked the other.

'I'm sorry, Mumma,' she kept repeating, so I said it too. 'I'm sorry, Cookie.' And then my mother looked at me and smiled, and we laughed. Then I remembered that I was touching the cold cheeks of a dead woman, and had the strong sense that she was no longer there in the room, and this made me happy, because I hoped she was with the other people she had loved as fiercely as she had loved us, on the other side.

I followed my parents back to their house and rang Moses on the way. I said to him, 'Sorry. I don't want to burden you with this. I just didn't know what to do, really.' He said he was glad I had called and he would fly back for the funeral. Then he said he loved me and I nodded, forgetting that he couldn't see me. Then I told him not to come, unsure whether I meant it or not, and by then I'd arrived at my parents' and said I needed to go.

A delivery person was leaving as I was entering and my father was by the door holding a huge bouquet of proteas and wattle. They were from his former law firm. The rabbi and funeral director came quickly after, as if they hadn't been in the middle of anything when the call came through. For this we were all very grateful.

My parents and I took turns saying things about Cookie and David – attitudes to God, Australia, politics, family, the ships they took and the trains they didn't, their lives before English and after, the many dead who appeared at the table, prodding their fingers into the rabbi's chest. 'I am just the vessel,' he said, at one with the ghosts. 'These are your stories, your loved ones. I can deliver all of this at the funeral, or you can. Whatever you feel comfortable with.'

My mother nodded and blew her nose. 'She was my mother. And he— He was my father.' Then the rabbi splayed his hands in the air and counted on his fingers a list of mourning rituals we may or may not wish to employ – sitting low, covering the mirrors, ripping our shirts, holding a minyan.

The funeral director asked if there was anyone we needed to wait for, or could they have the funeral the next day. Mum immediately answered that the next day would work. She wanted this to happen quickly. And how quickly and efficiently us Jews can bury our dead.

I looked at my hands, desperately wanting to tell Rabbi Grossman about Moses. This rabbi, who had chanted my Torah portion alongside me under his breath, who was known for falling asleep when the president of the shule delivered their weekly address to the congregation, who had been interviewed recently on a segment for ABC's *Compass* program about the origin of the word 'spiel'. I wanted to tell the rabbi that Moses hadn't been afraid of my grandparents, he hadn't gagged at the sight of mushed fish being spooned into David's mouth, or the cries for help in the room next door from a woman who was in constant pain. I wanted him to know that Moses had forgotten to pack his washbag when he'd left for Launceston and on the first night he'd gone I'd opened it and run my fingers inside the main pocket and found globs of toothpaste stuck to some headphones. I also wanted the rabbi to hold me and stroke my hair and bring me into his chest and tell me that he loved me. And maybe, if I would have just asked, Rabbi Grossman would have listened and held me as I'd wanted to be held.

After the rabbi left, I made sandwiches while my mother pored over photo albums and Dad went to the shops to buy only soft foods: cheese, sponge cake, jam, liver. Melanie came over at dinner time and brought her dog. The four of us shared two pizzas, a rocket salad and chips. Mum ate one bite of a margherita and then gave the rest of her slice to the dog, and Melanie said, 'Could you not do that, Mum?' I had four slices of pizza and still didn't feel full. At one point, Mum looked up from her plate and asked Dad if he'd told the Levinsons and the Rothfields and the Archers, and he nodded each time, eventually saying, 'They all know.'

'And did you put a note in the paper?'

'I did. And it's on the shule website.'

Then she looked at me and then looked around and said, 'Did you tell—' and then put her head in her hands.

At that, Melanie looked at Dad and asked if there was any wine and he went and got a bottle of shiraz from the cellar.

My mother asked me then where Moses was, perhaps out of kindness but more likely out of concern that he'd appear at any moment. I told her that he was in Launceston.

'You should stay here tonight then,' Mum said over the pizza, patting her eyelid with a finger. 'You don't want to be alone.'

I nodded and looked at my sister, expecting her to say something bitchy, but she said nothing and filled everyone's glasses with wine, and then Mum told a story about Cookie's first job in Melbourne and how she'd put salt instead of sugar into her boss's coffee because she couldn't read the English labels and we all laughed.

After Melanie left, I went to lie with Mum in her bed and we spoke of nothing, and the room grew dim like an empty womb. Dad came in and lay on the other side of me, and then Mum said that when she had been pregnant with Melanie, her obstetrician told her that she would likely go into labour in the night. 'You're just an animal,' he'd said, and she hadn't been offended by that, maybe because it was the 1970s or maybe because she did think of herself as an animal. 'And,' he'd continued, 'animals instinctively like to give birth when they feel safe and sheltered. And when you are home, safely in bed and in the dark, your body will begin to labour. Don't search for the signs during the day. Don't walk ten laps of the oval or eat bitter fruits. Wait till the night.' Mum looked over my head to Dad, who was listening with closed eyes and she said, 'Maybe death is the same. Maybe we will all die at night in our beds.'

Dad stretched his hand out over my stomach and Mum caught it there, in the rise and fall, and he said, 'We can only hope. We can only hope to have the deaths they had.'

Mum got up to take a bath and I retreated to my old bedroom that I had left and then returned to and left again.

In the morning Mum lent me something to wear, Melanie arrived, and then it was time to leave. The four of us bundled into Dad's car, on the way to the Jewish cemetery at Springvale. The funeral director had offered to drive us in a mourners' car but Dad had firmly declined, saying, 'No, no. I will take my girls.'

We hadn't been like this, the four of us in the car, since I was in high school. I closed my eyes and felt Melanie's bag wedged between us, rubbing against my leg, and was reminded of school backpacks and padlocked diaries. I thought of Cookie's fondness for Melanie, the firstborn grandchild. I opened my eyes and looked over at my sister, who may have been crying beneath sunglasses. I knew better than to reach out to her.

At the cemetery, I was goosebump cold and Melanie gave me a woollen cardigan to wear. Mum and I held hands as Rabbi Grossman talked about shtetls and Surfers Paradise, business ventures and bridge clubs, worlds that expanded beyond kingdoms and queendoms and then shrank to the confines of a single bed. Halfway through I looked around and saw Gemma. I'd forgotten to call her but there she was, standing a little back from the two large pits in the ground and the rumble of people: friends of Mum's and Dad's, and even a handful of nurses from the home who had come on their days off. I kept looking for Moses but stopped not long after Melanie finished singing a Leonard Cohen song acapella, slightly off tune. Mum had wanted to speak but found she couldn't, and Dad read the eulogy on her behalf. I also wanted to speak but found I couldn't. And then the four of us recited Kaddish and shovelled dirt onto the graves.

The cemetery smelled like paper and eucalyptus. The sun stung my eyes, which were red from weeping.

When Rabbi Grossman was done, people began to move in towards Mum, forming a semi-circle queue around her. I moved away from her slightly and felt a hand on my shoulder. I turned around and saw Julian Blume standing in front of me.

'Oh, Julian,' I said.

'Wish you long life, Naomi.'

People had been saying that to me all day. *Long life. Long life. Long life. May you live to 120*. I didn't know how I was supposed to respond. 'Thank you.'

'I hope it's okay that I came. My mum saw the notice in the *Jewish News* and told me.'

'The trusty *Jewish News*,' I said, and we both laughed a little. I hugged him and he was pepper and vanilla and smooth.

'Thank you,' I said, squeezing his arm. Before I could say any more, Gemma pushed through and reached her arms around me and pulled me in close. Gemma was crying and said, 'Cookie and David were the best.'

'I know.'

'I'm obsessed with that rabbi by the way.'

I laughed a little. 'I'm so glad you're here.'

Melanie pulled at my arm to speak to a relative and I told Gemma to come back to my parents' place.

Gradually, everyone but the four of us and Rabbi Grossman left. He told us we could stay as long as we needed and then Mum lifted her glasses and said, 'I need a stone. No. Two stones.' And we all began scouring the ground for stones. I picked one up. It was the colour of rust, smooth and reflective, and I placed it on the mound of dirt that was covering Cookie's small coffin. And then found another one, rough and glimmering, and placed it on David's. We all did this with stones of various shapes and hues, even Rabbi Grossman joined in. My grandmother had always wanted to hide her religion, and now here it was, on display for all to see as she returned to the earth.

As we walked back to the car, Mum said to me, 'You know, I never thought this would happen. I'm an idiot for thinking this would never happen.' She stopped in the middle of the road. 'These women, they didn't say half the things they could have, and it's still a mystery to me, all the things my mother couldn't say.'

I looked at my mother, who had no make-up on, still beautiful in grief. Regardless of what struggles they had known, Cookie and my mother had persisted, as my mother and I would. Was she saying all of what she could to me? Or only half? A quarter even? I leaned my temple against my mother's collarbone. *Your blood is in my blood, and therefore your blood will be in my children's blood and so on and so forth.* 'Please don't die, Mummy.'

She kissed the top of my head and heaved a heavy sigh and said, 'Okay. I won't.'

*

The front door was open and people were wandering in and then out. Family friends and relatives were scattered around the lounge and in the kitchen. Gemma found me in the garden, sitting alone on a perforated metal chair.

'Hey, Princess,' Gemma said. Behind her walked Julian Blume. 'Sorry, he kind of just invited himself along,' she whispered.

I squinted at the two of them. I felt pale and ghostly. 'I can't believe you took a plane to be here. It's so dramatic.'

'Shut up,' Gemma said, scraping a chair along the concrete pavers and plonking herself opposite. 'Come on, Julian, grab a chair.'

'I'm sure you two want to catch up. I just wanted to say, if you need anything—'

'It's fine,' I said. 'Sit.'

He nodded and lifted a chair from the opposite end of the outdoor table, placed it on the other side of me and sat down. Gemma bit into a bagel, leaving a splash of red lipstick.

'Who told you?' I asked Gemma.

'Moses texted me,' she said.

'Oh.' I suddenly felt very strange in my mother's clothes and my sister's cardigan.

The three of us sat in silence for a while, and then Gemma began asking Julian about his work and life, and he asked her the same. And there was something distinctly sanguine about

296

it. After some time, Julian put his hands on his legs and stood. I got up even though he said, 'Don't get up,' and gave him a hug. The fabric of his shirt was surprisingly soft. I wondered if he had worn it while working at the dental surgery. I wondered how many times it had been through the washing machine.

Gemma stayed until almost everyone had left, and the television had been turned on, and the dishwasher was thrumming. When she told me she was leaving, I asked her to wait for me.

'Really?' she asked. 'I figured you would stay here.'

'No. Do you want to come home with me?'

Shehecheyanu

The morning of the opening of the exhibition, Adele left a small posy of roses and tulips on my desk with a note: *Thank you for all your hard work. Looking forward to celebrating tonight. You've earned it! By the way, you have passed your three-month probation. I will be emailing you a new contract in due course. Mazel tov. A.*

Apart from the day of the funeral, I hadn't taken any time off. It seemed the death of grandparents didn't warrant it and it suited me to be as busy as I was. It had been a week since I'd heard from Moses, which suited me too – not to never hear from him again, only to be able to keep on keeping on and figure the rest out later. I was exhausted, running on adrenaline fuelled by both fear and mourning. The night before the opening, I'd stayed up till four am installing the exhibition with Charlotte and a small crew of tradespeople.

Now, the museum doors were open and the lights were on. My parents were there, as were most people who had received an invitation that was sent fourteen days late. Adele introduced me to the crowd. I stood in front of everyone and spoke about the exhibition and the inspiration behind it. 'The word kitsch derives from Yiddish. It means trash, but it is the trash we love. Now I'm not saying what you're seeing here tonight is trash …' I paused for laughter, but also because my hands were shaking, and I placed them on the podium to steady myself. 'I hope you take joy in these heirlooms that illuminate the formidable past, exciting present and hopeful future of this vibrant community.'

'Is this new?' my mother asked about my black dress, once the crowd began to disperse through the museum.

'We're so proud of you,' Dad said. 'You've done an excellent job.'

'Well, we haven't had a proper look yet,' Mum said.

I pointed to the exhibit entrance.

'Shall we?' she said, and I lingered a step behind as they headed towards the exhibition. On the way a volunteer approached to congratulate me and Mum pulled me in towards her, put her arm protectively around my shoulders and said firmly, 'Sorry, we're the parents. She's ours for the next five minutes.'

We entered the gallery and they immediately wandered off in different directions. Dad spent a long time in front of a perspex display detailing the history of the Caulfield Jewish Scouts Group, while Mum watched an interview with a young fashion designer that was playing on a loop.

I quietly thought that the gallery looked spectacular, small as it was, and I felt it wasn't Cookie's absence that made it so but rather her presence (not that she'd probably have come in the first place). At the last moment I'd managed to include a photo of her in the exhibition, slipped into a glass cabinet full of postcards near the exit. I wrote the following caption: *Photo of young woman wearing checked skirt suit and cat's eye glasses, 1957.* By then my mother would have been in primary school and Cookie would have been partnered with David. In the photo she had lowered her sunglasses and stared directly at the camera, looking neither happy nor sad. She was just there.

Next to Cookie's photo I had placed one of Paula Hohenberg's photos, the exterior of a typical Viennese coffee shop and a small girl licking her fingers. Adele had been intrigued by the inclusion, at which point I shared my proposal with her. She said it needed some work but we should present it at the next board meeting.

I had also included an extract from Paula's brother's donation statement.

My sister, Paula, was the artist of the family. She saw the things we could not see. Perhaps this is why she returned to Vienna after the war. To bear witness. Her untimely death forced an unwanted reckoning between us and the place of our childhood. May her art find new life here, in this museum of curiosities. I have long admired the work of this repository of Jewish life. Long may it continue after my death. Shehecheyanu. A beginning, again.

I went outside for some fresh air, intending to go back in, but with the faintest spittle of rain on my cheeks I felt more awake than God. I hadn't taken the car with the misplaced notion that I would be drinking, but I hadn't drunk a thing. I headed down Hotham Street, and turned at the cemetery, passing the noisy cacophony of spirits and memories. The night was black and silent. I clutched my keys in my hand as my mother had taught me. And I went home.

Acknowledgements

I wish to thank my agent Sarah McKenzie, and my publisher and editor Jo Mackay. Both of you held this book with love, never trying to change it, only ever making it more of what it needed to be. Sarah – your advice and care have been invaluable. Jo – the midwife of this novel who has made me laugh so much and feel ever so safe in your fine hands. Also to my magnificent copyeditor, Annabel Blay, who feels like an old friend (even though at the time of writing this we are still yet to meet), and all the team at HarperCollins HQ, I am eternally grateful.

I am indebted to and in awe of the Melbourne Jewish community arts organisations who over the years have supported me as an artist, in particular Melbourne Jewish Book Week, FOJAM, the Jewish Museum of Australia and the Kadimah Yiddish Theatre. Thank you for your dedication to celebrating and preserving the heartbeat of Jewish life and culture.

A huge thanks to those who read my writing in its early stages and offered reflections, insights and expertise, in particular Antoni Jach, Peter Kenneally. To Ginger Gorman for your generous introduction to Sarah. To Cantor Michel Laloum for your sound advice. To Phillip Kavanagh for always saying 'yes, and', to Jessica Murphy for your everlasting love.

To these powerful Jewish women writers who I am also proud to call friends: Tali Lavi, for your wisdom and generosity, and Sarah Krasnostein and Lee Kofman for your support and early endorsements. To my dear neighbour and friend Amanda Lux, who after meeting in the local playground became the first editor of my book, who rolled out the whiteboard for me followed by some much-needed showtunes.

To Jordan Barling and Siana Einfeld, LSCWL, exquisite writers, word-count-checkers, queens. The best writing group ever, even when we're not writing.

To my first reader, Vanessa Ackerman, my bosom friend across the seas, who has read everything I've ever written and knows the worst of me and the best of me. May we continue writing and sharing for all the mothers before us and the children to come.

Thank you to my family – brothers, sisters-in-law, uncles, aunts, nieces, nephews, cousins. And thank you to my friends. You have shared in my excitement and been my champions. It means the world to me.

To the long line of storytellers in my family: those I met and never met, I hear you in the voices of my family and in my dreams. My ancestors, my grandparents, my namesakes, I will never stop thinking about the journeys you took and the people, places and memories you left behind so that I could be here.

And to the greatest storyteller of all, my Babcia, who held court at every Shabbat table and family simcha until she had no more left to say.

To my parents, Susan and Gary, my first best friends, who have promised never to die, and in the unlikely event that they do must speak to me from beyond the grave. The best and most dedicated fan club, who have always encouraged and inspired me, and made every effort to come to every event I am involved in, no matter the rivers (Yarra) or oceans (all of them) they have had to cross. I would cross all the waters in the world to come to you.

To Wolf and Ziggy, my heart, my angel cubs. Your dad and I are your biggest fans, and so it continues.

To Rico. In a crowded restaurant you were the only one listening to me. You surprise me in every way. You astound me with your superhuman strength, internal and external. Thank you for everything. You are my love. The truest mensch there ever was. I hope you like my book.

Book club discussion questions

- Naomi is the grandchild of Holocaust survivors. How does the Holocaust impact her life as a third-generation descendant, and how does it affect the other members of her family? Does each generation experience it differently?

- This book is set in 2009. How does Naomi navigate her sexual and romantic life? How aware or unaware is she of power dynamics? If the book were set in 2023, would her behaviour or attitudes be different or impacted by movements like Me Too? What would you say to Naomi about her sexual and/or romantic life if you could?

- What is the role of the museum within the book, and how does the museum serve the book as a backdrop to the action?

- Jewish artists have historically used humour as a means of coping with immense trauma and violent antisemtism. How does the dark humour serve the novel? How did it make you feel?

- This book is largely about a Jewish family and their specific dynamic, but themes of intergenerational trauma, family relationships, sex and romance are common. How universal did you find the themes of the book? Which character or theme did you relate to most? Was there any part of the book that felt alienating or shocking? How many words did you have to google?

- What is Naomi's evolution by the end of the book? Are you hopeful for her, or do you think she will continue to make the same mistakes? How have her relationships with lovers and family members changed or stayed the same? Where do you hope to see her in five years?

- Naomi has a very close relationship with her mother, Vivienne, and her grandmother, Cookie. The matrilineal line pulses loudly throughout the novel. What is the significance of these relationships? How healthy or unhealthy do they appear? Did this make you reflect on your own connections to parents and grandparents?

talk about it

Let's talk about books.

Join the conversation:

 facebook.com/harlequinaustralia

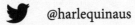 @harlequinaus

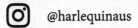 @harlequinaus

harpercollins.com.au/hq

If you love reading and want to know about our
authors and titles, then let's talk about it.